ELLA FINDS LOVE AGAIN

This Large Print Book carries the
Seal of Approval of N.A.V.H.

ELLA FINDS LOVE AGAIN

JERRY S. EICHER

THORNDIKE PRESS
A part of Gale, Cengage Learning

GALE
CENGAGE Learning·

Detroit • New York • San Francisco • New Haven, Conn • Waterville, Maine • London

GALE
CENGAGE Learning®

LIBRARY OF CONGRESS CATALOGING-IN-PUBLICATION DATA

Eicher, Jerry S.
  Ella finds love again / by Jerry S. Eicher. — Large print ed.
    p. cm. — (Thorndike Press large print Christian romance)
  "Little Valley Series #3."
  ISBN-13: 978-1-4104-4177-5 (hardcover)
  ISBN-10: 1-4104-4177-6 (hardcover)
  1. Amish women—Fiction. 2. Amish—Fiction. 3. Large type books.
I. Title.
PS3605.I34E44 2011b
813'.6—dc23   2011034950

Published in 2011 by arrangement with Harvest House Publishers.

Printed in the United States of America
1 2 3 4 5 6 7 15 14 13 12 11

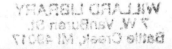

ELLA FINDS LOVE AGAIN

ONE

The light snow swirled around Ella Yoder's buggy, the drifts along the ditch already high for this early in winter. Ella pulled the waterproof buggy blanket higher over her legs. Oh, to be home at Seager Hill, sitting near the warmth of the old woodstove, the whole family gathered at the supper table under the hiss of a gas lantern. There to experience the long evening with the dishes done and nothing to do but enjoy reading a good book.

"I have to try!" Ella said, the words echoing in the empty buggy. "I have to make a real home for us. The girls deserve that much." Her thoughts wandered back to Aden and his untimely death. *I have to forget him and our dreams and hopes. I must move on.* Ella slapped the lines. *And yet I have no feelings for Ivan Stutzman. How can I marry him?*

Snowflakes drifted into the open storm

front. They perched like white crystal gems on her black shawl — fragile, breakable . . . breathless beauty sent from heaven. She shook her blanket and sent the snow flakes flying off her lap. The horse jerked his head with the movement on the lines, as if to tell her he was going as fast as he could in this weather. At least the wind was coming from behind. The return journey would be another matter, driving straight into the teeth of what was turning out to be a fierce winter storm.

How like her life. The time since Aden's death had flown like the wind at her back, pushing her along with its force and fury — and by men who proclaimed their love for her — Wayne Miller, the bishop, and Preacher Stutzman . . . *Ivan.*

Now the time had come to leave behind the memories of the past, to turn her heart toward love. And that journey looked to be as fierce as this trip home after supper at Ivan's house. She could have said no to the invitation . . . but the girls . . . It was always about the girls, really. They needed a mother and a home. They needed *her,* and she could make the decision that would make her their mother. She would surely marry Ivan.

"You can love him, and the feelings will come later," Ella's mamm had said, her voice firm. "He's a *gut* man of God. He loves you. And Aden's gone forever. You can make a home for Ivan's girls. They need that from you, and you do love them."

From behind her she heard the sound of an *Englisha* vehicle approaching even though the engine was muffled by the snowdrifts on either side and the heavy cloud cover. The noise was approaching much too swiftly. She tensed. Headlights reflected off the snowbanks. Her horse turned its head sideways and his blinder slipped, leaving him blinded on that side. Ella tightened the reins to keep him away from the ditch.

The vehicle behind her sounded like it was accelerating, the motor much louder now. Ella checked her lights outside the buggy with a quick sideways glance. Were they working? The intensity of the headlights behind her drowned the feeble glow her buggy lights were putting out. Surely the driver could see her. The road behind her was a straight stretch — no curves to hide the buggy's profile.

Ella pulled right, her horse protesting with an arch of his neck, hesitating to follow her directions. She held him to the side of the road with the sheer force of her hands on the lines.

"Slow boy," she hollered, hoping he could hear her above the roar of the motor. "It's safe. Come on over — just a little more, Moonbeam. Give that driver plenty of room."

Surely it was a man in the *Englisha* vehicle behind her. There were women who drove as they pleased, even among the Amish. Yet it was hard to imagine that anyone but a man would drive so recklessly on slippery, snow-covered roads.

The headlights wavered and then moved away from the buggy. Ella drew in a deep breath and willed the pounding of her heart to slow down. Surely she had been spotted, and the driver was turning out in time.

She waited for the crunch of tires beside her and the swirl of snow as the vehicle passed her. Instead, it slowed as it drew alongside her, keeping pace with the horse's slow gait. She glanced out the small buggy window. The pickup truck window was rolled down, but no faces were visible in the darkness inside the cab. Was she about to be waylaid on this lonely stretch of road during this cold winter night? Ivan's place was still at least a mile ahead, and she would never be able to outrun a truck.

"Are you by yourself?" the question came. The voice was female, and Ella opened the buggy door, pushing it aside. Not that it would have done much good, but if it had been a man's voice, she would have let out on the lines, whipping the horse with her cries and at least made a dash for Ivan's place.

"I don't have far to go," she said, hoping her weak voice carried to the speaker.

"There's a big storm comin'," a male voice said from the other side of the truck. "Straight off the lake, the radio said. It's supposed to dump the worst in a few hours. You'd best get off the road. It's bound to be dangerous weather . . . especially for you Amish folks."

"*Ach,* thanks," Ella said. "I'm just goin' another mile or so."

"You're not driving back tonight?" the man asked.

"I had thought I would, but I imagine I can stay over if things look too bad."

"We'd best be getting inside ourselves," the woman said. The motor roared again. Quickly the red taillights bounced and faded in the falling snow before disappearing into the blinding whiteness.

So the approaching storm was a bad one. She'd been suspecting as much the last fifteen minutes or so. Her initial hopes had gotten the best of her. She didn't want to stay with Susanna, Ivan's sister, but surely she could if she must. Certainly, she couldn't stay at the main house. Should she turn back now? Yet going back was farther than moving ahead, and Ivan would worry. He would think she had gotten stuck in some ditch and would set out to find her.

She slapped the reins. There was no choice but to go on. Perhaps Moonbeam could increase his pace. He shook his head, but lifted his feet faster, his hoofbeats all but soundless on the snowy road.

In the heavy darkness, Ella stayed in the center of the road. Already the drifts were sending tentative feelers out from the edges of the banks. She kept the lines tight, glad to see a house come up ahead. The soft shine of a gas lantern glowed from the window and across the sparkling snow.

It looked Amish, the familiarity a *gut* thing. Like the feeling of a warm blanket at night, making the darkness beyond the glow seem less deep, the distance yet to travel closer. Inside the house would be people like her, who saw the world as she did, who experienced life in a way she could understand. Surely the *Englisha* felt the same about their people.

Ella drove on. No other headlights appeared, the darkness of the woods deepening on either side of her, the snow increasing by the minute. This invitation to supper from Ivan had seemed such a wise idea at the time. If only they had put the occasion off until next week. She opened the buggy door again, glancing out. There was no doubt the *Englisha* man had been correct — she would not be returning tonight. She would surely be spending the night at Susanna's place. But perhaps it wouldn't be too bad. Maybe it was *Da Hah*'s way to expose her to Ivan's extended family.

Her mamm often said, "*Da Hah* makes use of all things for His own good."

Since Mamm was usually right, she would simply accept tonight's change of plans. The snowstorm was none of her doing.

Ella peered into the falling snow, recognizing the turn toward Ivan's farm. She dodged a long stringy snowdrift, pulling sharply left, before turning into Ivan's lane. Before her rose the familiar outlines of his white, paint-peeling home and the brown barn, both of them standing like ghostly forms in the falling snow. A light was still on in the barn, and Ella drove toward its door, pulling past the hitching post, which sat closer to the house. Moonbeam would need to be taken inside on a night like this, and since Ivan wasn't likely to notice her arrival, Ella

13

pulled the buggy to a stop and climbed out, preparing to unhitch by herself.

One tug was off, the leather frozen under her gloves, when the barn door swung open. Ivan rushed out, leaving the door swinging in the wind, the warm glow of the barn lantern flooding the yard and reaching the buggy. Ella blinked, her head bent against the sting of the snow.

"*Ach,* I didn't hear you drive in," Ivan said, quickly unhitching the other side of the horse. "I'm sorry about that. I half expected you to turn back."

"The storm came up faster than I thought it would," Ella said. "Someone did stop to warn me on the road, but I was closer here than home."

"I'd hoped to have a better welcome for you," Ivan said, smiling through the snow-flakes that were settling on his eyebrows and beard.

"It is awful tonight," Ella said, forcing a laugh.

Ivan grabbed the horse's bridle, and Ella shut the buggy doors against the force and howl of the wind. She paused, opening her mouth on impulse, feeling the cold snow-flakes against her tongue. How strange this evening was — so cold and yet joy stirred within from the snow. She felt young again, perhaps even ready to move on with life.

"Makes me feel like a child again," Ella said into the wind, repeating the gesture, her mouth open longer this time. Ivan would surely think her silly, would he not?

But Ivan laughed easily with her as he led the horse forward, the shafts dropping softly onto the ground. He had paused while watching her. "*Da Hah* gives pleasure even in snow, doesn't He? I just don't look forward to all the shovelin' tomorrow morning."

"If it even stops by tomorrow. The *Englisha* couple said the storm was a bad one."

"I think they're right. The barometer is falling fast. I don't think you'll be able to get back home tonight, Ella."

"No, I don't suppose I can," she said as they entered the barn. She shut the door behind them. "Can I keep Moonbeam in here for the night? And perhaps Susanna can put me up?"

Ivan turned to look at her over the horse's mane. "I see my invitation put you in a pickle. I'm sorry about that. Susanna has room for you. I guess we could have called supper off if the storm hadn't come so suddenly."

"It's not a problem," Ella said with a nervous smile. "I really wanted to come —

15

snowstorm or not. And this will give me more time to spend with the girls . . . and you. And perhaps get used to the place."

Thankfully Ivan seemed to understand. He nodded his head. The horse bumped him, reaching its head toward the stall and the wisps of hay hanging in the manger.

Ella waited for Ivan, standing under the lantern as he led the horse forward and into the stall. He came out and shut the latch on the stall before pulling more hay down into the manger with a pitchfork.

"There!" he said. "That should keep him satisfied for the night."

Ella rubbed her gloved hands together, the little warmth from the gas lantern on the ceiling not reaching her.

Ivan walked toward her, his face fully visible now. The snow melted from his beard, leaving wet spots that glittered in the glare of the lantern light. He seemed burdened, worried, the lines on his face longer than usual.

Two

Ivan's eyes searched Ella's face, and she blushed under his gaze, her neck warm under the folds of her bonnet. She kept her eyes on the barn floor as Ivan's bare fingers took her gloved hands in his.

"I'm glad you came tonight . . . even in this storm. It shows me you're serious about us — me and the girls."

"I'm tryin' to be," Ella said, meeting his eyes, their intense blueness bright tonight. Oh, if only this moment would cause her heart to pound with the emotion she once knew with Aden. If only she could bring herself to long for him to put his arms around her, crushing her to his chest.

"For this, for your willingness, *Da Hah* has blessed me more than you know," Ivan said, his voice breaking. "More than you will ever know."

"You are a *gut* man," Ella said. "I hope

someday I can be a proper mother to your girls."

"Then you have decided?" he asked, his eyes lighting up, his fingers so tight on her gloved hands that they hurt.

She shook her head, hoping her face didn't show the sorrow deep inside. "Will you have as a wife one whose brother has left the faith and plans to marry an *Englisha* girl?"

"Your brother is not you, Ella. And no one will hold your family to account."

"They always do," Ella said. Thankfully she could allow her distress to show now, and offering her brother's situation as an excuse was easier than having to explain the real reason.

"Perhaps, but I am not bothered."

"Yah," Ella said, meeting his eyes again. "You are *gut* in that way."

"Surely, then, we can be settin' the weddin' day soon? Perhaps in the spring? Before the plantin' starts? I know it's not like the young ones do, but we aren't so young," he said, his voice low.

"Yah, Ivan, I know. And I wish I could. And I thought tonight I might have the answer for you. But I know now I'm still not ready yet. I hope you don't hold that against me. Can you understand? Perhaps a little? I still need more time."

His head had fallen now, his fingers losing their grip. "You have given me great joy, even with such an answer," he whispered. "Just to have you here is enough for now, and I can wait as long as necessary. I can wait until *Da Hah* moves on your heart."

He smiled.

She slowly took her glove off, the leather now drying, her fingers sliding out easily. With her bare hand she removed the other, dropping them both to the floor. She reached for his hands, letting her fingers run over his cold calluses, feeling the warmth rush into them.

"It's best you understand me," she said, her voice barely above the hiss of the gas lantern. "Ivan, I do not love you in the way I loved Aden. But I know I have to move on with my life as best I can. Our people believe in love, in hope. And I do love your girls. I want a home for them again . . . not just having them live in my big house during the week. Whatever will happen between the two of us . . . only *Da Hah* knows. But I am willin' to keep trying. If you will have patience with me."

"Then in time, you might come to love me?"

Ella glanced up to meet his eyes. "I can

only say that I no longer sorrow as much for what I've lost. But I do still sorrow for what hasn't come back — the ability to love another in that way." She watched him waver, but then he smiled again.

"I would not push you into anything you're not ready for. So we will wait. Is that a *gut* enough answer from me?"

Ella lowered her head. "More than *gut* enough. It's an answer worthy of your wonderful girls. It is I who am not worthy of you."

"Don't say that," Ivan said. "You are much more than you can ever know. It's me who is unworthy of you."

"It will take some time before I can walk the way of our people."

"If my love for you were not so great," Ivan said, "then perhaps I could let you go, but the truth is that I love you too much."

His eyes found hers again, holding her gaze steady.

"I wish it weren't so for your sake." Ella managed a smile. "I wish I didn't need so much time."

Ivan leaned forward as if he would kiss her. She would not resist if he did. Perhaps it would help. Maybe even rekindle the fire that once burned in her heart. She felt his fingers tighten on her hands. *Will he?* Her breath quickened. *What would it be like if he did, bringing his lips down to meet mine?*

She dared to look up, but Ivan's gaze was far away now, seeing past barn ceilings and horse stalls. His grip lessened on her hands as the lantern hissed above them.

Ella waited, but Ivan said nothing.

What is he remembering, that light shining in his eyes, that little smile on his face, that joy I so rarely see flickering in his eyes? she wondered.

He sighed, gripping her fingers again.

"I'm sorry," he said. "I guess I have my own sorrows. But I do dream of the day when we will exchange the vows, when you will be ready to be my wife and a mother to my girls."

"And we can all be in one place together," she said. "In a house I can really call home."

"So that's why you're considering me," he teased, a twinkle playing in his eyes. "You want my farm."

"Ivan Stutzman!" she said in mock accusation. "How can you say that? What an awful woman you must think I am!"

"You are nothing but *gut*," he said as he pulled her close to his side with one arm. He walked forward with her at his side as they made their way to the barn door.

Her bonnet whacked against his shoulder

and she laughed.

"I guess I'm clumsy around a *gut* woman," he said. "I hope that doesn't drive you back home again."

"Nee," she said. "Not in this snowstorm!"

He laughed, suddenly stopping short.

"Ach, here I am so taken up with you, I'm forgettin' the lantern. I'll burn the barn down like a young boy in love," he said. Walking back, he lifted the lantern off the hook, carrying the light swinging at his other side.

"Neither of us is that young," Ella said, retrieving her gloves. She pulled them on, waiting for him to take her hand again . . . but he didn't.

"Sorrow makes us both seem old, Ella. But *Da Hah* will help us."

He shut the barn door, the intensity of the snowstorm choking back any words they might have said. Snowflakes shifted before the lantern's light like a living wall in motion.

"We'd best run," Ella shouted through the whirling white stinging her cheeks. She slapped her hands together in front of her face.

"No runnin' in this snow," Ivan said, waving his lantern forward, the light illuminating drifts already high between the house and barn. "Soon I'll need to carry you in."

"You'll do no such thing!" she said, stepping forward quickly.

He laughed and followed with his lantern. At the side door, he held it open for her, pushing the swinging screen door against the wall until she had passed through to the washroom. The water basin was frozen solid, and Ivan motioned for Ella to go on inside.

"I'll fix the water for you," she said instead, as he set the lantern on the counter. He looked at her in surprise as Ella took the basin outside, and with a quick whack on the porch rail removed the ice.

Entering the washroom again, Ella laughed at the look on his face. From the looks of things, the man sorely needed a woman doing things for him. She opened the kitchen door and saw Susanna standing near the large table, the evening supper spread out before her.

"Good evening, Susanna," Ella offered. "I made it through the snowstorm." She shook off the snow before stepping across the threshold.

"Good evening," Susanna said. "Quite some storm out there."

"Yah," Ella said, nodding. "Everything's frozen."

Susanna motioned with her chin toward the water bucket on the counter. Ella set the basin down, removed her gloves, and then reached to pick the basin up again. The cold metal stuck to her skin. She transferred the bowl quickly from one hand to the other and placed it back on the counter.

She grabbed the water bucket and filled the basin. She put the bucket down, picked up the basin and, careful not to spill the water, carried it back into the washroom where Ivan was still standing as if rooted to the spot.

"I have to wash too," she said as she set the basin down. She waited until Ivan was finished before she washed. He stood there watching her as she dried her hands on the cold towel. She could feel his eyes on her, and it felt strangely *gut* to be watched.

She left his gaze and stepped into the kitchen. Glancing at his still form, she gently shut the door.

"That storm sounds serious," Susanna said, a big bowl of white, fluffy mashed potatoes in her hands. "Can you get back home tonight?"

Ella shook her head, taking her bonnet off, and placing it on a chair.

"You're stayin' with me then?" Susanna asked.

"I was hopin' you would give me a place — even if it's just on the couch. An *Englisha* couple stopped me on the road. They said this would be quite a storm."

"Of course you can stay with me," Susanna affirmed. "There's always room for one more at the house."

"Are you sure? There's your parents, and here you've done all the work on this supper . . ."

"I'm glad to do it," Susanna said. "Ivan needed something special."

"Yah," Ella agreed, removing her shawl and draping it over a chair to dry. Behind her the washroom door opened, and soon she felt Ivan's hand lightly on her arm. Ella glanced at Susanna. What would she think of this open display of affection? That she was already promised to him? Susanna had turned her head, but not before Ella noticed a pleased smile on her face. Susanna obviously approved of the match.

"Where are the girls?" Ella asked.

"Mary and Sarah are upstairs in the big bedroom," Susanna said. "They like to play up there. And the baby's in the living room on a blanket by the stove."

"I'll call them," Ivan offered.

"Let me," Ella said, waiting for his approval. He nodded and pulled out the chair at the head of the table and sat down. Ella turned to go upstairs with the realization that she had looked to Ivan for his approval, not unlike she did her daett at home, but this man was to be her husband, not her father.

The thought caused a tremble in her hands as she entered the living room and approached baby Barbara beside the stove. The faint light from the kerosene lamp on the desk sent soft shadows across the baby's face. Barbara smiled happily, waving her arms and kicking her feet in the air at the sight of her.

"*Ach,* you are so happy tonight," Ella said, reaching down to brush her forehead.

"I'd best leave you here by the warm stove," she whispered. "I don't want you catching a winter flu bug. I'll go get your sisters. Then we'll go to supper."

The baby kicked her feet in gleeful agreement.

THREE

The stairwell was dark, and Ella was reminded of the thousand such trips up and down in her old home on Seager Hill. Tonight dim light was dancing on the walls at the top of the stairs. Soft little girl voices were coming from the bedroom. She drew a long breath. If *Da Hah* didn't intervene in some way, she would soon be their mamm — and a wife to Ivan.

But oddly, that thought no longer carried intense pain. In fact, she felt very little in the way of emotions. In some ways, that was how she wanted it to stay. Never again did she want to experience the heart-rending agony when love is torn from the heart. Perhaps it was just as *gut* her heart had become ice.

Ella deliberately stepped hard on the landing to alert the girls of her approach. There was no need for a surprise entrance and startling the girls. The door to the room was ajar, and Ella could hear the change of tone in their voices. The sound warmed her heart.

"Hi, girls!" she said, peeking around the edge of the door. A kerosene lamp burned on the dresser, two faceless ragtag dolls were lying on the bed, and Mary and Sarah were seated beside them.

"We were waitin' for you," Mary said, laughing.

Sarah nodded enthusiastically.

"So you made me climb all the way up here?" Ella said, teasing.

Their smiles broadened.

"It's really snowin' outside," Sarah said. "We can't even see out the window! It's even darker than dark."

"Oh, but the snow is beautiful," Ella said, giving them both a tight hug. "And so are you! I haven't seen you since yesterday."

"That was a long time ago," Mary said, her voice sober.

Again Sarah nodded vigorously.

"Oh, that's not so long," Ella said, laughing and squeezing them tighter.

"Well, it seemed so to us," Mary said. "We're glad you're here. Daett said you'd come. And Susanna has supper all ready for us, so we don't have to eat Daett's food."

"*Ach,* your daett's food isn't that bad," Ella said as she loosened her hug. *The poor little dears; they really do need a mother.*

"It's not like yours," Sarah said, exaggerating her smile, all her teeth showing.

"You'd better keep those teeth in your mouth," Ella said, pinching her cheek. "They might fall out."

"Oh no they won't," Sarah said, sticking her fingers in and pulling hard on one of them. "They're stuck in really tight!"

"So I see," Ella said. "I was just teasing you. You have really nice teeth."

"Do I have nice teeth?" Mary asked.

"Open up," Ella said. "Really wide now."

Mary complied, her mouth lifted high.

"Yes, sure 'nuff . . . you have *really* nice teeth," Ella said.

"Really?" Mary asked.

"You both do! Now come on down for supper. Susanna has everything ready."

"Will you have to go home after supper . . . in this big snow?" Sarah asked, her eyes big.

"What if you get stuck in a ditch?" Mary asked. "Who will help you out?"

Ella laughed. "Susanna is letting me stay at her house tonight. Come now, we need to go down for supper."

"Why don't you stay at *our* house?" Mary asked, her brown eyes fixed on Ella's face. "You're our mamm, aren't you?"

Sarah nodded slowly beside her.

Ella knelt down and wrapped her arms around the girls. "No, I just take care of you during the week. I've told you that before. You're mamm's in heaven."

"Then why are you here for supper?" Mary asked. "With Daett? That's how I know you're our mamm now."

"I'm just here on a visit," Ella said, her hands tight around their thin shoulders. "Then you'll see me on Monday again . . . for all of next week."

"Will you be our mamm someday?" Mary asked, her eyes hopeful.

"I don't know," Ella said, her breath catching.

"We would like to have you as our mamm," Mary said, laying her hand on Ella's cheek.

Sarah's little hand came up on the other side, her head nodding, her eyes eager.

"Look, sweethearts, perhaps *Da Hah* will give you a mamm someday. A real *gut* one. And maybe it will be me. But we'll just have to wait and see."

"Why do we always have to wait for the *gut* things?" Mary asked.

What was there to say to such an innocent question, to such hope raised from little hearts? Could God Himself deny them?

"I want a real mamm before I die," Mary said, taking Sarah's hand in hers. "Sarah does too."

"Yah, I know," Ella whispered as she rose to her feet. With the kerosene lamp in one hand and Sarah's hand in the other, Ella led the way into the hall. There Mary stepped forward, taking the lead, going down the stairs one step at a time. Ella stayed behind her, the lamp held aloft, as Sarah followed Mary.

They were so small, and so soon they would grow up. Why couldn't she tell them she would be their mamm? Hadn't she decided to speak the sacred vows with Ivan? Why was it so hard then for her to say so? Could her heart go on living if she missed this moment, a moment that might never come again? If she allowed the past to mar what could be so beautiful in the present?

At the bottom of the stairs Mary walked over to baby Barbara, bending over to whisper to her.

Ella paused, watching. How would she ever arrive at a decision with so many doubts and emotions tearing at her?

"Supper's ready!" Susanna called from the kitchen doorway.

Ella walked over and picked up baby Barbara, carrying her into the kitchen.

"I'm sure hungry!" Ivan said, already seated at the table,.

Susanna turned to Ella. "He's in a *gut* mood. You have that effect on him. I don't see him this happy very often."

Ella tried to smile as she helped the girls into their chairs. What would Ivan think if he knew her real thoughts? Her fears that she might never be able to love again.

Susanna brought a large bowl of mashed potatoes from the stove and then sat down herself.

Ivan looked around and asked, "Shall we pray?" His voice deepening into his Sunday tone, he led out, "Our Father, most gracious Lord and Savior. You who give life that man may live, bless now this meal which is prepared. Allow Your abundant grace to increase and abound in our lives . . ." His voice continued until at the end he added words Ella was certain had never been written in any prayer book: "And we thank You for bringing Ella to us. Amen."

Ella felt the blood creep up her neck. The emotion seemed so disconnected with any of her other feelings, like it stood by itself, the only part of her that touched the man.

Susanna passed the bowl of potatoes in Ivan's direction. He dipped a little out into Mary's bowl first and then Sarah's, one girl seated at his side, the other opposite him.

"Are you feeding the baby from the table yet?" Ella asked, wondering if she should reveal that she'd been doing so at her house.

"Oh, as much or as little as she wants," Ivan said, laughing. "I let her play with it when no one is here. I manage to get some in her mouth with a spoon."

"The baby needs a mamm," Susanna said plainly.

Ella felt the red creep up her neck again.

Ivan slapped a small portion of mashed potatoes on baby Barbara's plate, pulling his hand back in expectation. Barbara seemed to know the routine and stuck her fingers in the soft white and then sucked on them. Ivan laughed and added more potatoes.

"Now I have seen everything!" Susanna said, nearly jumping to her feet.

"I do believe it helps them grow faster when they take food in through the skin," Ivan said. "Now sit down. She'll live through it."

Susanna settled back into her chair, keeping her eyes away from the high chair.

They did make a cute though sloppy sight, the bearded father poised over the baby, his spoon held in the air, the child happily smearing mashed potatoes over her face, getting small portions in her mouth. Ella couldn't help but smile. After a brief silence, she asked, "How are your parents?"

"Mamm gets weaker every day it seems," Susanna said. "Daett's a lot stronger than she is. But winter's hard on both of them."

"I would suppose so," Ella said.

"Susanna does more than her duty with them," Ivan said. "I wish I could do more, and the rest of our brothers and sisters have large families, so they don't get over much either."

"I've been glad to help," Susanna said. "And I think it will be over soon. The old folks might not see another winter . . . at least not Mamm."

"It's that bad?" Ivan asked.

"I'm afraid so," Susanna said. "It's hard to tell with Mamm sick so much. Plus she's cold even when we keep the stove hot all night. Daett's probably sitting in front of the stove right now, keeping the fire hot for her."

"Are they okay alone if Mamm's in a bad way?" Ivan asked.

"She had the flu all week, but not much can be done except watch her. Daett's still able to do that. They don't eat much . . . soup mostly. I heated that before I came over."

"I want Ella to sleep in my room tonight," Mary said, apparently following her own train of thought.

"Ella can't," Susanna said. "She will be over to my place."

"But I want her with me," Mary said.

"You'll see her next week," Susanna said. "That's just the way things are."

Mary smiled when Ella patted her on the head.

Ivan didn't say anything. His plate was piled high with mashed potatoes and gravy, his youngest daughter beside him, her face covered with food from forehead to chin.

FOUR

The kerosene lamp cast shadows on the kitchen wall as little Mary stood with a white dishtowel and wiped diligently until every section of the plate in her hand was covered at least twice.

"That's dry now," Ella said. "Bring it over here to this side of the sink. Then you can have another one."

Susanna backed away from the stack of rinsed dishes, making room for Mary.

"I want to help too," Sarah protested from her perch on the kitchen table bench.

"Then take a towel and take a dish to the table. Do like Mary does," Ella told her.

"I don't want to do it at the table. You let us stand beside you at your house," Sarah said, her face in a pout.

"That's because there's more room at Ella's place. But I'm here now," Susanna said. "So do what Ella says."

"I like it best at Ella's house," Sarah said

with a frown.

Ella shrugged and smiled weakly at Susanna. "I just have my ways, I guess."

"It's high time they have one place," Susanna turned her head to whisper. "And one mamm."

Ella hung her head, feeling pale all the way down to her toes.

"It's nothin' to be ashamed of," Susanna said, glancing in Ella's direction. "Everyone knows my brother's seein' you . . . and most would have you married by this fall already. Let me tell you that I don't think Ivan can ever do any better. You are exactly what he needs."

"Thanks," Ella said with a nod, hoping this would suffice. She really didn't want to justify her hesitation — at least not to Ivan's sister.

"I'm done again," Mary said, raising a plate high above her head.

"Put it back here. Don't drop it," Ella said.

Mary laid the dish carefully on the countertop. "Are there anymore?" she asked, standing on tiptoes to search the counter.

"No, we're all done," Ella said. "Go on into the living room — and take Sarah with you. I'll be in for prayers soon."

Mary walked over to the end of the kitchen table and extracted Sarah from the bench with a pull on her arm. Sarah sleepily followed as the two girls went hand in hand to the living room.

"You're a good mamm already," Susanna said, approval in her voice.

"I try," Ella said. "Do you think Ivan's ready for evening prayers? I imagine we'd best get back to your place before it gets much later."

"Yah, we'd better get back," Susanna said, leading the way into the living room. Ivan was sitting in his rocker, a Bible open on his lap. He looked up and smiled when Ella entered, his blue eyes on her face. Ella lowered her head, keeping her eyes on Mary and Sarah.

"May I sit beside you?" she asked the two girls. When they nodded, she took a seat on the edge of the couch.

"We'd best have prayers now, Ivan," Susanna said. "Mamm and Daett have been alone long enough."

"I agree," Ivan said. "And thanks for the supper, Susanna."

Ella nodded her agreement. Already, Ivan and she were like a couple, the children gathered around, both of them thanking their guest for what she had brought. Ella sat back on the couch and let the feeling rush over her. Maybe this wouldn't be so bad. They would be the mistress and master of their own house, with the children *Da Hah* had already given, and then with the children *Da Hah* would surely give in the future.

Ivan opened the prayer book, and his eyes searched the pages as he turned them . . . until he seemed satisfied. He began to read slowly, about the Good Shepherd who cared for His sheep. The words were familiar to Ella. At the end, Ivan simply slid from the rocker, turned, and knelt beside it. Susanna and Ella immediately followed suit. Ella, while on her knees, helped Mary and Sarah turn around. Little baby Barbara was left to kick her legs on the blanket.

In a mellowed version of his preacher's voice, Ivan read the prayer through.

Ella listened. She liked the sound of his voice. This wasn't quite the way he used to sound during his Sunday sermons — before he changed. His old version of a sermon was to thunder against all the evils — real and imagined — that crossed his mind.

"Amen," Ivan said, closing his prayer.

Ella waited until he had gotten halfway to his feet before she took her hand off Mary's shoulder.

"Time for bed now," she said to both the girls. "Come and I'll tuck you in."

"The baby doesn't sleep in our bedroom," Mary announced. "Not like she does when we're with you."

Ella nodded. She hadn't known, but of course Ivan would keep the baby in his bedroom. It made perfect sense.

"Your daett has to watch her," Ella whispered in Mary's ear. "And he can't do that if she's upstairs and he's . . ."

"No, he can't," Mary said as Sarah nodded soberly.

Ella could feel Ivan's eyes on the back of her neck, but she didn't turn around. Quickly she took both girls' hands in hers. "I'll be right back," she said in Susanna's direction.

"They can put themselves to bed," Ivan said, his rocker creaking on the floor.

"I guess I like to spoil them," she said, turning to face him.

His eyes were friendly and warm, so perhaps he wouldn't complain that she had contradicted him. If she were to be his wife, he needed to know her ways.

"They can take some spoilin', I guess," he said, dropping his eyes to the open Bible on his lap.

Ella nodded. He hadn't disapproved, but that still left much unexplained. Did he tolerate public disagreements?

"I'll wait for you, so take your time," Susanna said, her voice low. "It's going to be rough walking home in the snow."

"Yah," Ella said. "The snowstorm. I guess I forgot." She glanced out the window where the snow was still falling heavily.

"Maybe you'd best both stay here?" Ivan questioned, concern on his face.

"I would," Susanna said, "but Mamm and Daett can't be left alone."

"Then let me shovel some sort of path for you," Ivan said, getting to his feet.

"I wouldn't trouble myself," Susanna said. "The wind will blow any path shut pretty quick."

"It'll last long enough for you to get to the house, " Ivan said, reaching for his coat and motioning with his head toward Ella.

"I can make it in snow," Ella said.

Susanna thought about it and then said, "But it would make it easier, yah?"

"It looks like we don't have much to say about it," Ella said as Ivan's back disappeared out the washroom door. She held open the stair door with Sarah's hand still in hers, contemplating the complete darkness up the steps.

"I'll get the light from the kitchen," Ella said. "Just wait for me here." She hurried off and quickly returned. With the kerosene lamp held high, Ella followed the girls' hesitant steps up the stairs. In the bedroom they quickly undressed themselves. Ella helped Sarah pull her nightgown over her head as Mary raced them. Ella noticed and slowed down for just a few seconds so Mary could gain ground.

"I got done first . . . and all by myself!" Mary proclaimed.

"Yah, you did," Ella said. "And that is *gut.*"

"I'll be fast too . . . when I'm big," Sarah said, jumping in the bed and snuggling under the covers.

"Yes, you will. Goodnight," Ella said tucking in both girls. She took the kerosene lamp, walked out of the room, and shut the door gently behind her. Quietly she returned downstairs.

Susanna was at the front door, her heavy black winter coat on. Ella retrieved her shawl and dress coat from the kitchen, slipping them on, along with her bonnet, and followed Susanna outside into the storm. Ivan was nowhere to be seen, but he had left a narrow path that disappeared into the swirl of snow.

"Here we go," Susanna said, laughing, her voice brave. "I guess we did need a path shoveled."

"Yah, I would say so," Ella said, gasping

as her foot nearly slipped.

She grabbed on to Susanna's heavy winter coat and hung on. Her balance regained, she tottered along, joining in with Susanna's giggles. Carefully they followed the little strip of path and were quickly swallowed up in the darkness.

"You think he's goin' in the right direction?" Susanna asked. "We could get lost out here."

"I think so," Ella said. "That's what my sense of direction says at least. Aren't we going downhill?"

"I guess so," Susanna said, moving forward again.

Time seemed to stand still in the shadowy darkness. The distance across was not far, but they had been walking for what seemed like ages. How quickly the world could change. Only hours ago she had arrived, and now the place could barely be recognized. Ella slipped again, saved by her grasp on Susanna's heavy coat.

"It must be my Sunday boots," Ella gasped. "I can't seem to keep on my feet."

"It's more than that," Susanna hollered into the wind. "But we'll make it."

Ivan's form appeared suddenly, like a ghost out of the whiteness.

Susanna cried in surprise, stopping so

quickly Ella bumped into her.

"It's my boots," Ella said again. "They're slick."

"Did you hurt yourself?" Susanna asked, her voice sounding frozen as she offered her hand until Ella was steady again.

"Nee," Ella whispered. "I'm fine."

"We're almost there," Ivan hollered above the storm. "I can see the house ahead."

"You sure you're taking us right?" Susanna hollered back.

"Yes," he replied.

"You're tired, Ivan. Let me take a turn," Susanna yelled at her brother's back.

"I can take a turn too," Ella said. "Anything to keep warm."

"I might take you up on that," Ivan yelled back, stepping off to the side and handing Susanna the shovel. She gamely attacked the drifts.

"The house is over there," Ivan said, pointing into the darkness.

Susanna adjusted her direction slightly.

"It's quite a night," Ivan said, turning to Ella. "I hope people are careful out on a night like this. No one could get far on these roads."

"You be careful yourself going back," Ella replied.

Ivan laughed heartily. "I will. But I do

think I'd better check the barn after I get you to the *dawdy haus.* One of the cows could be down."

"You think so?" Ella asked. "Were you having problems?"

"No," he said, glancing toward Susanna's back. "I'm just making certain."

"My turn," Ella said, slipping past him and tapping Susanna's coat.

Susanna handed her the shovel, blowing her breath out with a huge, "Whee!" She unhooked the top snaps of her heavy coat. "I was getting warm."

"That's more than I can say," Ella said, peering off into the darkness, faintly seeing the frame of a house ahead. She dug in with the shovel, heaving the snow downwind. She kept the path only a shovel wide. As they neared the front steps, she could still breathe easily. Gratefully she handed the shovel to Ivan when he offered to take it.

With a flourish he completed the last few feet.

Before the two women could open the front door, they heard Ivan say, "You girls take care of yourselves!" He disappeared quickly up the little path.

FIVE

As Susanna opened the door, the dim light of the kerosene lamp fell on her father, standing at the door to his bedroom. His mouth was working silently, his hand motioning for them to come.

"Daett, what's wrong?" Susanna called. "Is it Mamm?"

"She's not been well now . . . for over an hour," he whispered.

Susanna rushed past him.

As the elderly man tottered in the doorway, Ella took his arm, steadying his frail body.

"Joanna's been moanin' ever since we went to bed," the old man said. "I couldn't wake her. Now she can't talk. She can't even seem to move. She hasn't been well all week."

"Susanna will know what to do." Ella gently pulled on his arm, guiding him into the bedroom. Whatever the problem was, he might best be at his wife's side.

Susanna was bent over the slight form on the bed, her hand on her mamm's forehead. A low moan filled the eerie darkness.

Ella felt the fingers of Susanna's daett grip her arm.

"She's not doin' well," the old man whispered.

Susanna turned to Ella. "You'd best get Ivan . . . and quick."

"Of course," Ella said. "I think he was going to the barn, not the house."

"Maybe there's still a path he left you can follow. I'd go, but I'd better be stayin' with Mamm and Daett."

Ella nodded, gently loosening the old man's fingers from her arm. "I have to go for help," she whispered.

"She's really bad," he moaned.

"Perhaps we can get her some help." Ella glanced at the dark outside the windows. The storm outside would hardly allow any of them to reach the local clinic for help.

He seemed to realize the same thing and with a moan, moved slowly toward the bed.

"You had best go . . . quick," Susanna said, her voice raised just enough to carry across the room. "Her breathin' seems to be slowin' down."

Ella left the bedroom, her warm clothing still on, and searched quickly for some form of light. A trip all the way to the barn would be even more serious than the crossing had been from the main house. If she lost Ivan's trail . . . The thought sent a pang of fear through her.

A lower cupboard looked promising, but it contained only kettles and dishes. Ella tried a drawer, with the same result. She then glanced on top of the upper cabinets and saw the end of a flashlight. Grabbing the light, she made a fast exit out the door.

The storm had, if anything, increased. Great gusts of snow blew across the narrow path already half filled with snow. She was frightened at the thought the track might be completely filled in before she had time to return. With the wind in her face, Ella jumped down the last two steps. She rushed up the path, the flashlight of little help, her eyes open for any signs of a fresh path toward the barn.

Her hopes sank when she neared the house and found not a shoveled path but only footprints headed toward the barn. Here and there she found an occasional scuff off the side, made by Ivan's shovel as he propelled himself along. With no shovel herself, Ella forged ahead, occasionally tak-

ing a leap launching her to the next foot-
print.

Her light made meager stabs in the darkness as she maneuvered from hole to hole,
the snow overflowing her boots. At last she
saw the outline of the barn and, from inside,
a dim light.

Ella struggled with the door, and nearly
fell over backward when it opened from the
inside.

"What are you doin' here?" Ivan asked,
his lantern held high.

"Your mamm's in a bad way!" Ella gasped.
"You'd best come right away."

Ivan didn't hesitate. Shielding the lantern
with his coat, he started out the door. Ella,
feeling the sting of pain in her boots, held
up her hand to hold him back.

"I have to dump the snow out of my
boots," she said.

He bent over to help her loosen the boot
ties, bringing a three legged stool over for
her to sit on. Ella hurriedly removed the
boots, turned them upside down, and shook
out the offending snow.

Ivan waited till she was ready before
wrestling the barn door open again and
holding it from slamming shut until she was
outside. He took her hand and helped her
through the footprints, almost lifting her at

times with the vigor of his pulls.

At the path by the house, he released her hand, and Ella walked in front of him.

Minutes later they arrived at the shelter of the *dawdy haus* porch, the wind less severe there. Ivan stepped around her to open the front door. Ella followed him inside, his lantern now out of his coat, the living room flooded by its golden light.

Ella waited as Ivan set the lantern on the floor, threw his coat aside, and rushed toward the bedroom. Susanna appeared in the doorway as he got there, distress written all over her face.

"She's gone, Ivan," she said. "Mamm's gone."

"Is Daett with her?" Ivan asked, taking his sister gently in his arms.

Susanna mumbled a reply Ella understood as "Yes."

Ella took off her coat and slipped past the two. She sat by the old man, who was still perched on the edge of the bed, his wife's hands in his.

"She's gone," he whispered as Ella touched his shoulder in compassion. "Now she is with *Da Hah* . . . where the angels sing their songs. There never was a better woman in all the world."

Ella squeezed his shoulder tenderly, noticing how thin he was.

"If I could go with her tonight, I would gladly do so. We have been together so long . . . just the two of us. Do you think *Da Hah* would grant such a thing? I have no more use for this world with Joanna gone."

He turned his head toward the ceiling, and Ella could see his sunken eyes in the dim flicker of the kerosene lamp. They were brimming with tears.

"*Da Hah* has His reasons," she whispered, surprised at herself. "Reasons we cannot see."

His eyes blinked and fixed on her face. He pondered her for a long moment, and then recognition slowly came.

"You are Ella Yoder," he said, his voice rasping in the still room.

Behind her Ella heard movement at the bedroom door and then silence. Apparently Ivan and Susanna had noticed the conversation and decided to leave them alone for a moment.

"Yah," she whispered.

"You lost that Aden awhile back, didn't you? Before you could marry him?"

She nodded, afraid to trust her voice.

"Then you have also suffered — and so young," he said, nodding slowly, his eyes returning to the face on the bed. "My heart

51

can never be comforted though . . . not in this world. It is for you young people that life goes on. Do you think I will see her again soon?"

"Yes," Ella said, her voice trembling.

"I loved her," he whispered, barely able to say the words, struggling to gather himself. There followed moments of silence. No words were necessary. Then the old man spoke. "We must prepare her for the ground — as *Da Hah* has now taken her. I am too weak for such a thing, but Susanna will help you. And the people must be told."

"There's quite a storm outside," Ella said. "But Ivan will notify people in the morning. It may be that long before anyone can get out anyway."

"Yah," he said with a slow nod. "So it is. But *Da Hah* knows what He's doing."

Ella took her hand from his shoulder, ready to go.

He spoke again. "The clock must be stopped. Can you do that?"

"I can," Ella said. "Susanna will also know the time."

He nodded, his eyes steady on his wife's face.

Ella left him, stepping back into the bright glow of the living room and finding Ivan gone.

"He's gone back to check on the girls," Susanna said, answering the question in Ella's eyes.

"Perhaps I should stay with them, and Ivan should remain here," Ella said. "Oh, and your daett wants the clock stopped."

Susanna raised her eyes toward the tall old clock in the corner.

Ella looked. The big pendulum was no longer swinging.

"I stopped it while you were with him. Thank you for being there for him."

"He needed someone to talk to."

"And it was good that it was you, Ella. It's hard to talk with your children at times like these. He loved Mamm a lot."

"I could see that," Ella said. She noticed that Susanna had started a fire in the woodstove. A tub of water sat on the stove, steam already rising from it.

"I don't think I need help," Susanna said, following Ella's glance. "But perhaps you could stay with Daett. I don't want him alone or being in there when I clean Mamm."

Ella nodded and returned to the bedroom. She took the old man's arm gently.

"Why don't you come out to the living room with me while Susanna tends to the washing?"

He nodded and followed her without resistance.

Ella held on to his arm, wondering at the frailness of his body. She didn't remember him looking like this at last Sunday's preaching service. But perhaps she hadn't noticed. Did one grow older suddenly, in one night, when the loss was so great to bear? Ella paused, helping him into a rocker. She pulled out a chair from the kitchen table and sat down beside him.

He glanced at Susanna once as she went past with a bowl of water, a towel, and a washcloth draped over her arm. Then his eyes found the clock in the corner, and he seemed satisfied. His body sagged in the rocker.

"She was so beautiful," his hoarse voice whispered. "She came up for cousin Fred's wedding as one of the table waiters with some other boy I don't even remember anymore. Now she's crossed over before I have. It's because she was so much better than me."

After a few minutes of silence, save for the gentle creak of the rocker, the front door opened, mounds of snow spilling onto the hardwood floor. Ivan entered, bending over to brush the snow with his gloved hands, throwing it outside before carefully shutting the door.

"The storm's worse," he said, taking his heavy coat off. "The girls are all asleep, but, Ella, do you think you could stay with them for the night while I stay here with Daett?"

"Of course." Ella rose from her chair and pulled on her coat and shawl.

"You want me to walk over with you?" Ivan asked, his eyes searching her face.

Ella shook her head and offered a weary smile.

"I'm sure you can make it," Ivan said, his hand on the doorknob. "The path is still there."

Ella slipped her boots back on, and Ivan held the door open for her. With a quick glance at his face, she stepped out onto the porch. The wildness of the storm nearly overwhelmed her as Ivan pushed the door shut.

With a burst of energy she launched out, finding remnants of the path still clear enough to make her way, just as Ivan had said. Her breath almost gone, she reached the house and jerked the front door open. Light flickered across the floor from the kerosene lamp Ivan had left on the desk.

Ella shook off her coat at the front door, took her boots off, and then grabbed the lamp. She opened the bedroom door on the main floor and checked on baby Barbara. Then she took the lamp upstairs to check on the girls. Seeing they were okay, she glanced into another doorway — a guest room. She moved inside, took off her outer garments, and wearily crawled into the bed.

The night had been so much more than Ella had expected. But it was good and right that she was here. She drifted to sleep with the thought that surely *Da Hah* had known she would be needed here tonight.

SIX

When Ella awoke, the darkness was hanging heavily outside the bedroom window. Only the morning chill spoke of the soon breaking dawn. For a long moment she lay there, not remembering where she was. As the memory of the previous night returned, panic surged through her. *The girls! What will my early-morning presence in the house mean to the girls?* Always before she'd told them an overnight stay wasn't possible. Now, through no fault of her own, it suddenly had become possible. What would she tell them when they asked why she was there? And what would she say when they asked if she could stay another night . . . perhaps even tonight if the storm didn't let up?

What good would it do to think of that now? No good at all, she decided. She wearily got out of bed and searched in the unfamiliar dresser drawer, finding matches

57

where she expected them. She lit the kerosene lamp. With the wick turned as low as possible, she dressed. There was no choice but to wear the clothes from yesterday. With the storm apparently ended outside, she could surely go home. She would come back tomorrow for the funeral. Another night here was out of the question.

Ella left the lamp in the bedroom, keeping the door ajar to light the hall. She opened the girls' bedroom door. They slept as she had left them, tight under the covers with only their heads sticking out. She wanted to kiss them and take them into her arms, but she held back. They would awaken soon anyway.

Was it possible she could yet escape without them knowing she was still here? Desperation filled her — a desire to drive off in her buggy before the girls knew. That would prevent the questions over why she was there and why it couldn't happen again.

Maybe someday she would stay. Yes, she could marry Ivan, regardless of how she felt, and it would help the girls' situation. Ella sucked in her breath so loudly at the thought that she glanced at the girls. Thankfully they still breathed deeply, lost in slumber. She knew Ivan would be agreeable to marriage, whatever her terms. There was little question there.

But she needed more time. She must allow her heart to follow with its feelings. She could still have the girls during the week, and Ivan could continue to wait a few more months for a wife. They would soon enough have the rest of their lives to spend together. And her love for the girls would continue to grow. There would be no more suppers here at Ivan's house before then, of that she was determined.

Ella retrieved the kerosene lamp from across the hall and made her way downstairs. A quick glance through the window seemed to show a light in the barn. She continued to Ivan's room and quickly checked on baby Barbara. Then she moved back into the kitchen, left the lamp on the table, and returned to the living room window.

The sky had just the slightest hint of light on the horizon. The cloud cover was still heavy, but snow was no longer falling. When the barn door opened, a dim glow of light spilled onto the snow, revealing Ivan's form in the doorway.

He must be staring out toward the road, Ella thought. *Has he been able to get out and spread the news of his mamm's passing already?* She looked down. There were no footprints in the snow. No path shoveled to the road. The road itself still looked closed. So though he hadn't been out yet, he would surely leave soon. Necessity demanded it.

She would fix breakfast for the girls, and Ivan could eat over at the *dawdy haus.* This might keep the girls from further associating the two of them together. That decided, there really was no rush. This was a Sunday morning, and the girls would likely sleep for some time. She might as well make herself useful in some way, and helping with the milking seemed the most obvious choice. Since the snowstorm meant no one else knew about the death in the family, the neighbors weren't here to take over the duties of the house and farm.

What was she to wear? She certainly couldn't milk in her best dress. Ella paced the floor, thinking, watching the road for the headlights of county snowplows that would open the roads so Ivan could get out. *The front yard will need clearing for the funeral,* she thought. *When help finally comes there will certainly be plenty to do, the teams of horses pulling flip shovels, tossing and pushing snow into high banks.*

But for now she needed to help with the milking. First she had to find a chore dress. Perhaps there would be one in Ivan's bedroom. He would not likely have disposed of Lois's dresses. The thought of going through the closet in Ivan's room left her cold, but clothes were clothes, whoever had worn them in the past. She needed to be practical about this. Wasn't she already trying to be practical about her marriage plans? Wearing Lois's dress might help things along.

Ella retrieved the lamp from the kitchen and cautiously opened the bedroom door. The bedcovers were still thrown on the floor, and baby clothing was strewn around. Baby Barbara slept soundly in the crib. The man certainly could use a wife. But what would Ivan think if he knew she was in here? And wearing one of Lois's dresses was not something that could be hidden when she arrived in the barn.

Lois had been Ivan's wife — unlike what Ella had been to Aden. What would Ivan think about that? The difference between them was vast. Ella carefully set the kerosene lamp on a dresser. When she opened the closet door, the baby stirred. Ella froze until the even breathing started again. As she expected, one side of the closet still held dresses. *Are they the right size?* Ella couldn't remember exactly how Lois had looked, but she reached for a dress. A dark blue one looked worn enough for her purposes, and she took it off the rack.

Holding the dress up against her side, there seemed no reason the dress shouldn't fit. Perhaps a little long, but that wouldn't matter for chores. Now where to change? Ella glanced around. There was no way she could undress in here. She made a quick dash upstairs to the spare room, changed, and then came back down again.

Ella left the kerosene lamp burning in the living room in case the girls should awaken before she came back. A search in the closet by the front door revealed an old coat and boots, no doubt the ones Lois used to wear. Ivan apparently had never gotten rid of any of his wife's things.

A picture of Ivan's face rose before her. The distress in it, the words he had spoken to her in anguish, "I loved Lois too much. And this is why *Da Hah* has taken her from me."

Yet *Da Hah* had also taken Aden, and she loved him just as much. Perhaps that's why they were safe together, she and Ivan. Ella felt a touch of her old bitterness rising as she stood in the cold mudroom. What a messed-up world, but there was one small comfort. At least she would never be able to love Ivan as much as she had loved Aden.

With coat and boots on, Ella opened the

front door, kicking a small drift of snow away with her foot and finding the steps already cleaned. Ivan must have made another round through the path this morning after the snow stopped. At the junction toward the barn, Ella expected to follow only footsteps, but she found a freshly shoveled path. Gratefully she made her way to the barn door.

For a moment she paused to look toward the east. Gray clouds still hung heavy on the horizon, but she could see small patches of dark blue here and there. The sun would soon be up, and the snowfall obviously was over.

The smell of the barn greeted her as she opened the door and stepped inside. The scene was familiar, with the line of cows tied to stanchions. Ivan, sitting on a three-legged stool, had his back turned toward her and one knee was propped against a cow's leg. He must have heard her but likely thought she was Susanna.

"I told you I could handle the chores."

"It's me," Ella said. "I can help."

Ivan jerked his head up, scraping it on the cow's belly. The animal lurched forward. Only his knee held the cow's leg back long enough for him to snatch the half-filled bucket of milk to safety.

Ella laughed.

And Ivan turned red.

"That's not nice," Ivan said. "I wasn't expectin' you."

"I wasn't expectin' to come out, but I thought you could use help. And I hope you don't mind the dress. It was Lois's."

His eyes swept her figure. "You're wearing her dress *and* coat."

"Yah," she said. "Is it wrong? If so, I can change back into my own clothes. I only had my good clothes to wear."

He swallowed hard, his blue eyes finding her face. "No . . ." He forced a smile. "That's as it should be. Are the girls still asleep?"

"They were when I checked last, and I left the light on in the living room . . . just in case."

He nodded, seeming to approve, and turned back to the cow.

"Have you let people know yet?" Ella asked.

He shook his head but didn't turn around.

"Let me finish the milkin' then. And you can go tell them. The undertaker needs to be told."

"It's still early, and the roads aren't passable."

"The people need to be told. And the

undertaker can be called from the pay phone. Surely you can reach that far," she said, surprised at her boldness.

"Yah," he said, considering her words. "In this you are right. I guess I was still in my own world of chores and things."

"They would have come to help if you had let them know."

"The snow just quit, so I couldn't go before. It passed suddenly, like these storms do."

"Were you up all night?" she asked. "You poor man."

His back relaxed and he shrugged. "Maybe I got an hour or so in the rocker. Daett was mourning most of the night."

"Let me milk the rest of the cows then. I grew up around this."

"This one's almost done." He got up and pulled the milk pail away from the cow. "There's only four more to go."

"My hands still work," she said, kneading them to demonstrate and smiling.

He nodded, giving her the milk bucket.

Ella emptied it slowly into the strainer while Ivan watched.

When she finished, he took a deep breath and exhaled. He looked relieved.

"I know how to milk," Ella assured him, taking a three-legged stool off the wall and carefully sitting down next to a cow. She began the familiar rhythm of milking a cow by hand. Behind her the barn door opened and shut as Ivan left without further conversation.

Ella moved her fingers quickly, feeling the power in her hands, her muscles toned over the years.

"It's been a long time," she whispered. "I suppose it will be good to have cows to milk again, and to have a husband whom I can help with the chores." She let her thoughts wander as she milked . . . about being a wife and full-time mamm.

The cow was out of milk, and it turned its head back to Ella. With a jerk the cow brought its leg forward, and Ella would have lost the milk pail if she hadn't lunged forward, throwing her weight against the cow's leg.

"Easy there!" Ella laughed. "Sorry, bossy. I guess I got lost in my thoughts. You won't like me now will you? Maybe I can do better next time." *Next time. Will there be a next time?* Ella got to her feet and emptied the milk into the strainer. This could be her place in a few months. Her house and barn — if she desired it. "It's *gut,*" she whispered, "and right that I love the girls. But if only I could love the man."

SEVEN

As Ella emptied the last bucket of milk into the strainer, she heard the recognizable rattle of a snowplow on the road. When the milk had run through, she pulled the cloth screen out of the strainer, glancing around for Ivan's slop bucket. With a flip of her hand she tossed the dripping cloth in that direction. For a moment the cloth caught on the edge and then toppled inside.

"That's a good toss," she said, laughing as she realized she was talking to herself again. Being in the barn and milking the cows had awakened great waves of homesickness that now swept over her. She missed her family. If she were at home, Dora would be here helping her milk, and perhaps even Clara and Monroe. Eli too, though truth be told, he was gone now. Eli, with his stubborn heart, leaving to be near his *Englisha* girl-friend. The loss hung heavy in the damp air of the barn, and Ella set the milk bucket on the floor as tears formed, evidence to her sore heart.

Behind her a cow banged against the metal clasp holding her neck, reminding Ella of her present duties. That was *gut.* Responsibilities were a part of the flow of life, and they lifted a person out of despair and despondency. The cow mooed loudly, causing Ella to jump as she rushed to the front of the stalls to loosen the clasps. With the stanchions open, the cows seemed to know the way out, but they managed to bang their heads against the side boards anyway.

"Come on!" Ella hollered, slapping the backside of the nearest one. The slap was in vain as the animal didn't increase its speed but ambled along, swinging from side to side in her slow walk.

Ella paused, listening. *Are those voices? Yes. People are outside and coming closer to the barn.*

The barn door opened with a swoosh, snow flying everywhere. Ella flinched in surprise as two Amish boys entered, stomping their feet on the floor.

"Did we startle you?" the older teenager asked with a smile.

Ella didn't recognize the boys — neighbors likely, notified of the need by Ivan's report.

"You shouldn't come bargin' in like that," Ella said, trying to catch her breath. "You'll scare a poor soul senseless."

The boys laughed.

"Any choring still need doing?" the youngest asked.

"I milked the last cow," she said. "But the milk needs to be cooled. I don't really know what else. Is Ivan around anywhere?"

"Not now. He came by our place on his way to make a phone call. We'll look around," the older said. "Finish what we can find. Ivan might be back by then."

The boys looked around for work, and after a few moments the younger asked, "Say, are you Ivan's girlfriend?"

Ella felt her cheeks flush. She probably should answer as quickly as possible. Their amusement would only increase if she waited or denied the obvious. Instead she took her time, stepping through the stanchions to face them.

"Now, would that be any of your business?" She tried her best to sound put off by their question, but the truth was she almost wanted to laugh at their frank, youthful curiosity.

Both boys raised their eyebrows at her attempt to hide her smile, their own ensuing laughter filling the morning air.

"We didn't mean to stick our noses where they don't belong," the older said. "You know what I mean. We were just askin'."

"Well, then," Ella said, "I suppose I am. Now both of you get busy, and don't be askin' any other girls such questions. It's not fittin'."

The boys grabbed the heavy milk cans, showing little sign of the weight they contained, and disappeared toward the milk house and cooling tank.

Ella figured she should head back to the house in case the girls had awakened. As she stepped out of the barn, the first of the horse teams pulled in dragging a snow scoop. In the crisp morning air, with the sun just breaking out from behind the clouds, the young driver waved to her, his horses' nostrils spouting white streams of air.

"Get-up," Ella heard the driver yell as he held the huge snow scoop down. The horses knew what to do. At the end of the run, they turned sideways, and the driver flipped the scoop over, the snow tumbling into the beginnings of a pile.

Ella followed the snow path to the house, glancing over her shoulder. The driver was preparing for another run, and down the road another team was coming, the scoop tipped upside down and dragging behind. They would soon have the whole area between the house and barn cleared.

Figures appeared further down the road, walking. They looked like women, their forms gray and black against the white snow. They walked briskly, and Ella hurried to the house. At present no one was likely to come to the main house, but she needed to get inside to check on the girls.

Ella tossed her coat on a chair and opened the wood box in the kitchen, only to find it empty. Did Ivan keep the woodpile against the house replenished? At her house she had an outside opening directly into the wood box, but many of these older houses didn't. There was only one way to find out.

She pulled the boots back on, slipping into Lois's coat, and picked up a snow shovel leaning against the washroom wall. From the porch, she looked around the edge of the house. She didn't see an obvious wood-pile. Was it buried in the snow or did Ivan keep his wood somewhere else? Wherever the wood was, a long dig might be required. Ella looked down the side of the house and noticed a small rickety lean-to some yards away.

Yah, the woodpile. She headed in that direction, shoveling snow as she went. On the north side, the snow had drifted high against the lean-to, so she detoured around to the south side. Here the clear outlines of cut wood were evident under the snow. Carefully she knocked the shovel against the wood, dislodging the white piles. She filled her arms with wood and moved carefully back to the washroom door, making sure her feet didn't slip on the steps.

One load would have been enough for her purposes, but Ella went back for more. This might soon be her house, and already responsibility for it draped over her like a blanket. She only wished the necessary feelings for Ivan would envelop her as easily as the obvious needs for a woman in the family did. Oh, to just feel even a tingle in her emotions at the sight of Ivan. Would the time come when she would deeply desire his arms around her?

Aden's love had been like that, but the memory was almost faded now. With a sigh Ella dropped her load into the wood box. The pieces clattering loudly as they spilled against the walls of the box. She grabbed a few cut logs that seemed driest and put them in the stove. She pulled a few thin slivers of wood off the pieces, lit them with a match, and held them under the logs. Unexpected help came from the coals under the ashes, their warmth still there from last night. She found a small kettle, dipped water from the bucket into it, and slid it onto the stove. The fire would continue on its own, so she could now go upstairs to get the girls up.

At home on Chapman Road she would have let them sleep in, but with the preparations for the funeral, someone might need an item from the main house and stop by. Surely they would think it strange if the girls were still in bed. As their mother-to-be, she needed them awake and up.

Ella was halfway up the stairs when baby Barbara cried from the bedroom below. Something must have awakened her. Ella hurried back down and opened the door. Barbara was wide awake, kicking her feet, her diaper obviously heavy.

"Phew!" Ella said, laughing as she came closer. "So that's why you're up."

Barbara's face broke into a broad smile as her hands started going as energetically as her feet.

"So you're glad to see me?" Ella asked, smiling gently.

Lifting her out of her crib, Ella lay Barbara on the dresser top. Apparently this was where Ivan changed diapers. Nothing else looked suitable for that purpose. The baby continued to make chortling noises and kicked her legs as Ella worked.

At least Ivan knew how to change diapers. Not many men did — or were willing to try. He really wouldn't have to either. There were relatives who would take on the care of the three girls if Ivan consented to splitting them up. That Ivan wanted to keep them together as a family showed his heart. He was a *gut* man and would make a *gut* husband.

"I'll love him someday," Ella said out loud, and the baby laughed heartily, still kicking her feet.

"That comment wasn't meant for you, silly."

As Ella lifted the newly diapered Barbara from the dresser, she heard the patter of little feet coming down the stairs. She paused, listening with a warm heart to the familiar sound. Stepping outside the bedroom, she peeked up the stairs, but saw no one. Soft noises came from the kitchen. Ella entered to find both girls seated on the table bench rubbing their eyes sleepily.

"You're up — and all by yourselves."

They stared at her.

"Why are you here?" Mary asked. "You

said you couldn't stay."

Ella caught her breath, remembering the complications. She put baby Barbara in her high chair and sat down next to Mary.

"Mary, your grandmother died last night over at the *dawdy haus,*" Ella said as she gave her a hug. "That's why I'm here."

"What does 'died' mean?" Sarah asked.

"It means your *grossmamm* went to heaven," Ella said. "The angels came to get her last night."

"Like they did for our mamm," Mary said. "The angel came for her too. That's why we have another mamm now. One that lives down here with us."

Ella caught a glimpse of movement outside the living room window and took the opportunity to distract Mary.

"Come over here and see this," Ella said, taking Sarah's hand. Mary followed slowly behind them.

"See the long black car at the *dawdy haus?* They have come to pick up your *grossmamm*'s body."

The two girls watched in silence. They could see the front door of the *dawdy haus* held open by Susanna. Their father appeared first, followed by *Englisha* people, and then the stretcher covered with a white sheet.

"Is *grossmamm* covered up?" Mary asked.

"Yah, they will take her into town, and then bring her back this afternoon."

"I thought she went to heaven," Sarah said as the stretcher was slid into the black car.

"Her soul was taken by the angels. That's just her body," Ella said.

They watched as the doors to the black car closed and it pulled slowly across the snowy lawn and onto the main road.

"Now we need to get your breakfast," Ella said, turning away from the window. Soon she had oatmeal and eggs cooked. The girls ate eagerly but silently. Ella didn't try to get them talking. Heavy things had happened while they slept, and it was best to allow their minds time to absorb it. She fed and cleaned up Barbara and then took her into the living room and put her on a blanket by the woodstove.

When they were finished, Mary and Sarah climbed up on chairs, wanting to help with the dishes. Ella allowed it. With the kitchen and dishes cleaned, Ella changed back to her own dress and then helped put boots and coats on the two oldest girls. When they were ready, she picked up the baby and bundled her into a warm blanket after putting on her coat and cap. She blew out the kerosene lamp and guided the girls out the door and carefully through the snow to the *dawdy haus.*

The girls were instructed to sit quietly and behave themselves. Ella then offered to help where she was needed, checking on the girls as necessary, and eventually allowing them to play quietly in an upstairs bedroom.

Lunch was served by the neighbors while everyone visited and pitched in to help.

The *grossmamm*'s body was returned in the late evening. Ella watched as the hearse pulled in from the main road, and the body was carried into the main bedroom downstairs. Ella would bring the girls down later to take them through the viewing line. Already a few buggies had pulled in, and a line was forming outside.

EIGHT

The next day the funeral was held. Buggies were parked all along the road at the grave-yard, the snow cleared away from the ditches, and the horses tied to the fence posts. Only a small path remained where the *Englisha* cars could creep through. The drivers were mostly locals and respectful. At one point, Ella heard the impatient roar of a sports car, but when heads turned, the driver must have thought better of his speed and moved past the graveyard with hardly a sound.

The sky hung heavy with clouds, the low mountains in the west completely hidden from view. Ella, with Mary and Sarah beside her, was standing only a few feet from the open grave. Young Bishop Miller, from the neighboring district to the north, was get-ting ready to lead in the graveside prayer. It struck Ella as odd that he should be presid-ing at the funeral of the woman who might have become her mother-in-law. Bishop Miller had only months ago declared his love and asked for her hand in marriage. Ella had turned him down, much to the dismay of her mamm and daett. She glanced across the crowd to where her parents stood among the many mourners. They looked older than Ella remembered. She shuddered to think she would someday return here to see them buried.

Bishop Miller stared at the grave, his black hat in one hand, his prayer book in the other. He led out in a strong voice. He was a grand sight, really. He was confident as usual, his eyes focused on the white page. He was as good looking as ever. Ella couldn't help but hope he had asked some girl or widow for her hand in marriage by now — revealing that he had forsaken any dreams that she would change her mind. Yet from what she heard, the bishop was still single. Surely she had nothing to fear from him. Bishop Miller was a decent man, though a bit overconfident and eager in love. Surely he wouldn't bother her while she made up her mind about Ivan.

The bishop and Ella would have been wed this spring if she hadn't said no. She was the first woman who had resisted his advances. Perhaps he would find that hard to take. He was a man of great power among the people, yet there were guidelines for appropriate behavior — even for him — when it came to matters of the heart.

Bishop Miller concluded his prayer and placed his hat back on his head. A few of the young men stepped forward, and the soft thud of dirt against the wooden coffin began. Another body committed back to the earth from whence it had come.

Ella glanced down the line of gravestones. Aden's grave lay two rows over. She had avoided the spot when she came in with the girls. She'd noticed that Ivan had avoided the row of graves on the other side of the cemetery where his wife, Lois, was buried.

Two wounded hearts together, that's what they were. Perhaps *Da Hah* was trying to mend them both. Ella squeezed Mary's hand, who glanced up at her face, her eyes almost covered by her bonnet. The little girl shivered, and Ella quickly reached over to Sarah. She too was shivering. Ella pulled both girls against her and wrapped the bottom of her shawl over the top of them. Their shivers lessened.

Young boys and an occasional married man traded off with the shovels, and soon the mound was complete. Ella felt the move of the crowd as they slowly headed for their buggies. What did Ivan want done with his girls? He stood a few feet away, and she waited until she could catch his eye.

Naturally Ivan didn't stand beside her at the graveside. They weren't married yet, but now he approached her without hesitation. He knelt down to peek into his daughters' faces hidden under Ella's shawl and their bonnets.

"It's time to go," he whispered. "You'll go home with Ella from here. Then I'll pick you up as usual on Friday."

Mary nodded and Sarah shrugged her thin shoulders.

Ivan looked up at Ella and she nodded, her question answered. She needed to retrieve baby Barbara and get the girls out of the cold as soon as possible.

"They buried Mamm here too," Mary said, her hand pointing across the graveyard, her voice barely audible.

Ivan looked at her from eye level and reached to brush her cheek with his hand. "Mary, you do know that Mamm is in heaven, don't you? It's just her body that's in the grave."

"That's what Ella said," Mary whispered.

Ivan nodded.

Ella watched and wondered, *Oh, why can't I love this man? He has such a tender heart.*

"Why can't we all go home . . . back to *our* house?" Mary asked, a little louder now.

"Shhh . . ." Ivan whispered, brushing her cheek again. "You will go to Ella's place, and I'll pick you up there as usual. Be a good girl now."

Mary nodded, but it was obvious she hardly understood. How could she when even Ella didn't understand why *Da Hah* tore hearts apart and then tried to put them back together again so clumsily. Were the old people really right when they said *Da Hah* knew what was best? There sure wasn't much comfort in those words at the moment.

"I'll find Barbara," Ella said, as Ivan stood.

"Susanna has her," he said, motioning off to his left. "Thanks so much for what you've done. I know you didn't have to, and that it was hard. Especially stayin' overnight. I can only say *Da Hah* has been more than kind to me."

Ella nodded. That was a longer speech than he usually made, and she gave him a smile — warm, she hoped, and sincere.

He responded by moving his hand toward hers and then stopping. She could almost read his thoughts: *No. After all, this is public.*

Ivan finally nodded and moved away in silence, melting into the crowd.

Ella watched him go and then turned to where Susanna stood holding baby Barbara.

"They're sweet girls," Susanna said, handing Barbara over. "But they need a mamm."

Ella didn't respond, and Susanna apologized. "I'm so sorry. I didn't mean it quite so."

"Well, you're right. They do need a mamm. And perhaps someday I can be a real mamm to them."

"You would be just wonderful," Susanna said, looking relieved. "I really didn't mean anything by my careless words."

"I know," Ella said, shifting Barbara on her arm.

"I'll carry her to the buggy," Susanna said, offering to take the baby again.

Ella nodded and handed the baby back. They walked single file through the crowd, pulled along as everyone continued moving toward their buggies. Holding the girls' hands, Mary in front of her, and Sarah behind her, Ella pressed forward. A few people recognized them and nodded, but no one attempted conversation.

The clouds still hung heavily overhead and the mood was somber.

Ella helped the two girls into the buggy and reached back to Susanna for the baby. With Barbara inside, she was ready to climb in when a hand tugged on her arm.

"Ella!" her mamm said, gasping for air. "I thought I'd missed you . . . with all these people around."

"Mamm!" Ella said, turning with a cry of pleasure and embracing her mom. "I didn't know if I'd get a chance to talk with you. I did see you go through the viewing line."

"Yah, we sat out in the barn service," Lizzie said, gently releasing from their embrace. "It's been so long now. And we don't get to see much of you anymore."

Her daett stepped forward and said, "I guess our Ella is a big girl now."

"Oh Daett, it's so good to see you," Ella replied, uncertain whether to shake his hand or not. How did one greet one's father after not seeing him in a while? He nodded, giving her arm a quick squeeze.

"And the girls," Lizzie said, looking inside the buggy. "My, my . . . you two get bigger every day."

Mary and Sarah sat on the seat with broad smiles.

"Have you heard from Eli?" Ella asked. Wasn't that the question that lay close to all their hearts?

"He has an apartment in town," Lizzie whispered. She glanced around quickly. "They are talking of marriage, I'm afraid."

84

"The nurse . . . Pam?" Ella asked. But she knew the answer.

"It's for the best . . . that he's in town," Noah said, his head bent low. "I couldn't keep it from happening. And even another talk with Bishop Miller didn't do any good."

"It was when she came out on a Saturday night . . . right to the farm — that your daett put his foot down," Lizzie whispered.

"I don't blame you," Ella said to her father. "I knew there was some reason you asked him to leave, but I hadn't been told why."

"We didn't tell any of the other children," Lizzie said, glancing around again, her bonnet tilted back slightly for a better view. "Not even Dora knows, since they weren't home at the time, for which I am very thankful. What an example that would have set for the rest. And Eli knows better! I know he does, but he's so stubborn."

"I had to ask him to leave," her father said, speaking slowly, his shoulders bowed.

"I know, Daett," Ella said, reaching out to touch his arm. "No one blames you. And we all tried to speak with Eli. It's still up to each of us — the choices we make and answering for them."

"He's my son," Noah said, hanging his

head. "And it's a load almost too heavy to bear."

Ella hung on to the side of the buggy with her hand, keeping her eyes on the ground. What if they attracted attention with this conversation in public? Her mamm and daett were already suffering enough.

"Monroe doesn't seem to be affected much," Lizzie said, wiping her eyes. "At least for that we are thankful. And I think he has his eye on a girl in one of the south districts — Ezra Wagler's girl, Irene."

Ella searched her memory, but she came up with no familiar face. Still, she smiled. This was good news in the midst of the sorrow caused by Eli's actions.

"Dora's got a weddin' date next year," Lizzie said, attempting a smile through her tears. "She's doesn't say much about it, but I can tell she's happy."

"Norman always was a good match," Ella said.

"Are you going back to your house?" Noah asked.

Ella nodded.

"So you stayed at Stutzmans' last night?" he asked.

Ella nodded again. Surely her daett didn't think she would do anything inappropriate.

"With him in the house? Surely not. Not

even upstairs." Her father's voice rose.

Ella opened her mouth, but no sound came out. Apparently her daett did think her actions were questionable.

"Noah!" Lizzie whispered, her hand pulling on his arm. "Don't be ask'n such things. This is *Ella.*"

"Daett," Ella began, her voice trembling, "Ivan was over at the *dawdy haus* all night." Tears formed at the edges of her eyes. *How could he think . . .*

"It's because of Eli," Lizzie said, turning to Ella. "You must not hold this against your daett. He sees things wrong everywhere now. But he doesn't mean it — really."

"I am sorry," Noah said, squeezing her arm again. "I shouldn't allow my burden to spill over onto others. Will you forgive me, Ella?"

Ella felt her chest burning. Her daett had thought she would act inappropriately with Ivan. She met his eyes, still trying to hold back the tears.

"I am sorry," Noah said again, and Ella wiped her eyes, reaching for his arm.

"It's okay. I understand."

"Then let me get your horse on the road for you," Noah said, moving toward the front of the buggy.

"He loves you," Lizzie said, helping Ella

up the step.

Inside, Ella held the reins while her daett guided the horse onto the road. He slapped the horse's neck lightly, smiling, his hat pushed down on his head. The horse stepped forward and they were heading home.

Ella pulled Moonbeam to a complete stop at the main highway and glanced both ways. The road was completely empty of traffic. She slapped the reins and crossed, her horse trotting quickly and having no problem with the ice.

As she pulled up to Chapman Road and turned right, she could see that Joe had cleared the driveway all the way up to the barn. She had good renters in Joe and Ronda, and there was much to be thankful for. Pulling up to the hitching rail, she climbed down. As she reached for the tie rope under the seat, she turned to the girls and said, "Stay in the buggy."

Mary and Sarah nodded, staying on the seat while she unhitched. Once the horse was safely in the barn, she helped the two girls out. They walked carefully in front of her over the crusted snow, as Ella followed carrying baby Barbara.

As they went down the steps to the basement door, Ella wondered if this dear house that had come to mean so much to her in such a short time would be her house much longer. Would she soon be living at Ivan's place as his wife?

Nine

The early morning rush was over, and Ella had the second load of wash done. The dresses and diapers hung behind curtains in the basement, safe from the threat of the snow and moisture outside. Wearily she pulled out a kitchen chair and sat down. The warmth from the stove quickly embraced her. She realized she'd soon be asleep if she stayed put. Ella got to her feet again.

For a moment she was tempted to work on the new blanket. Mary and Sarah were playing quietly around her latest quilt project. Baby Barbara was on her special blanket behind her, and Ronda wouldn't be down to help with the quilt for another hour at least.

Yet Ella was determined to write in her journal today. She had wanted to ever since that evening at Ivan's place when his mother passed on. Now would be an excellent time.

She could take a few moments to begin her thoughts and then perhaps finish tonight after the girls were in bed.

So many emotions still swirled around her. Maybe clarity would come if she placed her thoughts on paper.

Ella added another piece of wood to the stove. With the damp wash hung to dry, the basement needed to stay warm enough. Even with the roaring fire she'd built, the moisture hung heavy in the air.

"We're playin' over here," Mary said, glancing up and catching her gaze from the other side of the room.

"Yah," Ella said, smiling toward the two of them. Baby Barbara's eyes focused on her as Ella pushed aside the curtain that partitioned off their sleeping quarters. Basement life would cease once she was Ivan's wife. That would be another *gut* thing to come out of their union.

What would she do with this house after the wedding? It had served her well, but more and more she was coming to see that it was meant for a husband and wife . . . not for her alone. Perhaps with her marriage to another man, she would give the house to Clara . . . or Dora. It didn't really matter, just so it was someone from the family. She would gladly give the place to

Eli if he would come back to the faith, but that chance seemed slim.

Ella returned to the table with the journal in her hand. Baby Barbara had turned over and was staring at the ceiling. Before Ella sat down, she moved Barbara closer to the light from the window. The child needed all the sunlight she could get. These winter days were dreary, and spring was still a long way off.

With the journal open, Ella squinted to read the words. She too needed more light. One could wash clothing, fix breakfast, and clean the kitchen in dim conditions, but writing was another matter. She would bring out the kerosene lamp. *Nee,* this was a day that needed plenty of light — only the gas lantern would do. Besides, she and Ronda could use the extra light to quilt with later in the day.

Ella pumped the air handle on the lantern until it wouldn't move anymore. She turned on the gas. With the lit match held a fraction of an inch from the mantle, the lantern popped into flame and was soon glowing with a steady hiss. She sat down, prepared to write.

So, I'm seriously considering love again. It's strange that I should come to this point, after I've vowed so many times I never would. And yet there's this conviction in me that I had best move forward because standing still no longer looks like a wise choice. It feels almost dangerous in a way. The funeral of Ivan's mother drove that home to me. We went to the graveyard, and there was the place where my wonderful Aden lies. I avoided it, of course, but I knew it was there, and the ache was still painful. But I could at least bear it for the first time. I think that's progress, or so it seems to me.

There was a time when I didn't dare have thoughts like this, let alone write them down. Aden was the most precious thing that had ever happened to me. It was Aden who taught me what love was, what it feels like, and yet he was taken from me. Why? I guess I will never know, but as our people say, Da Hah knows. One can but trust Him. And to doubt would be too terrible a thing to even imagine.

I suppose I'm wrong to think this, but I have to laugh when I remember Bishop Miller's face at the graveyard. He had the prayer, and he didn't look too happy to see me. He basically ignored me, which is fine. And I really can't say I blame him. I suppose he never had a girl stand up to him before. At least that's what was whispered to me in my thoughts.

He's a good-looking fellow — and confident as all get out — but it takes much more than that. To be honest, the bishop gave me nightmares. Oh, not that he's really a bad apple. It's just that life with him wasn't for me.

I would have disappointed him once he got to know me. Somewhere after the wedding vows, when it would have been too late, he would have had regrets. And how terrible would that be — to be married to a man knowing one can never meet his high standards.

The sacred vows make all things right, at least according to our people, but somehow I have a hard time believing it. I think Aden taught me that when he showed me what love was. Love can never be harnessed to a buggy like a horse. But really, I shouldn't be saying such things. I probably should burn this journal. What if someone else reads it someday? But I in the meantime, it does me good to keep writing.

I know that I love Ivan's girls. And

Ivan's okay, I guess. He's a tender-hearted man, and I'll love him in time, I guess, in my own feeble way. I know — I could never love another man like I loved Aden. It would seem almost a sin. At least Ivan doesn't give me nightmares like the bishop. He has never kissed me though. I think he doesn't quite dare, and I can't blame him, the poor man. He so wants to take me in his arms, but for some reason he doesn't. It's such a strange feeling in that I'm glad he doesn't. I don't like being so close to a man who wants me and being unable to respond one way or the other.

I have my hopes set on spring. I'm thinking that with the break of the weather, and when the birds begin singing again, a little love will come stealing back into my heart. Ivan already held my hands, and that wasn't too bad. It just wasn't like Aden. There was none of that feeling where my heart almost freezes with pain because I want him so much.

Ivan is so unsure of himself. His love seems all locked up inside of him. I've even seen alarm in his eyes, like he's scared of how he feels. It's almost like I draw him somewhere that he's forbidden to go. Perhaps that's because he's been married already and I haven't. He might be thinking about things I have never known.

Yet Aden held me and kissed me. It was pure heaven and contained not a moment of shame. I know how that feels. Can't Ivan go there? Is that too much to ask? Yet I can't blame him . . . really. I don't want to go there either. Because I know it won't be the same, and I know my heart will break all over again if it were.

Love will come again, I tell myself. Perhaps like a breeze, stealing my heart away. I might have to make the first move, like I did the other night, taking Ivan's hands in mine, showing him that I really want to try. That I believe love can happen for us. That we can both have joy on this earth again. That after our loss, two hearts can be mended and molded together.

When nothing more occurred to Ella, she closed the journal, the pages of the tablet falling together softly. For a moment she thought she heard someone drive in. It seemed like the sound made by an *Englisha* car driving on snow. But who would come today? Her quilt shop was open, but few people stopped by in the wintertime. Especially in this kind of weather.

Baby Barbara kicked her feet, and Ella walked past to look out the basement window. There was no sign of any vehicle. She must have imagined the sound. And it was time she prepared lunch for the girls. Ronda would be down soon, and their long afternoon of quilt work would begin.

Ella hid the journal behind a pile of folded dresses. It could stay there until she had time to put it away tonight. She was written out, and as tired as she felt, an early bedtime would be exactly what she needed.

She returned to the kitchen and paused, hearing the distinct sound of a knock on the first-floor door. Ronda's faint footsteps walked across the hardwood floor going to answer, and Ella listened to the muffled voices. The front door shut again, much too quickly for the person to have wanted anything with Ronda. She listened. Yah, there were footsteps crunching on her snow-covered basement steps. Quickly she bent over to straighten baby Barbara's blanket, pushing the journal deeper under the clothing. Obviously it was a customer she had heard driving in.

Male pant legs went past the window —

Englisha pants. Ella rushed to the basement door. Whatever he wanted, this visitor didn't need to come too far inside. Her wash hung behind the curtains, out of sight, but the smell was in the air. A woman would know why, but a man might think she kept a musty house.

He knocked on the door with a quick and decisive knock. Apparently he knew what he wanted.

"*Gut* morning," Ella said, pulling the door open slightly.

The snow made the dreary day brighter than it was, and Ella squinted.

"Ah . . ." the man said, smiling broadly. "Is this Ella's Quilt Shop?"

"Yah," she said, surprised. *What does a man want to see quilts for?* she thought.

"May I come inside?" he asked.

"You . . . you want quilts?" she asked.

He was a good-looking *Englisha* man, his chin straight, his jaw formed with straight lines, and his eyes had that twinkle some *Englisha* men had.

"Not really," he said, still smiling. "I'm sorry if I frightened you."

"Oh, no," Ella replied. "You didn't frighten me. I'm just not used to men asking after quilts."

He laughed and to her surprise, she really

wasn't frightened by this stranger. Still, it seemed that her heart was pounding with an awful energy all its own. She tried to keep breathing. This was an *Englisha* man, and there was no sense in acting like this at all.

"Ah," he said, his head tilted to the side. "Is it okay then if I come in? I have some questions that would be easier to ask with me not standing out here in the snow. I'm harmless. Really."

"What kind of questions? About quilts?"

"Well, no. About the Amish."

"Why are you coming to me?"

"Well, it all started when my mother visited here. Since she returned from her visit to the Amish country, we've all been fascinated by your people. I've done some research myself, and I'm very taken by your people. I would like to know a little more from something other than the Internet."

"The Internet?"

The man kept smiling and said, "Oh, sorry. The computer. Do you know about computers?"

These Englisha people. They think we are so ignorant. "Yes, I do know about computers."

After a brief silence, the man said, "Please. I won't be long. I promise."

With some hesitation, Ella stepped back from the door. He came in, glanced around, and pulled out a kitchen chair.

"Okay if I sit?"

What was there to say? No? What did one say when a strange *Englisha* man walked in and asked to sit at your table?

"Sure," she said, the word coming out in a rush.

He laughed again. "I'm sorry, ma'am. I really am, but I don't know how else to do this. Mom said you were one of the most decent Amish women she had ever met. She talked about you so much it's almost as if I know you."

"You know me?"

"Not really," he said. "Not in that sense, but I'm hoping this might be the place to start my journey."

"You said your mother visited here?"

"Yes. Mom bought a quilt from you. I think soon after you opened the shop, and you shipped it to her. I believe it was your first project, and it has your house drawing on it. In fact I found the place partly from the picture — even with the snow on the roof." He laughed again. "Mom couldn't be more pleased with your work. She's been showing the quilt to all her friends. And she talks her head off about the workmanship

100

and *you* . . . and it looks to me as if her judgment was correct."

"I'm not married," Ella said, blurting the words out and glancing at the girls. It didn't matter how this sounded, but the words suddenly needed saying.

"I didn't know," he said, raising his eyebrows as he looked at the girls. "I thought . . . Amish people married."

"It's not like that," she said, meeting his eyes, feeling warmth rushing into her cheeks. "I take care of the girls during the week. They are the daughters of Preacher Stutzman."

"Are you . . . uh . . . connected with him?" he asked. "Perhaps his relative?"

"No!" Ella said, the word coming out forcefully. "His wife died some time ago. I look after them weekdays . . . until he remarries."

"Oh," he said. "I didn't mean anything by my question. See I'm still learning the Amish ways and perhaps I seem a bit presumptuous. So is this how your people take care of each other?"

"He pays me for their care," Ella said.

"I see. Until he remarries, you said."

The red rushed to her cheeks again, but he was *Englisha,* so what harm could come from telling him?

101

"He has asked me to marry him."

"Well, congratulations," he said, half-standing before sitting back down. "I'm sure he's getting a wonderful wife. Sorry for all the questions. My name is Robert Hayes. I guess I didn't introduce myself, though it seems like I've known you for a long time."

"Ella Yoder," she said, suddenly feeling very weak in the knees. *But why?* she wondered.

TEN

"Ah, perhaps you'd best sit down," he said, standing and offering her a chair from the kitchen table.

Ella almost laughed. What a ridiculous situation this was. An unknown *Englisha* man in her kitchen, offering her a chair from her own table? Thankfully Joe and Ronda lived on the first floor or this could become a mighty uncomfortable situation to explain.

"Your mom's name is Marie? She lives in Maryland," Ella said, taking the chair.

"So you do remember," he said, pausing as Mary approached them.

"I'm hungry," Mary said, pulling on Ella's sleeve.

Ella froze. What was she supposed to do with this man and his questions? Lunch time had arrived, and she couldn't ask him to leave.

He cleared his throat. "As I said, I have a lot of questions about the Amish. I know

I'm imposing on you, but I really don't know where else to start. If you want to make lunch for the children, I can ask my questions while you work or I can come back some other time."

"No," she said, glancing at his face. "You can ask questions while I work, if you don't mind."

He looked quite determined, and she didn't want him to come back. This visit was bad enough.

"I'm hungry," Mary said again. Sarah had joined her and nodded in agreement.

"I really am sorry about this," he said. "May I help?"

"I'll fix sandwiches," she said, getting up. "The children are hungry, and you can eat with us. I don't know how much I can answer because some things aren't for *Englisha* ears, but ask away."

He laughed softly. "*Englisha,* yes. But we aren't from England."

"It is our way, and I don't know that it can be helped. I suppose that's the first answer to all things Amish. We do things our way, and that's just the way it is."

"I understand," he said. "Don't let me hold you back from fixing the girls' sandwiches."

"Oh, yah." What was wrong with her? She

was standing in the middle of the kitchen staring at him.

"You haven't eaten, have you?" she asked, turning and pulling homemade bread out of the cupboard.

"Not since breakfast," he said. "But I don't want to be a bother."

He already was a bother, but he didn't seem to know it.

"It'll be sandwiches then," she said, slicing the bread. "Think you can handle that?"

"With bread like that," he said, watching the thick slabs falling on the cutting board. "And homemade butter, I assume — and jam."

"Are you guessing?" she asked. "Or do they starve you where you come from?"

He laughed. "Of course not. They only starve you from the good things in life."

"Like homemade bread and butter?"

"That and much more." He stood to pull a chair out from under the kitchen table. Mary climbed on, and he scooted the chair back in.

"*Danki,*" Mary said, all smiles.

"Me too," Sarah said, lifting up her hands.

"Now, now," Ella said. "You shouldn't be bothering Mr. Hayes."

"Robert," he said. "And it's not a bother. I think I'm the one bothering you."

Ella took a few quick steps to pick Barbara up and lower her into the high chair. The baby slapped her arms up and down as she smiled at Robert.

"Hi, there," he said, leaning toward her. "You are a cute one."

Barbara jerked back, puckering up her face to cry. He backed away, throwing his hands up in mock surrender. "I'm sorry," he said.

"She doesn't like you," Mary said.

"I see that." He dropped his arms. "Why do you think she doesn't like me?"

"I don't know," Mary replied.

"She's a sweet baby," he said. "Perhaps I'm just new to her. Don't you think that's all it is?"

Mary shrugged.

"Time to eat," Ella said, placing the meat sandwiches on the table. She transferred the butter and jam over from the counter. "The girls like orange juice, and I make it fresh. Do you want some?"

"Fresh? Really? Of course." He smiled. "You don't have to do this for me, you know."

Ella ignored him and walked over to the root cellar, coming back with a handful of oranges.

Robert cooed softly at baby Barbara while

Ella cut the oranges in half, pressing the juice out with a hand juicer.

Even with her back turned, Ella could feel his eyes on her. She poured the juice into a pitcher, grabbed four glasses and set them on the table, and then sat down.

"We have prayer before meals," she said, waiting and watching him. Would he object?

He smiled, bowing his head with her and the girls as they prayed in silence.

What kind of man is he anyway? He seems to have no objections to praying at mealtimes, she noted.

"So your questions?" Ella asked, moments after the prayer. "We can talk while we eat."

"Yes, my questions," he echoed.

"Help yourself." She motioned toward the sandwiches and bread slices.

He carefully took a slice, spread butter and jam on the top, bit a piece off, and chewed slowly.

"You like it?" she asked and then realized it was really a dumb question to ask a visitor.

"Yes, it's very good," he said. "I haven't tasted anything so delicious in a long time."

"You're just saying so," Ella said, expecting warmth to creep up her neck again. Soon the redness would spread over her face until she'd feel like crawling under the table.

Even now her fingers were tingling.

"It really is good," he said, sighing. "You don't know how good it is."

"Well, we live with it," she said.

He definitely had gotten under her skin. But how? And how had she ever gotten herself into this situation? She ought to make a dash for the stairs, calling for help from Ronda. But that would be silly, and he'd think Amish women were insane for sure.

"I'm glad you like it." She broke a small piece off her sandwich and gave it to baby Barbara to chew on. Carefully she brought her glass of orange juice up to Barbara's lips for a long drink. Barbara gasped for air when she was done, a big smile breaking across her face.

"She likes it," Mary said. "And I do too."

"I'm glad," Ella said.

She could feel Robert's eyes on her face again. If he didn't ask his questions soon, she would ask him to leave.

"My questions," he said again, speaking softly. "What would a fellow do if he wanted to join the Amish?"

Ella almost choked on a bite of sandwich. "Join the Amish? You want to join the Amish?"

He looked puzzled at her response. "Why

not? Does that make one a weirdo?"

"You may want to join, but you can't just do that." Of course, Ella realized, sometimes people did indeed join the Amish, but not very often and not in their community. It just wasn't done.

"Really?" He leaned over the table. "Tell me why not."

Ella drew a quick breath. He had the quickest way of turning things back on her. "Well, for one thing, it's very, very hard."

He tilted his head sideways, staring at her.

"First, there's the language. Then all the things you'd have to give up. Your car for example, and your nice things. And music maybe. Then there are the rules we live by — lots of them. We grow up with those things, so they're relatively easy for us. We're accustomed to them. But you'd have to learn them — all of them — by heart. Then, of course, you'd have to get baptized. That's after six months of instruction class, and the ministers watching your life. Do you think you could live with that? I don't think so. My own brother is leaving the Amish. So how do you think you can make it?"

"Your brother?" he asked.

"Eli, yah. He's in love with an *Englisha* girl. She said she'd join the Amish . . . at first. But that's all changed. Now he's left us."

"I'm sorry to hear that," he said, biting into a sandwich.

"It just can't be done," she said again, meeting his eyes. Surely he would notice the pounding of her heart as she spoke, but even so, she kept his gaze. She would not look away. "Even when you love your family . . . it can't be done. Eli just proved that. And you would have no family here, so how would you make it?"

"You have a point," he said, his eyes looking away as they sat in momentary silence.

"I want another piece of sandwich," Mary said, and Ella took her knife and, cutting carefully, afraid she'd slice her finger with this strange man across the table from her, sliced off a section for her. Perhaps he would go now that his questions had been answered.

"Well, I'd like to try it," he said, his voice low. "As I said, for these past few months I've been learning what I could. And the more I've read, the more I seem to want it. I think I've known from the time Mother brought home your quilt. My heart has been turned in this direction since then. Perhaps God has turned it. Or perhaps by a longing for a simpler life from what I have. Perhaps from a desire to be with people who don't love the world. Would you deny me such a thing? Would you tell me that something like that . . . something perhaps from God . . . isn't possible? Don't your ministers believe there are those not born to Amish ways who are nonetheless destined to be with them?"

Ella shrugged. "If they do — at least around here — I've never heard about it."

"Where would I start?" he asked, his voice determined.

Baby Barbara slapped both her hands hard on the high chair and yelled.

Robert Hayes smiled.

He doesn't seem irritated by the interruption, which says something for him, doesn't it? Ella wondered. *Perhaps he is sincere. Perhaps his questions are coming from a good heart. Who could help this well-meaning but obviously confused young man?*

At once she realized what she should have said minutes earlier. "You need to speak with the young Bishop Miller. He lives a few miles down the road."

"Oh," he said. "Why the 'young'? Is it that by being young he might be more open-minded?"

"Yah," she said, "I suppose so. And he can handle himself well." Her heart was still pounding furiously. *Why doesn't it stay still?*

"Well, then, I will speak with your young bishop who can handle himself well."

"He's our best bishop . . . if we have a best bishop. He knows all about the *Martyr's Mirror,* and the history of our people. He helps out when one of us gets into spiritual trouble. Of course he couldn't help Eli, but he tried. Eli was too stubborn."

"Anything else about this bishop of yours?"

"He lives by himself. He farms. People love him. Respect him. He should be able to talk you out of this plan of yours," Ella said, forcing a weak smile.

Robert seemed to take no offense. "How do I find him?"

"Take a left at my driveway. Next right, then next left. Five miles or so, another left. There's an old red barn there. His is the third farm on the right."

The man seemed to process the information and then got to his feet. "So you really own this place?"

"Place?"

"This house where you live," he said.

"Oh, yah. I own it. I rent out the first floor. Why?"

He shrugged. "Mom thought you did, but I wondered. Isn't it kind of strange for a young, single Amish woman to have her own place?"

"Perhaps," she said, not looking at him.

"A story behind that, I assume."

"Yah."

"Well, we all have our stories. So one more question, and then I'm gone. Do you women vote for baptismal candidates?"

"What?"

"When your people are baptized. Do you vote for them, like an approval thing beforehand?"

"Yah, we do."

"Will you vote for me when my time comes?"

Ella laughed out loud. What a bold, in-your-face rascal this man was! It sure beat everything.

"I'll take that as a yes," he said, laughing heartily. "Thanks for lunch."

Ella got to her feet, but he was already at the door and had opened it. He gave her a little wave and he was gone. She listened to the snow crunching under his feet as he went past the window. Moments later his car started and the sound slowly faded as he drove down the driveway.

ELEVEN

Ella sat stunned for long moments until Mary pulled at her arm. "I'm done eating. Can we go play now?"

"Your naps," Ella said. "You have to take your naps."

Why couldn't she think clearly? Had the *Englisha* man been a dream, an angel's visit of some kind? Perhaps a message from heaven? But he hadn't left any message. And why was her heart still pounding? Was she . . . in some strange way *attracted* to the man? She could barely stand the thought. And yet there it was. Had Eli placed some awful curse on the family? Was there a fatal attraction to *Englisha* love somewhere in their history? Ella shuddered.

"I don't want a nap," Mary said.

"Mary, was there a man here? Did he just leave?" Ella asked, knowing full well the answer.

"He ate sandwiches with us," Mary said,

her voice matter-of-fact.

Out of the corner of her eye, Ella saw Mary moving slowly off the chair, her gaze on her doll.

"No, that's doesn't work," Ella said, taking her arm. "No escaping nap time. All three of you. I know how you become once we start quilting. Grouchy, grouchy, grouchy."

"But I don't want a nap," Mary protested, following meekly behind Ella, who had lifted little Barbara out of the high chair and was carrying her toward their curtained-off bedroom. Jumping on the bed, Mary and Sarah found their usual spots, and lay down, obviously more tired than they wanted to be. As they settled in, Ella prepared the baby's bottle.

With the girls down, Ella hurried to clean up the kitchen before Ronda came down. She hoped removing the evidence of the man's visit would also erase his presence. And yet could she also erase the hot flush that still remained on her cheeks? What on earth was wrong with her? And how was she to explain this to Ronda?

The man had spoken with Ronda before he came down. Had she noticed how long he stayed? Ella laughed out loud. Yes, Ronda would definitely notice something like that.

It was one of the reasons Ella liked her, why she was glad Ronda lived on the first floor — because she kept an eye out for anything out of the ordinary. Ivan couldn't even arrive late to pick up the girls without Ronda's comment the next day.

By the time she had the table clean, she heard Ronda's footsteps on the basement stairs.

Ronda had no sooner entered when she blurted out, "Who was that man?"

"A customer . . . kind of."

"He sure stayed a long time."

Ella smiled. What had this man done to her that her heart was still thumping this way? Thankfully he was an *Englisha* man, and she would never see him again. There was no more to it than that.

"You seem mighty pleased with yourself," Ronda continued, taking a chair by the table. "Did you make a sale? Is that why it took so long? You know we're already two quilts behind."

"His mom bought our first quilt," Ella said. Thankfully her mind still worked, and she knew exactly what to tell Ronda. Enough — but not too much. There was no need to spread rumors around about an *Englisha* man who wanted to join the faith. Such talk would do no one any good.

Bishop Miller would know enough to send the man on his way, and that would be the end of the matter.

"*Ach . . . vell* then," Ronda said, settling into the chair.

"Marie was his mother's name. She's from Maryland, and he said she liked the quilt a lot. That he could even pick the house out from the drawing. Can you believe that? And his mother said the workmanship was excellent."

"So he stopped in to say . . . what? Hello?"

"Not exactly. He didn't say what he wanted for a while. We talked about his mother and then the quilt. Then he said he had questions about the Amish."

"The *Englisha* always do. They're full of questions."

"Anyway, the girls were hungry so I invited him to eat lunch with us. We just had sandwiches."

"You *didn't!*" Ronda said, her eyes big. "Did he ask his questions?"

Ella laughed. "Yah. Big ones. I answered what I could."

"Well, I'm glad it wasn't me," Ronda said, taking a deep breath. "I wouldn't know what to say."

"He was nice enough. I guess this is part of doing business with the public. Though I didn't expect selling quilts to turn into visits from the *Englisha* customers' children."

"And a *man* at that," Ronda said, eying Ella intently. "You seem awful happy about something."

"It's good when our customers are so happy with our work," Ella said. "That's all." *Now, if Ronda will just drop the subject. More talk and I might say something I shouldn't.* Ella felt a deep chill go through her body.

Ronda seemed satisfied and got up to sit beside the quilt they'd been working on. "You need light back here," she said. "I was surprised to see your lantern on, but I see why."

"Yah," Ella said as she put some dishes away.

"I too have some news," Ronda said, turning toward her.

"Yah?" Ella said, keeping her back to Ronda.

"A *bobli!*" Ronda said. "I am going to have a baby."

"Oh, Ronda!" Ella turned to Ronda and, wiping her hands on a dish towel, said, "That is so wonderful!"

"Yah," Ronda said, all smiles, her eyes flitting around the edges of the quilt. "The child will come in late summer. How will that be — our first one . . . for Joe and me."

"My, that *is* good news."

"I had to tell you because you will be seeing it soon anyway," Ronda said, blushing.

"It will be *gut* to hear a baby's cry upstairs."

"That brings up the question of whether or not we'll be staying here. I haven't heard anything from you about your marriage plans."

Ella turned back to the last of the dishes. "Ivan and I don't have an exact date yet."

"I'm asking because Joe and I need to know if we'll need to find another house."

"I'll make sure you aren't cast out into the cold," Ella said, coming to sit beside Ronda. "We just haven't talked about that . . . Ivan and I. I would think I'd move to his place. I can't imagine he'd want the house here. There are way too few acres, and he's a farmer at heart. He has everything set up over there."

"So what will happen?" Ronda asked, her thread stopped in midair.

"The only thing that has come to me," Ella said, "is that Clara or Dora would have the place."

"You'd give them this house? The one Aden gave you?"

"Life goes on," Ella said. "I won't need it

anymore. And it has been a blessing to me, along with you and Joe, so I'm satisfied." She walked over to the quilt and sat opposite Ronda.

"You sure are cool about this." Ronda looked sharply at her. "You never were quite like this before. How can you walk away from the house just like that?"

"Well, I certainly can't sell the house. That would be wrong. How could I sell what Aden gave me?"

Ronda considered this for a moment. "Ella, tell me the truth. Will you be happy with Ivan?"

Ella glanced at Ronda's face in the soft light of the gas lantern. "What kind of question is that?"

"I mean, does your heart beat faster when you see him? Have you come to love him yet? Love him like a woman needs to love her husband?"

Ella hardly knew what to say. She took a deep breath. "I'm trying to work my way through some of those things. It's not easy, you know."

"Then it hasn't happened yet."

Ella shook her head. "Does it have to?"

"I would think so," Ronda said, meeting her eyes over the quilt. "But I've never been in your shoes. I know it must be hard."

Ella nodded, her eyes on her handwork. "I try, but then something happens to bring it all back. The memories of Aden. I know it's wrong to keep comparing my feelings for Ivan with what I felt for Aden, but as you say, it's hard."

"Is there a chance it would be easier to love a different man? Bishop Miller showed some interest in you. He's a fine, dashin' sight, even after you told him there was no hope for a marriage between you. That says a lot for a man — the way he stood up to what must have been a most painful disappointment. I expect he'd come racing back if someone dropped a little hint near him."

Ella laughed. "Don't you dare! I'm not interested in the bishop."

"Well, what about one of the other widowers? There aren't too many single boys left. In fact, none that I know of."

"Ronda, please don't be so silly. Besides, there's more than just my happiness to consider. When I think of Ivan and me, I can't help consider what would happen with the girls if I didn't marry their daett."

"Just because they need a mamm, doesn't mean it has to be you," Ronda said, glancing sharply at her. "Ivan can find some other woman, I'm sure."

"There's just one problem. The girls have

stolen my heart."

"And so you'd marry a man for his daughters?"

"No, of course not. There's also the fact that Ivan loves me. You ought to see the way he looks at me. Also, he needs me. Isn't that good enough?"

"Only if *you* love him."

Ella thought about Ronda's words before she said, "But perhaps I want a different kind of love this time." Her voice rose with passion. "I want a love that doesn't break my heart. One that isn't tearing it all up until I can't even find the little pieces. Perhaps I want a love that doesn't hurt. One that doesn't cause me to crawl on the ground with pain when *Da Hah* takes it away."

"Yah," Ronda said. "That makes sense. I don't know, of course, because I haven't been there. But losin' Joe would feel like that."

"At least you'd have his *bobli*," Ella said, hearing the bitterness in her voice. Where had all this come from? These were questions she thought were long settled in her mind. Had that *Englisha* man brought them back up? It could not be. She wanted desperately to wipe the imprint of the man's face from her memory. Faintly she heard

Ronda speaking. "What was that?" she asked.

"It would be harder now that I have his *bobli. Nee,* I know it would be harder. Losing Joe now would be worse than before," Ronda repeated.

Ella felt her eyes brimming with tears. She pulled her gaze away, hardly able to see the quilt. Her stitches under her fingers looked like blurred lines in the distance. Ella paused, wiping her eyes. "I'm sorry," she whispered. "I'm sure you're right."

"I wasn't tryin' to preach to you," Ronda said, wiping her eyes. "Ivan is a nice man."

"I know," Ella said, her stitches now visible again. Carefully she ran the needle around the line, the stitches so small her eyes strained to follow.

Ella hoped Ronda would turn the conversation to another topic.

Ronda did seem to realize enough had been said on the subject. The two women worked the rest of the afternoon mostly in silence, with a few words of idle conversation as they occurred.

The girls soon roused from their naps, and began playing with their dolls. Hours passed until the light grew dim with the approach of the evening. Joe could be heard returning home.

As Ronda went up the stairs to the first floor, Ella said, "Don't worry, Ronda. I'll make arrangements with whoever gets the house. I'll make sure you have enough time after the baby comes to find something else."

"You have always been more than kind," Ronda said. "*Danki* much."

Ella nodded, her eyes unaccountably brimming once again.

TWELVE

Ella simply could not sleep. She paced the floor, occasionally looking out the window at the freshly fallen snow. If only she could step outside for a few moments. She needed to think, and the pacing wasn't doing the trick. All three girls were asleep for the night, so why couldn't she go outside? She had to figure out why this *Englisha* stranger was driving sleep from her mind! Tomorrow she would pay for this foolishness, as she would surely be unable to stay awake when Ronda came to quilt. And this was all *his* fault.

In desperation, Ella peeked behind the curtains separating the beds from the larger room. The girls were still sound asleep. She listened for a moment before letting the curtains slide from her hand. Her coat and shawl hung by the stairs. Yes, she would go outside for a walk, snow or no snow.

At the kitchen table she turned the kerosene lamp down low. Its light cast crazy shadows on the basement ceiling, making the chair the *Englisha* man had been sitting in appear wobbly and crooked. Ella turned her eyes away. She wouldn't think about the chair — or the man.

Gently falling snow swirled around her as she stepped outside the door. It was much worse than it had appeared from inside. Already the basement steps were covered. She pushed the snow aside with her boots before she used each step, careful not to slip. Should she fall, Ronda would hear her cries for help — and wouldn't *that* be just the perfect end to this day.

Ella wrapped her shawl tightly around her head and neck. Each blast of wind seemed to drive flakes and cold right through her coat. Already the snow came halfway up her boots. Someone would have to shovel snow in the morning again. Ella tried to make out the barn, but she couldn't see that far in the darkness and swirls of snow.

He was here, right in this driveway with his Englisha *car. Where is he now? Over at Bishop Miller's?* Ella almost laughed out loud. *What will the bishop do? Welcome Robert in with open arms? Tell him his dream can be realized? That the Amish welcomed outsiders?*

Ella pushed forward through the snow. Perhaps if she reached the barn, she could sit and think without reminders of the *Englisha* man. Wasn't the man's name Robert? Yes, that was it. Robert Hayes. *Moonbeam will listen to my sorrows without being shocked. Should I have confided in Ronda this afternoon? Would she have understood?* Ella laughed again, the sound strangled by the wind. *No, Ronda would certainly* not *have understood. She would think I've lost my mind.*

Perhaps she *was* out of her mind. Ella shivered, wrapping her shawl even tighter around her neck. In front of her the faint outline of the barn appeared, and she stumbled against the door, reaching to turn the latch. It was frozen. Ella rattled the metal, trying harder. This time the door opened, and she rushed inside, feeling the dark warmth of the barn wrap around her.

Moonbeam neighed from his stall, but Ella couldn't even see her hand when she held it up to her face. Joe kept a lantern out here, but the light might attract attention. But with the snowstorm, surely she wouldn't be seen. Ella groped for the box stall where Joe kept the lantern and matches. Moonbeam nickered, a friendly, hopeful sound, as if he were glad to see her.

"It's just me," she whispered. "I'm trying

to find the matches."

Her horse banged loudly in his stall, and Ella smiled in the darkness. At least Moonbeam wasn't afraid to express his feelings. Not like she was. Afraid of feelings for, of all things, an *Englisha* man. The whole thing was just not possible. His promises to join the faith were as empty as those of Pam, Eli's beloved nurse. If she allowed it, he would surely try to lead her heart away from the faith the first chance he had. Bishop Miller probably had Robert well on his way already, sending him back to whatever town he had come from.

Ella found the matches with her cold fingers, and scraped one on a rough stall board. She pushed down too hard, hearing the wood stem snap under her fingers. With greater care, she flicked the second match over the board with a lighter touch. The match flared, and when she turned the knob on the lamp and held the match to it, it caught the gas fumes with a pop. Ella hung the lantern on a nail as light flooded the barn.

Moonbeam had his head out of his stall, blinking slowly, as if he couldn't believe his eyes.

"No, we're not going anywhere," Ella said.

128

"I'm only out here to think for a few minutes."

In the other stalls, Joe's two horses kept their heads inside, but one snorted and kicked against the wall.

Ella checked to see if the horse was okay. He bobbed his head in the light and shook himself. She carried the lantern to the furthest end of the barn and hung her shawl in front of it. Here the straw was stacked high to the ceiling with a few bales scattered around. Ella pulled two of them together. She could stretch out here, perhaps spend the night with the horses. Already she felt much better. Let it snow outside, she would rest here for a while. The girls would be okay. And Old Christmas wasn't far away, a night much like this, when the Christ child was born in a manger among the animals. So if Christ was born in a barn, surely it was okay for her to spend time here.

Ella let the peacefulness sweep over her. There were stories among her people of beasts that spoke on the Holy Night. Not that anyone ever heard them, but Ella lay back on the straw bales and thought of the stories from her childhood. They were easy to believe when sitting on straw bales in the middle of a snowstorm surrounded by lantern light shaded by a shawl.

"Can you talk on the Holy Night?" she asked Moonbeam. He turned to look at her, jerking his head up and down.

Ella laughed. "I meant a little more than that."

He jerked his head again.

"You horses have it easy. You don't have to worry about falling in love. You have no bad boys who steal your heart. Of course, Aden wasn't bad . . . not like this *Englisha* man.

"There, I said it! Now someone knows, at least, even if it is just you, Moonbeam. And it makes me feel a little better. Oh, I know I'll never see him again, but still I'll feel like my heart betrayed me. But of course you don't know anything about that. You're just a horse."

Just then a horrible thought gripped her, bringing her upright on the straw bale. Was it possible? Would the young Bishop Miller actually do such a thing? He could if he wanted to, and her blood ran cold at the thought. So her nightmare with the bishop might not be over with after all. Was the bishop really that kind of man? It was possible, wasn't it? As soon as Robert mentioned to the bishop where he had come from — a few more questions would pull all the information the bishop needed. Robert would tell him that Ivan had asked her hand in marriage. Robert wouldn't know enough not to give the information. Oh why did she tell him? *Stupid!* she thought.

She could see it all now, as clear as day. As soon as Robert mentioned his admiration for Ella and gave the bishop the same speech about joining the Amish that he had given her, the bishop would play along. Perhaps even encourage Robert, telling him the steps he needed to take, even take him under his wing for a few weeks. And in the bishop's care, the other ministers would allow Robert to stay. All the time, of course, Robert could be used by the bishop to come between her and Ivan. How Bishop Miller would do it, Ella wasn't certain, but it was possible. The man would set about his job with great glee. And he certainly understood women, didn't he?

With great indignation she rose to her feet, brushing the straw off her coat and taking the gas lantern back to the stall where it belonged. Setting the lantern carefully where it had been, Ella brushed the dust of her fingerprints from the top of the board. This night visit to the barn would stay between her and Moonbeam. The young bishop and whatever scheme he cooked up would not take her away from Ivan's girls, only to swoop in himself afterward to pick up her heart. And worse, if Ivan learned of any of this — of her unwanted attraction to the *Englisha* man or of any inappropriate action with an outside man, he would be obligated to cut off their relationship.

"You won't succeed!" Ella cried, casting the retort back toward her horse, as if he were the young bishop himself. "I told you no once, and I still mean it!"

The barn fell into darkness as Ella turned the valve on the lantern. She felt the heaviness descend on her. She reached out with her hands, lest she bump into something. The door handle was soon under her fingers, and she stepped outside. She was prepared to face the blast of the wind with the sting of snow but was surprised when only the wind came.

A quick glance up showed the scurry of clouds already broken up by the strong wind. Stars twinkled through in spots, and then they were covered up again in the race of the clouds. The temperature had dropped rapidly, making the night much clearer.

Had she been seen? Well, if so, she would simply tell Ronda the truth. At least part of it. That she had gone to the barn to be with Moonbeam. A sort of therapy that Ronda might understand. A lecture might follow no doubt, along the lines of Ella needing a *husband* for therapy, but she could bear up under that. She would tell Ronda, "I'm trying," although Ronda wouldn't know how hard she was — or wasn't — trying.

Her trip to the barn had helped, but it also had raised a new dilemma. How was she to know for sure of the bishop's plans? He lived in a different district from hers and could take any visitors to church with him and she wouldn't know. She might not know for weeks if Robert were still around.

Ella tried to run through the snow, but had to slow down. Then, reaching the concrete steps down to her basement door, she slipped on the top step and missed the next two before her hands caught anything solid. With a jar, she landed hard.

"Dumb . . . dumb . . . dumb . . ." she muttered. "Do be more careful, woman!"

Slowly she moved. Thankfully there was no pain. A quick glance upward revealed no faces in one of the first floor windows. Ella got up and took the rest of the steps more carefully.

Inside, with the door shut tightly behind her, she first checked behind the curtains and found the girls still sound asleep. She then added extra wood to the fire. Even more would be needed later, as arctic as the temperature was outside. She would know when the fire died down by the cold creeping in and awakening her.

For a long moment Ella paused, thinking, and then made a quick dash for her journal. Tomorrow morning she would be too tired to think, but right now the thoughts raced clearly through her head. She turned the kerosene wick up as high as it would go and wrote quickly.

I fear that my heart has betrayed me to an Englisha man. And yet how can that be? On top of that, I think the bishop will try to help him — for his own reasons of course. Part of me wants to think this can't be true, that even though the bishop had his feelings hurt by my refusal to marry him, he would still have enough sense to know that I won't reconsider under any circumstances.

Another part of me — the stronger part — tells me I am right. That the bishop will help out the Englisha man. He will give Robert the shelter and the direction he needs until a division between me and Ivan can be created. Bishop Miller is a very wise man. He among all people knows how much I loved Aden and that I don't have the same feelings for Ivan yet.

I know I'm right, and yet I can't even tell Ivan, like I feel I should. If I were to confess my attraction to an Englisha man, that would be exactly what Bishop Miller wants. See, already his plan is working! I do so wish Da Hah would help me somehow. I don't want to turn out like Eli.

Ella wrote the last words in a heavy hand, the pencil pressed down so hard the lead almost went through the paper. Then she closed the tablet, took it with her, hid it behind the clothes as usual, and wearily climbed into bed.

THIRTEEN

It was Friday, and Ivan would be coming for the girls. But Ella had a better idea — one that had her rushing around her basement kitchen packing food for the supper she would take to him. She'd best hurry though. Otherwise he would be on his way to her place. Just as she packed the last of the food, Mary announced that she couldn't find her shoes and Sarah, out on the basement steps, began to bawl like a wounded calf.

Ella opened the basement door and asked, "What happened, dear? We're tryin' to rush."

"I slipped and fell," Sarah said through tears as she clasped her knee.

"Let me see," Ella said. "Pull your hand away so I can see."

Ella saw no blood, just a little white scuff where the concrete had rubbed.

"It hurts!" Sarah said, pulling in

sharp sniffles.

Ella puckered her lips and blew a long breath on the scraped knee. A look of delight crept over Sarah's face and she laughed.

"There we go. All better now?" Ella asked.

Sarah nodded vigorously.

How strange that real pain could be fixed simply by blowing air on it. Did *Da Hah* not know the secret? If He did, she had hurts He could blow on anytime now. But perhaps He was too busy?

"Somebody hurt herself?" Ronda asked, raising the upstairs window and peering down through the screen. "I thought I heard cries."

"I hurt my knee," Sarah said, pointing.

"Tsk tsk," Ronda cooed.

Ella smiled. Ronda already had the air of a young mother, even though the birth of her first *bobli* was still months away.

"Stay right there . . . don't move," Ella said in Sarah's direction, as she looked back for Mary, who was proudly holding up her shoes.

"That's good!" Ella said, rushing to her. "Let me help you put them on. We have to go. And do you think you can carry something out to the buggy for me?"

"Yah, something big," Mary said without

hesitation.

Ella looked over her small body. "I think I'll make extra trips. You can save time by putting your shoes on by yourself. Can you do that?"

Mary nodded. "But I can't tie them."

"Then we'll have to practice that later. I'll tie them when you're ready."

Mary sat down on the concrete floor, grabbing her shoes. She stuck her right foot into one. Thankfully, she knew how to place the right shoe on the right foot.

Ella turned to go load the food into the buggy. There was so much though. Perhaps Ronda could help her? That might entail questions, but right now she wasn't afraid of questions. She was taking supper to Ivan, and that was nothing to be ashamed of.

"Ronda!" she called up the stairs.

"Is Ronda going to our house?" Mary asked.

"No," Ella said. "I need her help with the food."

The front door opened, and Ronda appeared. "Yah?"

"Will you help me carry some things out to the buggy? Please? I may be late already. Getting ready took longer than I expected."

Ronda laughed. "Sure, I'd be glad to."

She came downstairs quickly, and the

questions started just as fast.

"Isn't Ivan comin' for the girls? Are you leavin' for the evening? Runnin' away with his little ones?"

Ella laughed. Ronda was a dear.

"Come on now," Ronda said, teasing. "Spill the beans with me. You know I won't tell! Or do you want me to tell him where you have taken them?"

"Ronda, I'm goin' to his place and takin' supper in," Ella said. "I got the idea sudden like, and that's what's throwing me behind. Still, I thought I had plenty of time, but I don't want him drivin' all the way over here for nothin'."

"*Ach* . . . you are serious," Ronda beamed. "But surely you won't be by yourself in the house with him and the girls. You know how that could look since you're not married yet."

"I've already thought of that," Ella said. "Susanna and her daett will be invited over. That's another reason I have to hurry. I need to get there before they make supper. And if they can't come over, I'll leave the food with Ivan and come home."

"I'll give you something to eat, if you have to come back," Ronda said with a short laugh. "I won't let you go hungry, but my guess is Susanna will jump at the chance not to cook. And I heard she really appreciated how you helped out at her mamm's funeral."

"I was only helpin'," Ella said, lifting the heavy casserole container, as Ronda grabbed a salad and two pies. "It was nothing special."

"Being part of the family . . . that's what it's all about," Ronda said, holding the basement door for Ella. "Aren't you takin' bread, jam, and butter? You know how men like hot food. It works your way right into his heart."

"Yah," Ella said laughing.

If Ronda only knew. She already was in Ivan's heart. It was her own heart that was the problem. Hopefully this meal would help. Maybe it would bring her into the routine of Ivan's life . . . or something like that.

When they got to the buggy, Sarah following along behind, Ella placed the food in the back and reached for what Ronda carried.

"Your horse ready?" Ronda asked with a glance toward the barn.

"I harnessed him earlier and gave him a half bucket of grain to keep him happy."

"You spoil Moonbeam, you do know that?"

"I like to use him well," Ella said. "If he's spoiled . . . well, it won't kill him."

"Ivan's gettin' a good wife . . . you know that too. He'll be so spoiled, he'll get so fat, he won't be able to preach over his stomach on Sundays."

Ella laughed. Ivan kept himself in shape, not too thin, but sized down. The image of a bulge around his stomach while preaching was hilarious. He hadn't preached in a while, but she hadn't forgotten.

"You will spoil him," Ronda said. "Even if it seems impossible to you, you will. I know you."

"Can you watch Sarah for a minute?" Ella asked, swinging the child onto the buggy seat. "I'll be right back with Mary and the baby."

"I'm right . . ." Ronda said. "And you'd better remember I said so when it happens."

Ella smiled and hurried back to the basement door. Mary sat beside the baby waiting.

"You sweet darlings," she said, bending over to tie Mary's shoes before she picked up Barbara. "Okay, let's go. We have to get over to your daett's place."

Mary held the basement door open and pulled it shut behind them.

Ella took her hand going up the steps. She

141

loved these girls, and her love for Ivan needed to grow. And there was no reason it couldn't. *Da Hah* had already planted the seed with her love for Ivan's girls, and a little water added to the soil should do wonders. By summertime the garden would be growing into a fruitful crop.

Ronda was trying to bridle Moonbeam when Ella arrived back at the buggy, but she was struggling.

"He won't open his mouth," Ronda said.

Ella set Barbara on the buggy seat and asked Sarah to hold her, and then helped Mary up before she went to help Ronda.

"Open up!" Ella commanded, slapping the horse on his neck. Moonbeam promptly popped his mouth open and the bit slid in.

"The spoiled rascal," Ronda said. "That's what comes from too many oats."

"He just does that for strangers now," Ella said. "He doesn't like my whacks on his neck. Other than that little trick, he's one of the easiest horses I've ever had to harness."

"Well," Ronda said, still glaring, "I don't like horses taking advantage of me."

"Just whack him on the neck if it ever happens again," Ella said, leading Moonbeam outside.

Ronda lifted the shafts as Ella swung the horse under. They both pulled on the tugs, snapping them in place. Ella tossed the lines into the buggy, leaving Ronda holding the bridle while she climbed in.

As Ronda let go, Ella slapped the reins and headed down the drive. With a backward wave, she turned onto the main road, hanging on to the lines as the horse pulled hard. He was a little ornery tonight. Perhaps he was a little spoiled. Maybe Ronda was right, and she had better cut back on the oats.

"Whee!" Mary sang beside her, the wind streaming past her little bonnet.

Ella pulled to a stop at the corner and turned right. With a gentle slap of the reins she urged the horse on, pulling up the wool buggy blanket tight under the girls' chins. Moonbeam was still tugging at the bit.

Well, she was in a hurry, so why not? Her horse sensed her desire. He picked up the pace and loped down the gravel road.

Several *Englisha* cars passed her, the drivers turning to look back with strange expressions on their faces at her speed. Ella laughed. They could think what they wanted — that she was a young Amish woman out with her children for a fast ride or that she had simply taken leave of her senses. Mary and Sarah were thrilled and laughed at the ride.

The girls deserved to get out more. They needed a taste of life. Before long they would be grown with sweethearts calling for them. When the time came, their boyfriends would drive fast to impress them, but she would already have placed the girls one step ahead of the game.

Ella threw her head back, laughing cheerily along with Mary and Sarah. Going fast was still fun, even for her as a grown woman. She just hoped no one could see her getting so much enjoyment out of speed. A turn came up ahead, and she pulled back on the lines. There was no sense in causing an accident. An overturned buggy in a snowy ditch wouldn't be a pretty sight. That would be just what she needed on her conscience. Ella pulled back harder on the reins.

"Fast ride over," she said, even with another stretch of open snowy road in front of her. Perhaps it would be best to leave fast rides for the boys to impress them after all.

"We *like* to go fast," Mary said. "That was really fun."

"Well, it's enough fun for today," Ella said, her voice firm.

They settled slowly back into the seat. She couldn't see their faces under the bonnets. The little dears. Perhaps she should humor them, but no, she wouldn't. Ivan's place lay just ahead. He would think she had lost her mind if she drove dashing into his lane with their bonnet strings flying.

She laughed when she thought of the look on his face. How unlike her, and yet how like her. It had been a long time since she had done anything like this. Would Ivan love this side of her? The side Aden used to bring out when he let out the lines on warm Sunday evenings on their way home from the hymn sing? Aden often let her drive, and his horse was one of the fastest among the young people. She could drive his horse almost as well as he could — a fact Aden knew and didn't seem bothered by. That was one of the wonderful things about him.

They would sit close together, her hands clutching the lines, as the land went speed-ing past the buggy door. If another buggy came up, she would turn out for it. No ditch was too scary or night too dark as they raced past. They went over the roads, moving at times as if the buggies ahead of them were standing still.

What had brought such thoughts to her as she was on her way to the man who would surely be her future husband? This was not the time or place to think of days gone by. She now had another life to live — one that didn't include fast buggy rides.

"It's Daett's house!" Mary hollered.

"Yah," Ella said, with a catch in her voice. "We're almost there."

FOURTEEN

The snow had gathered in the yard since the funeral — a foot deep in places. Ivan was keeping the path open from the barn to the houses and a large area in front of the barn. Ella pulled back on the lines as they bounced into the lane. The place looked deserted. Several horse tracks went around to the back of the barn, as if Ivan had driven them across the yard. Perhaps they had broken out, and that was the closest way to the pasture. She glanced toward the ditch by the road. Human footprints circled around, and then went up the back to the fence line.

Ella pulled to a stop by the barn door, stepping carefully down into the snow.

"Mary, can you get down by yourself?" she asked the older girl, who had followed her, bravely placing both feet on the buggy step. "The steps are slippery."

Ella held back on her instinct to grab the

girl. Mary had tried this before and always called for help. Perhaps tonight she would take the plunge and get down herself. Each girl needed her own rite of passage when it came to buggy steps. She remembered well her own surge of delight when her mamm no longer helped her down.

"I want down too," Sarah said, calling from the seat, holding baby Barbara beside her. Ella left Mary standing on the buggy steps, wavering as to whether to attempt the long step down, while she tied the horse to the hitching post. She walked around to the other side of the buggy and reached up to help Sarah down.

"Now, just wait here," Ella said, motioning toward a spot in the snow, "while I get Barbara down."

She reached up for Barbara and pulled her into her arms. She looked around. Still there was no sign of anyone. Likely Ivan was in the barn, as it was already chore time. She heard Mary pull in her breath from the other side of the buggy, followed by a soft thud in the snow.

"I got down by myself!" Mary yelled, her voice triumphant.

"Wow! You're a big girl now," Ella praised. "But just remember, you still have to be careful. Take things slowly so you don't fall."

Mary looked back up at the buggy step, letting her breath out slowly. "At least I did it once, and now I can practice some more."

"That's the idea," Ella said. "Come around now, and I'll take all of you into the house. Then I'll come back for the food."

Mary trudged along behind as they made their way up the shoveled path toward the *dawdy haus.* She might as well try there first, since there was no sign of Ivan near the main house. She looked around the yard, remembering that just days ago it had been full of buggies and men and women dressed in black. Now few signs were left from the occasion and some were, no doubt, hidden under the freshly fallen snow. How like life, the endless move forward even in the face of death.

Ella pushed her dark thoughts aside and knocked on the *dawdy haus* door. Quick steps came across the floor.

Susanna opened the door, a surprised look crossed her face. "I thought someone drove in, but I figured they'd come to help Ivan."

"It's just me," Ella said. "I've brought supper over, and I thought you and your daett might want to join us."

"How wonderful!" Susanna said. "We'd love to."

"Have you made supper yet?"

"A little soup, but that I can save till tomorrow. This is so *gut* of you."

"Did I hear you say Ivan needed help?" Ella asked.

"Yah," Susanna said. "The poor man. He's been having all kinds of trouble today. Young Bishop Miller was here earlier and talked with him for the longest time out in the barn. Then that young colt of his broke down the fence. It must have pushed the gate out with his chest. He took all the horses with him down the road for a joy run."

"Young Bishop Miller was here?" Ella asked, unable to disguise her shock.

"You act surprised? Do you know anything about it?" Susanna asked, looking strangely at her.

Ella's mind whirled. What was she to say? She really didn't know anything — she only had suspicions.

"Not really. Well, no . . . I don't."

"Well, if you do, you don't have to tell me," Susanna said with a laugh. "I thought it was probably church business. But it must be serious to have Ivan involved instead of the deacon."

"He didn't tell me anything." Ella took a deep breath. "It's just . . . well . . . you know how things go . . . I thought perhaps . . ."

"Oh, they'll get it worked out," Susanna said, tickling baby Barbara under the chin till the babe broke into a big smile. "So what's the occasion for supper? Did you think to save Ivan from the trip over to pick the girls up?"

"Yes. And I just wanted to bring supper. And from the sounds of it, I'm glad I did."

"Already reading each other's troubles," Susanna commented. "I like that. I think it's a *gut* sign. A hot supper hits the spot for me, and certainly for Ivan, after his day."

"Then I'll take the girls over to the main house and get them settled in. I still have to bring in the food and warm the casserole."

"Do you need help?" Susanna glanced out toward the buggy. "You still have your horse tied up, and Ivan's probably just starting with the milking."

"Well, help would be nice," Ella said. "Ronda helped with the loading, and we still had to make several trips."

Ella waited while Susanna pulled her heavy coat on.

"We're going over to the main house," Susanna hollered toward the living room. For the first time, Ella saw the old man in the rocker. He was sitting in silence, his feet planted on the floor.

"Oh, hello," Ella said. "I didn't see you."

He nodded but said nothing.

"I'll help Daett over later," Susanna said, gathering baby Barbara up. "He needs to get out more. He misses Mamm a lot."

"I can imagine," Ella said, holding open the door as Mary ran ahead on the snowy path, Sarah's hand in hers. A few moments later, Susanna opened the front door at the main house, and they settled the girls in the living room.

"We'll be right back," Ella told them. "Mary, you keep the baby happy. You can see us through the window."

Mary didn't looked concerned and spread out on the floor. Sarah followed suit. Baby Barbara laughed out loud with both of her sisters at eye level. Ella quickly shut the door and ran to catch up with Susanna.

"So what's troubling Ivan?" she asked, gasping to catch her breath in the chilly air.

"I don't know for sure," Susanna said. "He's always been the tender one of the family. I suppose that's hard to believe what with the way he used to preach Sundays. It's still strange that he should stop that now, as I'm sure you've noticed."

"Yes, I have noticed, but I thought that was *gut.* Don't you?"

"I think so, but I'm still not sure what's up."

"Do you think I should ask him?"

"If he'll tell you," Susanna said. "I dug around a little bit this morning, but not a word did he speak about it. The man worries me."

"Maybe a good hot supper will help," Ella said. But then she thought of young Bishop Miller having been here. *It might take a whole lot more than a hot meal to cheer Ivan,* she decided.

Ella lifted the food out of the back of the buggy and handed the casserole to Susanna. She balanced the two pies and salad on her hands and arms. Behind them the barn door opened with a swirl of snow.

Ivan stood in the doorway, his boots snowy and his hat covered with loose straw. His eyes looked sunken into this face. "Good evening," he said, his eyes taking in the casserole in Susanna's hands. "To what do we owe this surprise? Supper is it?"

"You guessed it!" Ella said with a nervous smile. "I thought I'd bring supper over — special . . . for you."

"With how my afternoon has been going, you know how to hit the spot. I just started the milking and haven't even gotten to my other chores. And the young colt took the whole team out for a run down the road. I'll be a while."

"That's what Susanna said. Perhaps you could use help with the chores?"

"That would be nice, but what about supper?"

"I can manage to get the supper ready," Susanna said. "Ella's done the hard part."

"I'll be right back — as soon as I get the casserole into the oven," Ella said, seeing a look of hope flash across Ivan's face. The man looked more than tired.

He nodded, went back into the barn, and closed the door behind him.

"I'll bring Daett over," Susanna said as they struggled back up the path. "Then I can watch the food. Don't you think that's a better idea than leaving a woodstove to warm a casserole?"

"I'm sure you're right," Ella said, holding open the front door. "I was trying to make as little work as possible."

"It's not a problem, and Daett will be glad to get out of the house," Susanna said, greeting the girls on the living room floor with a smile. She set the casserole on the kitchen table and turned to go.

Ella filled the stove with wood. The kindling caught quickly, and the fire was burning with a dull roar when Ella heard steps crunch the snow outside.

Walking to the front door, she held the

door open as Susanna brought her father up the steps. The old man tottered, nearly slipping, but Susanna kept a firm grip.

"This world's a rough place," he said, resting on the top step. "A man gets old fast."

"You've had a good life," Susanna said. "Now don't be complainin' because I have to get you out and movin' around. And Ella has got a *gut* supper waiting for us."

"The food would have tasted the same down there," he said. "Right on my rocker. Now is that too much to ask?"

"There's a rocker over here," Ella said, laughing and pointing.

The old man chuckled. "Thanks for bringin' the supper," he said.

"You're welcome!"

As Grandpa walked slowly across the room, he paused for a moment near the girls, waving his hand at them. "You girls okay tonight?" he asked.

He didn't wait for an answer as they nodded at him, but took a few steps and reached for the rocker arms. He turned and lowered himself to the seat.

"He's just a tease," Susanna said. "Although I suspect I'll be complainin' myself when I'm that age and someone drags me out into the cold."

"I know," Ella said, pulling on her coat.

155

"I'll see you in a bit. I'm going to help Ivan"

She opened the front door and stepped out on the step. Old age was still a long ways off, and many waters would run under her bridge before then. If *Da Hah* allowed her to live, perhaps her end would also be blessed, as the old man's was, surrounded by family he loved. Carefully she went down the steps, working on not slipping on the icy treads.

FIFTEEN

Ella pushed the barn door open, entered, and then turned around and with both hands lifted the door back in place until the latch snapped. Ivan hadn't lit a lantern yet, but he would need one soon with the early winter dusk hanging heavily in the barn. A cow mooed from the stanchions, twisting her head around to get a good look at the intruder.

Ella walked past, watching for a quick flick of the cow's tail. From somewhere down the row of cows, the steady hiss of milk streaming into foam rose softly.

"I'm down here!" Ivan called, his hat coming into view.

Ella glanced around, searching for a milk pail. Several three-legged stools leaned against the barn wall.

"Milk buckets," she said. "Where do I find them?"

"They're in the milk house," Ivan said, his

voice muffled.

Ella pushed open a side door and made her way down a long dark hall, running her hands along the wall to find her way until she reached the door to the milk house. Once inside, she selected two milk buckets and made her way back up the long hallway. The barn burst into light, just before she pushed open the last door. Ivan had the lantern hung on the ceiling when she stepped inside. His face was now bathed in the soft light. Ella frowned at the sight of dark circles under his eyes.

"Ivan, you're working too hard," she said. "I can see it in your face."

He shook his head. "*Nee*, but I am thankful for the help tonight . . . and for supper."

Was now the time to ask him what the young bishop wanted? *Nee*, there were chores to be done.

"Which cow first?" she asked.

He pointed. "That one. The black spotted. Then we move on up the line."

Ella sat on her stool and quickly found the rhythm this cow liked — a slow, steady pull. She felt the cow relax against her shoulder, the udder filling with milk until it bulged. Quickly her bucket filled.

Ella emptied the bucket into the strainer, pouring slowly as the milk worked its way through. She glanced around. Why did the barn have no cats? Usually there were a few around these old places, half wild at times, but wise enough to show up for free milk at chore time.

Her sister Dora made an art out of squirting an occasional stream of milk at a cat's face. This scared them off at first, but they quickly learned to open their mouths. A cat would sit on its dignity, allowing its face to be reduced to milky whiskers for a few drops of delicious milk. It was a funny sight.

How she missed her family! She sighed and moved on to the next cow, who wouldn't relax, her strokes bringing out little milk. Ella spoke to the cow softly, "Come on, girl. You'll be okay. I know I'm a stranger, but you'll feel better with the milk out. Now how about it? Will you let it down?"

When nothing happened, Ella stopped and gently ran her hand along the cow's side, her eyes on the udder. A smile crossed her face, as the milk began to squirt from a teat. She still had her farm girl's touch. With long strokes, she started filling the pail, standing to empty the bucket when she was done.

"That one's always been a little skittish," Ivan said over her shoulder.

Ella jumped, feeling the red rush to her cheeks. He had surely heard her talking to the cow as she milked.

He laughed softly, motioning toward her now full milk bucket. "Looks like you talked her down."

"Daett taught me how," she said, keeping her eyes away from his.

"He did a good job then, but I already knew that."

A strong urge gripped her. Now was the time to ask the question, whether the cows were milked or not.

"Ivan, what did Bishop Miller want?" she asked, glancing at his face.

"*Ach,* Susanna must have said something," he commented, his eyes looking to the floor.

"Yah, she's worried. And so am I."

"I guess you have a right to know," he said, his voice trembling. "Perhaps I can tell you while we milk since there are still four cows to go."

Ella's heart hurt at the sight of his troubled face, but she moved to the next cow.

Ivan took his three-legged stool, sitting down beside the cow next to her.

Had the bishop already told Ivan about Robert? Had he passed on the news that she had entertained an *Englisha* man alone in her house for lunch? If so, perhaps the bishop didn't even need to help Robert in order to use him against her. He could just as easily send him away and still use the information obtained from Robert. Ivan would surely have to support any church action that might be taken against her.

But she could defend herself. Ronda had been in the house the whole time, and Robert was a son of a customer. That would supply justification for her actions. Ella drew in a deep breath, gathering herself together.

"The bishop has a problem with me — and a serious one, I'm afraid," Ivan said, his voice so low Ella almost missed it.

"A what?" she asked, pulling her head away from the cow. The swish of Ivan's milk strokes were echoing in the barn. Surely she had heard wrong.

"The bishop has a serious problem with me," he said, louder this time.

"With *you?*" Ella tried to keep her milk strokes going but failed.

"He wants to know why I don't preach like I used to. He says he's concerned, as are some of the other ministers. They think I might have acquired liberal ideas or that I am drifting away from the church."

So was this a new angle on the bishop's

attack to separate them? Accuse Ivan of going liberal? If it was, the argument seemed weak to her.

"Who has the right to tell a minister what his style of preaching should be?" she asked.

"There's more. He found out I have some current Amish writings in the house," Ivan said, his voice muffled again.

"I didn't know you read any Amish writings."

"I started after Lois died. I guess the bishop figured that out or perhaps he got it out of me. I can't remember."

"I still don't see why that's a problem," Ella said. "It's not even worth a visit. Not if they're *Amish* writings."

"Normally it wouldn't," Ivan said. "But with everything put together, even I have to admit it doesn't look good."

"What do you mean?"

"He wanted to see the papers, and I showed him," Ivan said, his voice tense. "I couldn't hide what I had been readin' — and I didn't want to."

"In the Amish papers?"

"Yah, they've been runnin' articles — lots of them — against tobacco use. I've read them and had some marked, sentences underlined and the like. Somehow Bishop Miller must have heard about it, and the evidence was there."

"So what does that mean? Our people use tobacco, but that's always been true, hasn't it?"

"Yes, but it's become a big controversy among the Amish. A lot of strong feelings are involved. I suppose you aren't aware of that."

"No, I'm not," Ella said, finishing the cow and standing up. Her stool clattered backward, tumbling under the cow behind her. That cow brought her foot forward, kicking the stool out into the aisle on the other side. Quickly Ella set the milk bucket on the concrete floor and chased the errant stool.

Ivan muttered something.

"I didn't hear that," she said, picking up the stool.

"Many of the Amish are questioning the old ways, thinking that perhaps the forefathers weren't aware of the dangers of tobacco. They think the practice should be stopped, and these writers are leading the charge."

"Is that bad? They're Amish. Isn't that good enough?"

Ivan got to his feet. "I suppose it depends. Bishop Miller said this community wouldn't follow what he called an *Englisha* liberal trend."

"What do *you* think?" she asked, searching his dark, shadowed eyes under the lantern's soft glow.

He smiled wearily. "I have my sympathies for the articles."

"But not that long ago you wouldn't have had."

He nodded, "See, even you can see what's been happening to me."

"But that is *gut*," she said. "I like how your sermons are more gentle."

"Yah, and I'm sorry it's happened after Aden's death and not before. I still feel bad about the way I preached at his funeral. I should never have spoken such harsh words while your heart was broken."

"I know that," Ella said, reaching out to touch his arm. "You have said before that you are sorry, and I have forgiven you. So please don't let the bishop's words tear you down. There should be nothing wrong with being against tobacco. It sounds as if other Amish are."

"He's a *gut* man, Bishop Miller is. He's only looking out for the church's interest and for my soul. He means no harm."

If she could only tell him what she suspected, perhaps he would be on his guard in the future. But there was no way she could question Bishop Miller's motives without revealing her repudiation of his love.

"I scare myself," Ivan said, his eyes searching her face. "I see things in the Bible now — things I never knew were there."

"Like what?" she asked as she looked over the cows.

He shook his head. "Mostly things to do with tobacco use, and other verses the articles quoted. They make for trouble, Bishop Miller says. If it were simply a matter of opinion, perhaps the danger wouldn't be so great. But to see the matter in Scripture is nothing but trouble. I know that, and Bishop Miller has an obligation to keep the peace in the community."

"What is to be done then? Surely this matter will go no further?"

"Bishop Miller doesn't know. But there will be talk between the ministers. And I will abide by their decision, whatever it is."

"Then why don't you preach hard and rough at the next preachin' Sunday? You don't have to worry about me, I will understand. It might help your position greatly."

"You have some wild ideas that wouldn't help," Ivan said, still looking down to the floor. "But there is more to tell you."

"Yah?" Ella asked, reaching out to squeeze his arm and boldly touching his cheek with her fingertips.

"I have had dreams of her. In the night-time. I saw her in the skies last night, holding out her arms for me. She's calling for me to come."

"Her?"

"Lois," he said, his voice barely a whisper.

Sixteen

Ella stood a long moment, the silence broken only by the hiss of the lantern and the quiet munching of the cows. Finally she said, "It was just a dream. We all have dreams. They come and they go."

"But I wished to be with her," Ivan said, his eyes meeting hers. "I shouldn't be sayin' these things to you. It's not decent when we need to be thinking of a life together. But . . ."

"You're needed here," Ella stated. "Here for the girls' sake. It's not time for you to go."

"I know, but have you ever dreamed of such things, Ella? About being with Aden?"

"*Nee,* but I thought I saw him once."

"Was he calling you from the heavens?"

Ella shook her head.

"Come," Ivan said, taking her hands in his. "We must not think of such things on a night like this when you've brought supper over. You came to bring me joy and gladness, and I have nothing but trouble to offer you."

"It's life, I guess. Like they say, it goes on."

"Yah," Ivan smiled weakly, the lantern throwing light halfway across his face.

She reached up to touch his beard, running her fingers down the full length.

His fingers tightened on her hands.

"We have not yet spoken the vows," he said, his voice husky with emotion, his free hand brushing her face. "We must not sin against *Da Hah*."

"We are not sinning, Ivan."

"You bring light to a very dark world," he said, touching her lips with one hand.

Ella felt warmth across her cheeks, and let go of his other hand. Why was she so embarrassed around him?

"I was meanin' no rebuke," Ivan said, his fingers touching her cheek again, pushing her chin upward, his smile gentle as her eyes met his. "It's my own heart I fear, not yours. You are much too *gut* for me."

Ella laughed shakily. "Don't be sayin' such things, Ivan. You are a *gut* man."

"I am not wrong in what I say. *Da Hah* says no man is good. We all fall short."

"Will you preach to me now?" Ella asked,

her face tilted. "Practicing for Sunday perhaps?"

He laughed then, full and hearty, bending to pick up his milk pail. "I guess we'll have to see if your plan works. Preaching Sunday is this week, and they won't do anything that soon. Bishop Miller will be here some Saturday afternoon before long, and we will talk about it then. And I wonder what he'd do if I really let go with my preaching again?"

"Do it then! Let him hear the old Ivan in all his holy glory. I can see the look on Bishop Miller's face now!"

Ivan laughed softly but sobered quickly.

Ella glanced at him. *Where did this sudden change come from? His hand is trembling, even while gripping the handle of the milk bucket.* "What's wrong?" she asked.

"I fear I can never go back to my old way of preachin'. So much has happened."

"Then don't," Ella said, touching his arm. "Eventually Bishop Miller will see that the change is for the good. You are a much better man since the changes. Anyone can see that. I want to support you in whatever you decide."

"Yah," he said, managing a smile. "Now we must get these last two cows milked or Susanna will think we have fallen in a snowbank and come looking for us."

"Which ones are still to be done?" Ella asked. "I've lost track."

"These." He motioned with his hand. "I see you have kept up with me. Are you *gut* or am I getting old?"

"I'm *gut!* And thanks. I wasn't raised a farm girl for nothing."

Ivan's stool scraped on the floor, and Ella pushed gently on the haunches of the cow she intended to milk, running her hand down its leg to check for nervousness. When no reaction came, she set the milk bucket down and began. Quickly the gentle swish of milk streaming into buckets of foaming liquid filled the barn.

Ella finished first and emptied her bucket slowly, watching the milk swirl around the container. Her hands ached a little. She was out of practice, but that would change when she married Ivan. Even if a *bobli* should soon be on the way, she would have time to help with the chores for many months.

She glanced toward Ivan, feeling the red coming up her neck again. What if he had heard her thoughts about a *bobli?* She really should not think such things yet.

"He won't make it," she said, and started laughing at the look on Ivan's face when he whirled around to face her.

"Whose making what?"

"The bishop," she said. "He's just tryin' to make trouble. It won't work."

Ivan smiled gently. "I'm grateful for your support, but my heart may not be as pure as you think. Bishop Miller is a wise man. Now I have to get these milk cans out to the water cooler, and if you would let the cows loose, that's all the help I need. I'm sure Susanna can use your help in the house."

Ella nodded. Ivan seemed more like himself now, so perhaps with a *gut* supper he would recover fully. The man disappeared down the hallway and out a door while she loosened the stanchions around the cows' necks. They bumped around, got themselves tangled up in each other in their haste, but eventually formed a single-file line and moved out to the field behind the barn.

Ella tightened her coat and plunged into the night and back to the house. The air had gotten colder but was still bearable. Under her boots the snow crunched. The winter had been hard already. Hopefully the weather would eventually break. If not, they would just have to endure.

She left her coat and boots in the cold washroom. Someone had lit a kerosene lamp, but the water bowl was frozen. She broke the ice, tossing it outside. She opened the kitchen door, went inside, grabbed the tea kettle, and refilled the wash basin, leaving the door cracked open to allow some of the kitchen warmth to seep out as she washed.

"All done?" Susanna asked when she came back inside.

"Ivan's putting the milk in the cooler and should be right in."

"The girls are with Daett." Susanna motioned toward the living room.

"Can you use some help in here?"

"*Nee*, I'm almost done."

"Then I'll see what the girls are doing," Ella said, walking into the living room.

Mary and Sarah were gathered around the old man's rocker. He was at the end of a story, his voice husky. Their faces turned up toward him.

"Then your *grossmamm* said we should let her in the house for just a few days. I didn't know about the plan, but your daett agreed for once. I thought he wouldn't, since he hardly ever gave in to his sister's wishes. So they kind of ran over me on that choice, even if I had wanted to say no. They got to stay — all of them — until the mother cat was well again."

Mary's eyes shone. "They took care of

them in the house when the mother cat broke her foot."

"She had kittens," the old man said, smiling warmly. "We never allowed cats in the house, but it was wintertime, really cold that year, about as bad as this one. So I gave in on that one, and *Grossmamm* had her way."

"Can we have kittens in the house?" Mary asked.

"Yah, I want them too," Sarah echoed.

"Under no condition," Ella said. "Cats belong in the barn."

"Then in the barn?" Mary asked, pleading. "You have a barn."

"No," Ella said. "My barn isn't set up for cats. You need milk cows for cats."

"I don't know about that," the old man said, laughing.

"Why aren't there any cats in your barn?" she asked Ivan's father.

"They all seemed to have left," he said. "They were her cats . . . Lois's."

"They just left after she died? But old barns always have cats."

The old man nodded. "I know. But the ones Lois had are gone, and no others have come to take their place."

"Well," Ella said, "it's time for supper. Susanna has everything ready. By the time we're ready, Ivan should be in."

She helped the old man up from his chair and held on to his arm as the girls skipped ahead and took their chairs. Ella helped Ivan's father into his chair and returned for the baby, sliding her into her high chair.

"I want our barn to have a cat," Mary said, returning to the subject.

"Perhaps we can get one for your barn," Ella said, patting her arm.

"I wouldn't," the old man said, shaking his head. "Not yet at least. It will just run away and break the girls' hearts. Once you come to live here, Ella, then perhaps a cat might stay."

Just then the outside washroom door slammed shut, announcing Ivan's arrival.

"Are we ready for supper then?" Ella asked.

"My stomach's right hungry," the old man hollered toward the washroom. "Hurry up there, son."

"I'm coming!" Ivan called. He pushed the door open moments later. He took his seat at the head of the table, bowed his head, and led out in prayer, his voice strong.

Has something happened to strengthen him? Ella wondered. *Have, perhaps, my presence and words made a difference?*

"Amen," Ivan said.

Everyone looked up, and Susanna started

the casserole around. The old man took his helping first and then Ivan did. Ella helped the girls with their plates.

"Have you got that colt settled down, son?" the old man asked.

"Not yet. I think he needs more work. But it's hard in the wintertime. Spring can't come soon enough for me. I don't know what's wrong with the colt. I thought I had him well broken last fall."

"They're all like that," the old man said. "Young horses always have minds of their own, and it takes a while for them to settle down."

"This one's a little wild," Ivan said. "I had high hopes for him. I can't really afford another horse if he goes bad. You don't get much for an unruly horse at the auctions."

"Yah," the old man nodded. "I know. Farm life's hard, and it has always been hard."

The table got quiet as everyone focused on the delicious food. Soon everyone had eaten their fill.

"Would you like some pie?" Ella asked Ivan's father.

"I might," he said. "I think there's still room. And I must say you cook *gut* food."

"It's nothing special — just food," Ella said. "But I'm glad you like it."

"Susanna also cooks *gut* food," he said. "When she has time."

"Hey, Daett!" Susanna objected. "You make it sound like I'm starving you."

"I know," he said. "I was trying to tease, but I guess I'm getting too old for even that."

They ate pie in silence, the moments slipping by like water in a slow-but-steady brook. When they were finished, Ivan said, "Let's pray." He bowed his head in silence. When they were done, the girls helped with the dishes, and Ella prepared to leave for home. She gave each of the girls a kiss, and then Ivan walked her out to her buggy. He untied her horse as she climbed in. He let go of the bridle and came up to the buggy door. Ella gripped the reins as Moonbeam pulled on the bit.

"Goodnight," Ivan said, his hand on the side of the buggy door.

"Goodnight," she said. "I wish there were more I could do for you."

"You're doing plenty, and don't worry about this problem with the bishop. I'll have it worked out soon."

"I can't help but be worried. You know that, don't you?"

"Yes. Will this issue with the bishop give

you doubts about what your answer will be?"

"*Nee.* I still want it to be yes," she said, the horse jerking on the lines in her hands.

"That is *gut,*" he said. "And thanks again for supper."

"Goodnight," she said, letting the horse go.

Moonbeam dashed forward, nearly throwing Ivan into a snowbank. She looked back and saw him standing, waving toward her, as she managed to make the turn at the main road without flipping the buggy over.

SEVENTEEN

The night air had turned icy, and Ella pulled the winter blanket up as far as it would go. With a single hand she held the reins, the other clutched the blanket. In the dim buggy lights, the horse's breath blew in great blasts as he climbed the hill toward Chapman Road. The night mirrored her emotions — cold, unsettled, frozen.

Making the turn into her drive, she slapped the reins once when the horse slowed down. She saw lights shining brightly in the living room of the white house. *Joe and Ronda must still be up,* she decided.

Moonbeam walked slowly up the driveway, pulling up as close to the barn as he could get. Ella waited for a moment. Perhaps Ronda would send Joe out to help unhitch. The front door remained closed.

She finally climbed down, the buggy lights still on, the tugs feeling like icebergs under her fingers. Carefully she pulled them off and dropped the shafts gently onto the snowy drive. Opening the barn door and going inside, the light from the buggy reached far enough for her to see. She took the harness off Moonbeam, hung it up on the wall, and led her horse into his stall. His manger contained enough hay, so she exited and pulled the stall door shut with a solid click. He was safe inside for the night. She decided he didn't need any oats tonight.

Ella took the basement steps sideways, thankful for the light glowing through the living room window. A faint warmth from the stove greeted her as she entered through the basement door. The fire had not gone completely out. She lit a kerosene lamp, removed her coat, and stirred the coals. Fresh wood brought the flame to life. Ella held her hands over the kitchen stove and rubbed them briskly together. She thought back on the night . . . the words spoken, the stirrings of emotion she'd felt.

They would make it — she and Ivan. Bishop Miller would soon give up his attempts to break them up. Robert was likely gone by now, back to Maryland to be with his mother.

Ella took a deep, cleansing breath as she enjoyed the heat from the stove.

She'd help Ivan through his church

troubles — whatever they were. At least no one would ever know that the *Englisha* man — Robert — had moved her heart.

She pulled the curtain back from the bedroom so the warmth from the stove would move through, undressed, and climbed wearily into bed. Sleep came quickly enough, and she dreamed of wide open spaces where flowers swept across fields as far as her eye could see. The beauty took her breath away, and she stood trans-fixed.

Off in the distance someone came toward her, walking slowly at first. Then she could see him running. *Who is it?* Caught up in the wonder, Ella ran toward him. *Is it Aden?* Her heart pounded until it hurt, and her breath came in gasps.

When his face came close enough to see, she saw it was Ivan. She slowed to a walk. He waved and continued to run. In her exhaustion, she waved back, hoping he didn't notice her disappointment. Then she heard a voice calling his name. *Is it my voice?* Ivan also heard, but he looked skyward. When she followed his gaze, light had broken from the sky, and a figure was form-ing — a woman, her arms outstretched.

Ivan answered with upraised arms, with more joy on his face than she'd ever seen.

His name was called — distinctly pronounced — and Ella realized it was not her voice. *Lois* was calling to Ivan. Time seemed to stand still around them, the figure hanging in the sky, the light shining, and Ivan's face lifted toward the heavens until her own name was called. Quietly the sound came at first, growing louder and louder.

With a start Ella awoke, trembling.

"Ella! Ella! Can you hear me? Ronda needs you. She's in a bad way."

Joe's voice came clearly from the kitchen area, apparently as near as he would approach.

"Yah!" she called, still shaking. "I'll be right there."

"Sorry to bother you," Joe shouted. "I brought the lamp with me, and you can bring it with you. Ronda's in our bedroom. Hurry!"

Ella heard his footsteps retreating. She dressed in haste. What could be Ronda's trouble at this hour? Everything had seemed fine when she'd arrived home.

With her slippers on, she grabbed the lamp Joe left and raced up the basement steps two at a time. Her dream lingered in the back of her mind, taking more of her breath away than the climb upstairs.

She had no reason to be jealous of Lois.

Ivan had loved Lois, and she had wished Ivan were Aden. What difference was there between them? None.

Ella rushed into the living room and headed for the open bedroom door.

"Ach . . ." Ronda said, her face white. "Ella, I need help."

Joe sat on the other side of the bed, and Ronda motioned with her hand for him to leave.

"What's wrong?" Ella asked when he had closed the door behind him.

"I think I've lost the baby. I'm sure I have," Ronda whispered, tears in her eyes. "The bleedin' won't stop. I don't know what to do, Ella."

"I don't know either," Ella said. "I've never dealt with something like this before. Is it very bad?"

What had she heard about such cases? What did the midwives do when a woman miscarried? "When did it start?" Ella asked. "And how much blood is there?"

"There's a lot," Ronda whispered. "The sheets are soaked. I lost the baby before you came back from Ivan's, but I thought that's all there was to it. I haven't told Joe."

Ella lifted the blanket, took one look, turned quickly away, and called for Joe.

When he opened the door with a jerk, Ella

said, "We have to get Ronda to the clinic right now. Ronda, you're going to have to be brave. Joe, you'll have to drive us in the wagon."

Joe looked bewildered. "What's happened?"

Ella lifted the blanket again. "She lost the baby, Joe. I'm so sorry. And she's bleeding a lot."

"It's after midnight, and the wind has picked up. Perhaps I should ride for the midwife. I'm sure my horse can make that trip, but I'm not so sure about the wagon. My horse is half lame, and Daett won't have the *gut* one back until tomorrow."

"Joe, there's no time to get the midwife. We have to take the chance on getting Ronda to the clinic. We'll use my horse."

Joe nodded and disappeared, the swift sound of running work shoes on the hardwood floor echoing in the house.

Ella ran her hand over Ronda's forehead, now beaded with sweat. "I'm sorry we have to take you out into this weather."

"I know. I'll bear up," Ronda said through her tears.

"Let's get you ready then. You'll need all the clothes you can get on to stay warm."

"I'll never get the blood out of these sheets," Ronda said, trying to get up.

"Don't worry about the blood," Ella said. "Think about Joe, about hanging on. Can you do that? Joe needs you."

"I'll try," Ronda said. "But our *bobli* is gone."

Ella couldn't think of words to say. Quickly she took a white sheet and wrapped Ronda's lower body as tightly as she could. She found socks in the dresser, pulled them on Ronda's feet and then added another pair on top of that. Ronda's thick Sunday coat came out of the closet, and a quick race to the front door produced Ronda's rough, everyday coat.

"I'll not be able to move," Ronda whispered.

"You're not supposed to," Ella said. "We'll carry you."

Ella laid three blankets on the bed, and paused to think. "I'll be right back," she said. She raced downstairs with the kerosene lamp to grab the coats and boots she wanted. Joe was already in the bedroom when she came back up, and she noticed he left heavy snow tracks across the floor.

"I'll take her feet," she said as Joe carefully lifted Ronda by the shoulders.

"Hang on, sweetheart!"

They moved through the bedroom door. Joe had tears in his eyes, understanding the seriousness of the moment. As they hurried out the front door, Ella cautioned, "Don't run, Joe. I'll slip and fall."

Carefully they slid Ronda headfirst onto the bed of the open spring wagon, Ella pushed two blankets under her, and laid the rest on top. Joe was already on the seat. Ella climbed up, holding a blanket in front of them as a windbreak. Joe clucked to Moonbeam, and the wagon headed toward the main road.

How Joe survived in the open spring wagon without freezing seemed like a miracle to Ella. The icy wind cut through them like a newly sharpened knife. For her part, she finally lay on top of Ronda, a blanket wrapped over both of them, her open coat tucked down the sides. She needed to keep Ronda warm. She began to pray. *Da Hah* must help them. Joe drove down the snowy roads like a mad man, and Ella's heart swelled with pride for her horse. He must have known a life depended on him because his pace never slackened.

For a moment, Ella wondered if this was how Ivan had driven that summer night with Lois in the back of the wagon. He had permitted no one to ride with them, she'd heard, in order to lighten the load, but even that hadn't been enough to save his wife.

Finally Ella saw the lights of the clinic ahead. She thanked God that Ronda still breathed steadily under her.

Joe drove as close to the front door as he could and then leaped over the wagon wheel. He ran through the door of the clinic to get help. Moments later a nurse appeared, followed by two men who quickly transferred Ronda to a gurney and wheeled her away.

When they were gone, Ella allowed the tears to come. She could cry now that her duty had been done and the matter was out of her hands. After a few minutes, she walked over to her horse, his breath still coming in great heaving gasps, foam from sweating bubbling over his chest strap. Grabbing a blanket from the back of the wagon, she rubbed him down slowly.

Soon there was a flurry of activity behind her. A parked ambulance turned on its lights. Joe came over to Ella and said that Ronda was being taken to the hospital. The doctor at the clinic had stabilized her for the trip as much as possible. Joe quickly turned and made his way to the ambulance Ronda had been placed in. He climbed in. Ella went to a white clad nurse who had accompanied Ronda to the ambulance and was about to return through the clinic door.

"How is she?" Ella asked.

"She'll be okay, ma'am. Her blood pressure was still high enough, so they'll wait until she gets to the hospital for the necessary blood transfusion."

"What caused the problem? Was it more than a miscarriage?"

"The doctor thought it was cervical shock," she added cautiously. Ella knew it was probably against the rules for the nurse to say much, but sometimes with the Amish community, the medical personnel bent the rules.

The nurse added, "You and that man of hers did good work tonight."

"Thank you," Ella said, as the nurse, her teeth chattering, disappeared back into the building.

Now what am I to do? Ella wondered. *Moonbeam is near exhaustion, and home is a long way. Yet there is little choice in the matter. We have to return home.*

"Are you up to it, old boy?" she whispered to Moonbeam.

He snorted.

She climbed into the open wagon. She allowed Moonbeam to take his time on the road. She pulled the blankets up to her chin, reaching back later for the one she had rubbed him down with. What did it matter in this cold? Even when she saw blood splatters by the light of the faint starlight, she pulled the blankets tighter around her body.

They made the last hill up Chapman Road at a walk. Ella's hands were almost numb. When they got to the barn, she managed to unhitch the horse without lights, guided by memory and the light from the stars. She quickly wiped Moonbeam down and put him into his stall. Finding the grain by groping with her hands in the darkness, she gave the horse a huge scoop. She heard his rapid chewing as she left and shut the barn door. He had earned the extra food and then some. Glancing at the wagon on her way to the house, Ella walked on past. Tomorrow she would take care of the cleaning.

The kerosene lamp still burned on the first floor, so Ella entered by the upper door, retrieved the light, and carried it downstairs to her own quarters. Tomorrow would be another day, full and urgent as usual, but now she needed to sleep.

EIGHTEEN

Saturday Ella baked bread and tended to the cleaning up of Ronda's blood-soaked sheets from her miscarriage. She did the washing and, every so often, glanced out the window toward the road in the hopes someone would arrive with some news. By evening she was resigned that no news was probably good news and went to bed early.

Sunday morning she awoke before the sunrise. She stirred under the covers, sat up slowly, and reached for a match to light the kerosene lamp. With the wick lit, she wrapped herself in a blanket and moved from the bed to the stove. Ella tried to open the stove, but the lid slipped out of her hand and clattered to the concrete floor. Peering into the stove, she saw a few live coals left in the ash bed. She added small slivers of wood first, then larger ones as the flames steadily grew. Picking up the fallen lid, she waved her hand to drive back the stream of smoke before replacing it.

She returned to the bedroom and chose a dress to wear. She put it on while standing as close to the stove as she could. Today was preaching Sunday, and she likely would hear news of Ronda there, if someone didn't stop by this morning. In the hopes that Joe might bring Ronda home today, Ella went upstairs and lit the fire in the stove. At least it would take the chill out of the house.

She opened the front door to check on the weather. The slight warming trend from yesterday had held overnight, the frost-covered thermometer reading twenty degrees. Faint streaks of light touched the cloudless horizon. She wanted to step outside to watch the sunrise. Surely that would calm her spirit for the Lord's day, but instead, she closed the front door and walked to the front window. The view was the same, and here she could enjoy the faint warmth from the stove. She didn't want to get chilled or catch cold. Ella watched as the light grew slowly, flooding the horizon with pale colors of red and orange. The blaze of the rays grew brighter and brighter until the sun peeked over the horizon. She glanced away.

Was that how *Da Hah* was? Did He give a little hope, and then a little more, and then help would finally arrive? Her mind turned to the problem of Robert. What should she do about the *Englisha* visitor? Was there even anything she *could* do? She gathered her courage. She needed to know what was going on with that man. Today was the day to find out just how far Bishop Miller's plans had gone. Had he listened to Robert's story and then sent him on his way afterward? Or had the bishop led the man on to thwart her plans?

No word had reached her of a strange *Englisha* man in the area, but she might not hear. She rarely got out, and Bishop Miller lived two districts north. The simplest solution would be to attend church in Bishop Miller's district and see for herself. Her presence would cause no undue questions, as many people visited friends and relatives across district lines.

The sun was now fully up, and Ella took a deep breath. It was a beautiful morning, perfect for a day trip north. But what if Robert were there? She held her hand against her pounding heart. That would only mean one thing: He really was joining the Amish. That was something that couldn't happen without the bishop's extraordinary support.

Do I dare go? Ella let her breath out

slowly. *Yes, I will! The house can keep itself for the day.*

She walked over to Ronda's stove and added a few pieces of wood, making sure the damper was tightly closed. Going downstairs, she gathered the eggs and bacon for breakfast. A good breakfast might build her courage. The water bucket was empty. She'd planned to replenish the bucket last night but had forgotten. Pulling on her coat and boots, she ran outside, pausing at the sight of the barnyard. She should harness Moonbeam now. He could wait in the stall, and she would be saved time later.

She left the bucket sitting in the snow and headed to the barn. If Joe and Ronda had been in the house, she wouldn't have continued running. Joe might consider it improper. Breathless, she arrived, pulling in deep breaths of the morning air. Joy surged through her. Was this a sign her trip would be a *gut* one today? That no surprises would be revealed? Wouldn't that be a relief? If that happened, perhaps she could even believe the bishop meant no harm in his pursuit of Ivan's discipline.

Moonbeam greeted her with a shake of his head. Ella rubbed his neck. "Have you recovered from the race to the clinic the other night? You're a *gut* horse. Did you know that? You did really well. I'm thinking Ronda has much to thank you for."

He whinnied as if he understood, and she laughed. The harness went on quickly, and Ella stepped out and shut the stall door. "No oats this morning." She shook her finger at him. "You don't have to run like that again, and I hope not for a long time. And I don't want you taking me for a fast ride on a Sunday morning."

He bobbed his head, and she rubbed his neck again, the glossy hair under her fingers hiding ripples of muscle. Ella blew a breath of air at him, patting his nose. "You be a good boy now. In a little bit you and I are off to Bishop Miller's church. What do you think of that?"

He snorted loudly, bobbing his head again. Ella laughed again and slapped him gently on his withers. She definitely needed a grown-up to talk to — anyone other than children and horses. *Is Ivan the talkative type? Aden had been, but Ivan?* She really didn't know yet. At times he seemed to have secrets inside that produced long moments of silence.

When she returned to the water bucket, the snow underneath had melted, leaving little mounds of slush clinging to the bottom. Ella wiped them off with her hand as she walked to the outside spigot, breaking off the ice hanging from the spout before pulling up the handle to fill the bucket.

Back inside the house, she set a pot of water on the stove to heat before fixing her breakfast. She ate, cleaned the table, washed the dishes, and checked the stove one more time. A glance at the clock showed the time was still early, but why not leave now and perhaps drive a little slower and enjoy the beautiful morning? It sure beat waiting alone in a quiet house.

On the walk to the barn Ella paused, struck with doubt. Was this a foolish thing to do? What if someone asked her why she had come? "Just visiting" might not be such a good answer after all. Did she have any relatives in that district who might serve as an excuse? *There is an uncle on Mamm's side of the family who lives in the northern districts, but not in Bishop Miller's. Well, I'll think of something,* she decided.

Ella continued to the barn. She led Moonbeam out of his stall. He held his head high when she tried to slip the bridle on. "Come on, boy! It's going to be a nice drive."

He shook his head, but lowered it when Ella tugged on his mane. She slipped the bit into his mouth and the headstall over his ears. She led him to the buggy. She held the shafts up, guiding Moonbeam underneath with the other hand in one clean motion. Fastening the tugs, she threw the lines inside and climbed up. She tightened the lines, and Moonbeam took off with a jerk, lifting his feet high. Turning left at the driveway, Ella pulled the buggy blanket up tight and settled in for the long ride.

The wind had driven the snow into tall drifts wherever trees stood in the ditches. The snowplows had made matters worse by piling the snow higher. Four miles north, the little creek looked frozen solid, without even a bubble of water popping up.

Ella held back on the reins as several buggies came up behind her and passed when the road widened. Most of the drivers were young boys, and she used her bonnet to shield her face. When they were out of sight, Ella pulled back even more on the reins. Moonbeam shook his head, but gave in, slowing down.

Dull hoofbeats came from behind, and she slapped the reins, startling her horse. He leaped forward. Keeping a good pace now, she drove down the side roads, the line of buggies becoming longer the closer she came to the house where church was being held. At the next road she turned, pulling into a barnyard already filled with buggies.

Her presence as a single female was immediately noticed when she passed the front sidewalks and parked by the barn. Before she stepped out of the buggy, three young boys made a quick dash in her direction. Ella welcomed them with a smile.

"Good morning," they said in unison.

"Good morning to you. And my, that is fast help."

"*Ach . . .*" one of them said. "*Gut* lookin' girls are worth it."

He looked young and harmless, so Ella joined their laughter.

"You'd better not let Lucille hear that!" one of the others cautioned.

"You got that right," the first young man muttered. "But it's still true."

"Just put my horse someplace where I can find him easily," Ella said turning to go. "Not all the way back in the barn."

"Don't worry," the third one said, smiling. "We'll take care of you."

Ella wrapped her shawl tightly around her shoulders, pulled her bonnet forward, and walked in front of the long line of men and boys. Hopefully Bishop Miller wouldn't notice her in all the comings and goings. She didn't dare look for Robert. Would he really be here? The idea was preposterous. He'd have to learn the language. He'd have to learn and obey all the rules of the church, many of them recited by memory as the need arose. It would be enough to drive anyone to distraction — unless they had been raised in the faith.

The screen door slammed repeatedly ahead of her as shawl-clad women in a long line entered. Ella stood behind the last one, returning the muffled "Good morning." The woman turned to look at her because her voice and face were only slightly familiar.

Inside, most of the women were stacking their shawls and bonnets on the washroom table, the pile high already. Ella placed her wraps to the side on the floor. Hopefully she would be able to find them easier after the noon meal as the rush began for home. The pile on the washroom table could easily become a jumbled mess when someone pulled their items from the middle or bottom.

In the kitchen, the women lined up against the wall, the young girls off to one side. Ella shook hands with a few of them, and then took her place among the women her age. As a visitor, it was the other women's place to come to her. Not that she felt like a visitor. She knew enough of the faces to feel at home.

As if by an invisible signal, the line began

moving toward the benches. Ella followed. *Is Robert here?* Her heart pounded as she kept her gaze focused away from the line of boys already seated on the other side.

NINETEEN

The first song was announced by a firm male voice that echoed through the house. In the rustle of the pages, Ella dared look around for the first time. The young boys sat on the first benches; the older ones further back. She recognized the faces of the three young men who had helped her unhitch. They were looking nervously at each other, likely still in the aftereffects of boy-talk from outside.

Ella saw no one with the familiar face of Robert Hayes. Why she had even imagined he'd be here seemed laughable now. And how would she know him if he was, since he'd have to be in Amish clothing?

The song began, and Ella found the words on the page. The girl beside her shifted on the bench, her fingers wrapped around her side of the songbook, a slight smile on her face. Ella could easily see the girl had been watching the older boys' bench. Involuntarily, Ella glanced in that direction.

It was hard to tell which came first — the shock of what she saw or the immediate racing of her heart. There, amid the single young men, sat the *Englisha* Robert! He was focused on the songbook, so Ella had plenty of time to fully take in his odd appearance. He was dressed in full Amish dress, his white shirt buttoned all the way to the collar. His black vest and pants were obviously new. His smile was triumphant and mischievous when he suddenly raised his eyes and caught her looking at him.

Ella's fingers lost their hold on the songbook, and she knocked the book out of the other girl's fingers. It clattered to the floor. Snickers rose from several children behind her. They were quickly muffled by their mothers. Ella had a sudden urge to leap up and declare her personhood violated by the affront of being stared at by Robert, but she froze instead. The girl beside her glanced strangely at her. She picked up the book from the floor and offered Ella her side again. It was a gesture of grace. Ella took it, but it seemed that nothing could still the pounding of her heart.

So the bishop was up to exactly what she had imagined. He was going to help Robert join the Amish — something that would surely take a long time. The bishop would use that time to tempt her, and then he would pull the rug out from under Robert when she fell. Robert, in his innocence, had said too much, and he would be the one to pay the most. Ella set her lips firmly and held her hand to her heart, hoping to still it. Bishop Miller would never separate Ivan and her through this transparent ruse. How the bishop figured she would marry him after this was all over was indeed a puzzle. Of course, he had always been confident of himself. But this pushed the limits even for him.

The girl beside her glanced up, and Ella was sure she made a strange sight, her face no doubt as white as a sheet. She tried to join in the singing as if nothing had happened. Her eyes fixed on the white page in front of her. She sang of the martyrs who gave all for their faith, but her mind wouldn't allow the words to register. She only saw Robert's face and his happy smile. If he could only see what lay ahead, he wouldn't smile like that. She certainly couldn't tell him without an admission of her attraction toward him. That would no doubt shatter his faith about as much as would her accusations against Bishop Miller.

The ministers came back downstairs, a long line of dark suit coats and somber faces. Bishop Miller didn't preach. Apparently this Sunday wasn't his turn. Ella kept her gaze on the speaker or the floor — and as far away from Robert's bench as possible. What he thought of this wasn't her concern. She hadn't approved of his venture, had indeed made that plain at her place. He was now on his own.

With the last sermon finished, testimonies were asked for — from Bishop Miller and two older men from the congregation. Bishop Miller gave his quickly, and so did the next man. The last man took his task as guardian of sermon purity more seriously. He spoke at length, summarizing the sermons, adding a few points of his own, and then pronouncing his blessing. The clock on the wall showed a quarter after twelve, and the last song still wasn't sung.

Ella wondered what Robert thought of the service. *How does he like the hard benches?* If he was staying with Bishop Miller since he left her place, this couldn't be his first Sunday service. What kind of man would attempt such a great and radical change in his life? She mustn't think about him! She'd already shown too much concern for a strange man. He was making his own way.

Her concern was Ivan, his church troubles, the girls, and how to make sense out of her life in that regard.

The last song was announced and begun. By the time the first two stanzas were sung, the clock read half past twelve. Ella could hear the sighs of relief from the children behind her when the last note died. Bishop Miller announced the close of the service, and the boys filed out first, followed by the girls.

Ella presented herself at the kitchen for table duty — visitor or not. The tables had already been set up by the men. Ella chose to wait on the women's table. As Bishop Miller's guest, Robert was likely to make the first table, and he was to be avoided at all costs.

In the buzz of the women's conversation, Ella picked up snatches here and there.

"He's stayin' at Bishop Miller's place."

"He just came in from nowhere. Something about his mother knew some Amish people."

"Yah, I can't believe it either. Who would have thought such a thing possible? He's actually planning to join."

"Our own boys are tempted to leave . . . and here is someone from the outside . . ."

"Bishop Miller says he believes his story,

so I guess that's good enough for Bert and me."

"What if he's after one of our girls? Who knows what *Englisha* boys think. Look at what happened to Noah Yoder's boy, Eli."

"I heard the girl swept him right off his feet."

"I'm glad my Naomi is taken already and is gettin' safely married now she's twenty-one. At least she's stayin' in the faith like most of our people, though even the wild ones usually come back."

"Bishop Miller says he's learnin' the language. 'A real natural,' he said. I guess it makes things easier that way."

Ella slid the filled peanut butter containers onto the table and picked up the empty ones. So Robert was serious and had made quite an impression already.

An older woman pulled on her arm, smiling when she turned around.

"You shouldn't be puttin' yourself out like this, you being a visitor and all. You be sure now and get on the next table."

"I'm fine," Ella said, returning her smile. "I'm not really a visitor. I just live two districts down on Chapman Road."

"You're Ella Yoder, aren't you? My name is Susie Bender," the girl said. "Yah, you're the one with the new house. The one built after Aden Wengerd died."

"Yah," Ella said, feeling a slight stab of pain at the mention of Aden's name.

"You're seein' that Preacher Stutzman," Susie added, nodding. "I thought that's who you were. Noah and Lizzie are your parents."

Ella kept her smile firmly in place. She knew what hadn't been said. That Eli was her brother.

"They're settin' the table now," Susie said, getting up to guide Ella by the elbow to the table. Several women smiled at them on the way over. Apparently Susie often took young women firmly in hand. "You settle down and eat now."

Ella slid onto the bench and waited quietly until Bishop Miller announced prayer. The room settled into silence as a prayer was recited from memory. Ella breathed a prayer of thanks that somehow she had gone unnoticed by the bishop so far. Ella opened her eyes and spread peanut butter on a piece of bread as younger girls bustled down the length of the table, keeping the bowls filled. Ella's section quickly ran out of bread, but a quick wave from one of the women's hands brought a fresh supply.

With the meal over, Ella didn't linger. She wanted to get home. It seemed like the only safe place left for her. Bishop Miller had invaded so much of her life, even after she had rejected his advances. He seemed to be everywhere.

She located her bonnet and shawl in the washroom and walked outside. The barnyard was oddly empty. The only male voices were coming from the pole barn. Perhaps the boys had kept their promise and put her horse where she could get to him easily, but who knew for sure. She could ask for help at the pole barn, but *nee,* that was going too far. A quick glance inside the barn showed Moonbeam was tied just inside the front door. So the boys were true to their word. She smiled.

With her horse in tow, Ella headed for her buggy. She finally attracted attention from the pole barn. Two of the same boys from earlier raced toward her, making stay-away motions with their hands to the other heads that had glanced out.

"We wouldn't leave you stranded," one of them said. "Why didn't you yell for help?"

"What was I to do? Holler in the door?"

"*Ach,* yah," they said together. "We would have loved that."

"Well, dream on," she said.

They laughed and soon had Moonbeam hitched in the rapid and efficient manner of people who had been doing it their entire lives.

"Thanks!" Ella said, smiling and taking the reins. They stood back, watching her go. She let her horse have his head on the way home so he set the pace. *The sooner I arrive back at the house the better,* she thought.

As Ella pulled in the driveway she noticed *Englisha* car tracks made in the snow since she'd left that morning. Ronda must have arrived home.

Ella unhitched in haste, almost running toward the house. She knocked gently on the door and right away Joe answered, a weak smile on his face and dark rings under his eyes.

"You're back!" Ella said. "I'm so glad."

"Yes, we're home," Joe said, holding open the front door. "Come in."

"May I see Ronda? Is she well enough?"

"So, so," Joe said, his smile strengthening a bit. "They released her this morning. Ronda's mom arranged for a driver to bring us home. We arrived here around noon."

Ella took her boots off, leaving them by the front door, and rushed into the living room. There was no sign of Ronda.

"She's in the bedroom," Joe said, his footsteps behind her. "Just go on in."

Ella entered slowly and saw Ronda sitting

upright on the bed, propped up with pillows. Ella moved to her, wrapping her in a tight hug. "Oh, it's so good to see you! I was so worried."

Ronda squeezed her hand. "Thanks so much for what you did for me the other night. I don't remember much except I stayed warm. Joe said you took all kinds of measures. And you even cleaned our bed from the mess. I'm so grateful."

"You would have done the same for me," Ella said. "It's so good that you're back and looking so much better. Do you have something for supper?"

"Mom would have sent something along, but we didn't know for sure if I'd be out today."

"It was that bad then?"

"I'd lost a lot of blood, but you already know that. They had to clean things up and give me blood. I was weak for a while, and the doctor wanted to make sure nothing else came up. 'Infection is a worry,' he said. So he kept me in the hospital until this morning."

"I'll get supper for you and Joe then," Ella said, feeling invigorated. Thoughts of Bishop Miller disappeared.

"That's so good of you," Ronda said. "But at least use the kitchen up here. It's easier, and I'll enjoy hearing you out there. It'll help me get better just being around you."

TWENTY

"What would you like for supper?" Ella asked.

"Oh my. Anything homemade will be nice after the hospital," Ronda replied. "But, really, Ella, you don't have to do this. You've done enough already."

"Oh, shush," Ella said, holding her finger to her friend's mouth.

Ronda looked at Joe and after a moment said, "Well, last week you made ham gravy and potatoes for the girls. Would that be too much to ask?"

"If you can wait," Ella said. "The mashed potatoes take the most time."

"For that I'll gladly wait," Ronda said.

Joe's smiled indicated he would be happy to wait too.

Ella went to work right away. The potatoes and ham were in her basement root cellar, which worked as well as any *Englisha*'s refrigerator. She quickly gathered the potatoes in a bowl and the ham on a plate and went upstairs to start the meal. It wasn't long before she had the stove so hot she needed to open the kitchen window.

By the time the water was boiling, the potatoes were peeled. Next, she cut them into chunks and put them into a pot on the stove. The ham could wait to be cut later.

What about a dessert? Ella thought. Ronda probably wouldn't expect a dessert, and that seemed all the more reason to fix one. Ella would make a favorite: German Sour Cream Twists. They took two hours to rise, but the baking time was just fifteen minutes.

Ella set more water on to boil, and when the dough had been made and stirred, she set it close to the warm stove to rise. In an hour she would shape the dough into twists and let them rise for another hour. If nothing else, they could begin supper while the twists baked.

When the potatoes were soft enough, Ella poured the hot water down the drain, and quickly mashed the potatoes into white mounds. Next she chopped up the ham.

She spent ten minutes dealing with the thermometer inside the oven, adjusting the fire with smaller chunks of wood until the temperature was reasonably stable. Her mamm could do this without the thermometer, but she didn't dare do that yet. Besides, her mamm did occasionally overheat a dish.

"Supper's almost ready," Ella called toward the bedroom. Joe emerged from the room a moment later with Ronda leaning heavily on his arm.

It didn't take long for Ronda to spot the rising dough. "You're making a dessert too? Oh, Ella, you shouldn't have!"

Ella nodded with a smile. "It's nothing. I had to do something special for your welcome home, you know."

"Sounds good to me!" Joe said with hearty approval as he guided Ronda to the couch in the living room.

Ella laughed. "I think you'll both like it." She set the table for three, all the while keeping an eye on Ronda. She still looked weak, white-faced . . . but happy. Ella realized how hard it must be for her to recover from the physical strain she was under and the loss of the *bobli.*

While the ham gravy warmed, Ella starting working on the twists now that the dough had risen.

"They look like some kind of doughnuts, right?" Ronda asked.

"German Sour Cream Twists," Ella replied, spreading waxed paper on the counter and rolling the dough out.

"I wish I could help," Ronda said, making as if to rise, but Joe gently pulled her back onto the couch.

"You'll have plenty of time to work later, dear," he said, his voice gentle. "Right now you have to get better fast."

"I know," Ronda said wearily as she sank back into her seat. "It would just feel so much better if I could do something."

"I have an idea," Ella said. "What if I bring over the breadboard, and you can form the dough into the twists?"

"Oh!" Ronda said. "I'm sure I can do that. I wouldn't have to get up."

"It'll give you something to do," Ella said, bringing the board over. "And soon you'll be back on your feet, perfectly well."

Working at the counter, Ella still watched Ronda out of the corner of her eye. She was forming the neatest little twists in the dough. *She would be so* gut *with a child, tender, her touch a comfort for any little one,* she thought. *Why had* Da Hah *chosen to take away what she wanted so badly? Was that a principle of His? But,* nee, *I shouldn't question, should I? No matter how little things make sense.*

The ham gravy was already on the table, so Ella said, "Come, we'd better eat before the gravy gets cold.

"Just cover it and it'll stay warm," Ronda said. "I'd like to get the twists in first. Then they can bake while we eat."

"Okay," Ella said with a shrug. "They have to rise for a while first, but I guess I can reheat the gravy."

Ronda worked quickly, not taking as long as Ella had expected.

After Ella set the twists aside to rise, they all took their seats at the table and bowed their heads in prayer. Joe looked like he wanted to pray out loud, but he didn't. He simply announced the end of prayer with a soft "Amen." Ella started things off by passing the sliced bread, making sure the butter plate was handy in the middle of the table.

After Joe and Ronda helped themselves to the ham gravy, Ella took spoonfuls for the mashed potatoes on her plate. She glanced at the clock, aware of the waiting twists. It was hard to relax with them not yet in the oven. Unfinished business. She rose and went over to see if they had risen enough. Not quite.

Ella added another piece of wood to the stove and returned to the table.

"This is *gut* food, Ella," Joe grunted, his mouth full.

Ronda nodded, her smile weary. "Thanks, Ella. This is exactly what I needed."

"You'll be up on your feet in no time," Ella said, getting up to put the twists in the oven.

The last of the meal consumed, Joe said, "I better get to my chores." They bowed again in prayer. As Joe put on his boots, Ella promised, "I'll have the twists ready with powdered sugar frosting when you're done."

Joe grunted again and pulled on his coat. He headed out the door.

Ella poured some powdered sugar into a small bowl, added a splash of vanilla, and stirred in milk until the proper consistency was achieved. She checked the twists in the oven. Almost done. While she waited, she cleared the table and put the food away.

The first pan of twists was done, and Ella took them out of the oven and slipped a second pan in, making sure the oven was still hot enough.

Taking the bowl of frosting to the table, Ella and Ronda took turns dipping their knives in the soft white frosting and spreading it over the twists.

With Joe choring, Ella felt an urge to talk to Ronda about what was on her heart. *Is Ronda up to it?* she wondered. She studied her friend's face and took the plunge.

"Do you mind hearin' about my troubles,

Ronda?" she asked. "It seems like I need to talk to someone."

"Of course I don't mind," Ronda said, holding the twist in her hand still.

"I think Bishop Miller is trying to break up Ivan and me."

Ronda raised her eyebrows.

Ella went on. "You know he had his heart so set on winning my hand. He didn't take it well when I said no. And now I don't think he's wanting to take my no at all. You know how he is, confident and all."

"So what's he doin' to make you think this?" Ronda asked, taking another twist and spreading on frosting.

"He's after Ivan about some church issues," Ella said. There was no need to mention Robert yet — perhaps not at all. If she were wrong in one thing, she might be wrong in the other.

"Ivan?" Ronda responded, laughing. "He's usually after other people, so how did he get in trouble with Bishop Miller?"

"That's just it. That's why I think it's mostly made up. He's spoken to Ivan in private, and now there's to be a ministers' meeting about it soon."

"What did Ivan do to rile Bishop Miller? I mean, it has to be something."

"Well, you might have noticed that Ivan

doesn't preach like he used to. He's not as rough anymore. I happen to like him not so rough, but Bishop Miller is believing Ivan is getting liberal ideas. Also Ivan has writings in his house that speak out against tobacco use among the Amish."

"Is that all?"

"Yah." Ella searched Ronda's face, waiting. "So what do you think?"

"It could be serious, I guess. Especially the tobacco thing. I know Daett doesn't like it either, but they've never said anything to him about it."

"He's not a preacher, and Ivan thinks there might be scriptural grounds against tobacco use."

"He told Bishop Miller that?"

"Yah . . . or Bishop Miller got it out of him somehow."

"I don't know," Ronda said. "I think Ivan can handle himself. I don't think you need to worry."

"So you think it's reasonable?"

"Of course not. These things happen though, and they're mostly never reasonable. But I don't think Bishop Miller would do something like trying to break you two up using church trouble. That would be really lowdown, don't you think?"

Ella drew a long breath. "Ronda, if I tell

you something else, will you promise to tell no one? I mean *no one!*" Ella whispered. "Not even Joe."

"So there's more to this. I thought so," Ronda said, touching Ella's hand.

"Do you remember the *Englisha* man who came through here a while back?"

Ronda nodded. "The good lookin' one."

"Yah," Ella said. "I didn't tell you, but he said he wanted to join the Amish. He was asking me who he could contact about joining, and I sent him over to Bishop Miller. I told him such a thing just wasn't done and figured that would be the end to the matter."

"That makes sense. I would have said the same thing."

"Well, he's still here. I went up to Bishop Miller's meeting today and saw the *Englisha* man in church. He was in full Amish dress, and everyone's talking highly of him. He's learnin' the language and staying at Bishop Miller's place. He clearly has Bishop Miller's full support."

"Why would Bishop Miller take such a big chance? If the *Englisha* man fails, the bishop won't live that down for a long time."

Ella wondered if she dare venture on. Did her sins need to be brought to the light? "Ronda, there's more." She hesitated for only a moment, then let it out. "Ronda, the truth is that this *Englisha* man . . . he gave me the same feelin's Aden used to. It happened that day he was here, and that's why I helped him out and gave him lunch. I thought it wouldn't go anywhere, that I'd never see him again. But I'm worried Bishop Miller has figured it out. Maybe Robert even said something to him."

"Oh, Ella," Ronda laughed, "that doesn't make sense at all. Bishop Miller wouldn't do something like that."

"I don't know," Ella said, trying to catch her breath. "So you think this is all my imagination?"

"Really, Ella, it is. It must be." Ronda touched her hand again. "You can't suddenly have feelings for a man you don't know, and an *Englisha* man at that. I think you and Ivan need to get married as soon as possible. It's not *gut* for a woman your age to be alone. If you want me to, I can get help from someone. Tell them what is going on. Perhaps I could speak to your mamm or daett."

"My daett?" Ella gasped. "*Nee!* After what Eli has done? He'd think another of his children has fallen for an *Englisha* for sure. No, I can't have him knowing any of this. He might die before his time, and it would be my fault. This can't go any further than you, Ronda. I'm not going to do to Daett what Eli did, I promise you."

"Come . . . come," Ronda said, stroking her arm. "It's not really as bad as you might think. Once you and Ivan have said your vows, you'll be safe and sound in his arms."

"I keep telling myself that," Ella said, trying to breathe normally. "But what if this church trouble sticks? And they might just make it stick. Then there will be no wedding plans because everything will stop dead in its tracks."

"Ach . . ." Ronda shook her head. "There will be a way around this. Ivan isn't dumb. He'll know what to do with Bishop Miller."

"But what about my heart?" Ella asked, laying her hand on her chest.

"Your heart has been broken . . . greatly broken," Ronda said. "It still needs a lot of healing, and Ivan can help you with that. You need to be loved by a man, Ella. It does a woman *gut."*

The front door swung open and Joe entered. He bellowed, "Are those twisty things done yet?"

"Not so loud!" Ronda chided with a smile.

Joe came over to the table, took off his coat, and took the two twists Ronda offered him. They disappeared quickly into his mouth. With a look of delight he helped himself to another before taking his chair.

Ella stood to finish up in the kitchen while Joe and Ronda talked about their plans for the next week.

The girls would return. Ella wondered if Ivan would say anything to her about his troubles when he brought them. Likely not.

"I'm leaving you the food, Ronda," Ella said as she finished. "I suppose Joe can store it where you want it."

"He can. And thanks so much," Ronda said.

Ella left them, finding her way downstairs in the darkness by the feel of her hands. She struck a match at the counter and lit the kerosene lamp. Wearily she sat down at the table and, in the flickering light, Ella stared at the wall. Her heart pounded furiously now that she was alone . . . and remembering the face of the *Englisha* man.

TWENTY-ONE

Unable to sleep, Ella paced the floor, her thoughts spinning wildly. Above her she heard faint shuffled steps, probably Joe helping Ronda to their bedroom. He was a good man. *Da Hah* had blessed Ronda when Joe came into her life. *Will I ever have such a blessing in my life again?*

There had been Aden, but *Da Hah* took him. Now there was Ivan and his girls. They were surely a blessing. But then there was the *Englisha* man. Could she ever think of him as a blessing? No, she could not. She thought of Eli. What would happen if she went down the same path he had taken? Her family would be disgraced twice over. An Amish boy's transgressions with a forbidden girl were at least understood. An Amish girl who fell for an outsider was not soon forgotten, her name a blot on the family forever.

Did this *Englisha* man Robert even care

for her? Ella steeled herself at the question. It had no meaning whatsoever. It could never be. She would have to depend on the girls to keep her from the insanity of giving life to the idea of loving an *Englisha* man. Would they be enough to stop her wayward thoughts?

She despised herself for this weakness, for this reliance on innocents to right her world. Where was Aden when she needed him? She sat down. The house around her was still now, no sound coming from Joe and Ronda upstairs. They must be asleep — at peace, while she wrestled alone. The unfairness of her situation brought tears that stung her cheeks. Ella wiped them away angrily.

What was worth anything? Loyalty? Trust? Love? And what was love? Ivan at least had his dreams of Lois. She had nothing but memories, and now even they seemed distant.

She gazed at the lamp. The flame was constant yet moving, as if it were alive. She watched for a long moment and then stood to pace the floor. What was it about Aden that she had loved? The answer lay in the memories, but did she really wish to go there? Perhaps it would be best to bury them and think only of the present.

With a flourish, she loosened her hair,

pulled the wire pins out, and ran her fingers through its full length. Her hair flowed over her shoulders, a dark mass that gleamed in the lamplight as it extended past her waist. She would not stay away from what she'd loved. Aden was gone, yah, but he had shown her the way to love. He had left her that much, and there was nothing to be ashamed of.

She sought Aden's face, allowing the memory to return and pushing the fear of Bishop Miller's schemes out of her mind. She remembered the trembling of her heart when she looked into Aden's eyes. His whole face would light up, with that crinkle of his cheek, reflecting the love he held for her. No, she had not dreamed such a thing.

Their love had been real, obvious in those moments when he had touched her face with his calloused hands that were weathered by the outdoors. She had longed for his hands on her neck, in her hair, the joy of his touch, but always honor held him back from that which was wrong. Honor was all that made sense then or now. Yet honor had cost them their world together. The future she had seen in his eyes had never come to pass.

Her thoughts turned to the night he first took her home . . . the night of their first kiss. She had served him shoofly pie, which he'd eaten even after admitting it wasn't his favorite. Was that why she had never baked another shoofly pie since? Yes, no doubt.

Ella pulled on her coat and walked outside into the clear night. Aden had loved the stars. Together they had watched, counted, and named them. They had done so while standing beside his buggy or on the walk from the buggy to the front door of her home on Seager Hill. The view to the heavens was better up there, Aden had said, because it was higher. She'd laughed at him, telling him the distance to the stars couldn't be measured by such things.

Her fingers reached for the snowbank along the basement steps and grabbed a handful. Squeezing it, the cold stung as the flakes turned into a piece of ice and then water. Snow. They had made snowmen one Sunday afternoon. Her mamm said they were silly. All people in love were silly. They must just be careful. *Da Hah* would help them. Careful about what? Careful about pain that wouldn't go away? Careful about this agony from the hole in her heart? Careful about this memory of what was and never would be again? Was that how she was to be careful?

She didn't feel careful — not at the moment. Reckless perhaps? Her eyes were wide open to what Bishop Miller might have planned for her. Could he really do what she was thinking?

Ella picked up more snow — two handfuls this time. She squeezed and her fingers felt on fire. Did the bishop actually hope to win her consent to say the sacred vows with him? Ronda didn't think so, but how would she know? Ronda hadn't sat with him, been close to him. She hadn't heard his voice, feeling the firmness of his hands on hers and the certainty in his voice.

So clever the bishop thought he was, and Ivan was playing right into his plans. Should she warn Ivan? Would he listen if she did? Not likely. He would think her mind full of imaginings, just as Ronda had. Ella stared at the stars, the night air cold on her face and gently blowing her hair over her shoulders.

Beyond her memories of Aden and her worries about the bishop were her troublesome feelings for the strange *Englisha* man. They had come on their own, and surely they would leave on their own. Only after they had done their damage, it looked like. Why would an *Englisha* man come in from the outside like this? So out of the blue and with a story of his mother's quilt. Ella laughed. There was no way Bishop Miller swallowed that story. She knew him well enough for that.

Ella easily turned to tears. Great waves of them came, stinging her cold cheeks. How was she to stop them? The world seemed to be careening at the moment. Only the house behind her seemed solid with its presence and comfort. Aden's house. He had given it to her — even from beyond the grave, so to speak. From it she had found a reason to go on, a purpose in life. Now it and the land stood with her, solid and steady.

She had been thought brave by others to build the house. Ronda admired her for it. But was the building in vain? She would soon live with Ivan as his wife. She was supposedly not secure until there was a man beside her. Ivan.

She pulled her coat tightly around her and gathered fresh courage. "Ivan's home will be mine," she whispered. "Ivan, the girls, and me. I will do it for love, for his love and for the girls, because what Aden has left me won't be enough. These feelings for the *Englisha* man will be my secret, hidden away in my heart all the days of my life because it can never be."

Ella waited. Surely the bitterness would come, the edges laced with poison, but she felt only sorrow. The kind that came from death and from dirt thrown on bodies that would never breathe in this world again.

"It's just as well," Ella said out loud. "Perhaps I will learn my lesson this time. This kind of love doesn't do anyone any *gut*." Her voice caught, and her eyes searched skyward again. "But, oh Aden, you were so real! Why couldn't you have stayed with me?"

A streak of light, fast and furious, raced across the sky — a star falling from the heavens. Her gaze followed its fiery trace. Was this a message from Aden? Did he still care about her from afar? No, Aden would be beside her. He wouldn't send a star in his place. She was on her own, there was no question about that.

As for Robert, she would stay away from him. Certainly she wouldn't make more trips to the bishop's district to scout things out. She could stay here — hunkered down — until Robert was gone. If she saw him, she was certain he would know her heart from the look in her eyes. She would not be able to hide it.

With great weariness, Ella returned to the basement. Stepping inside, she felt a gladness for the wave of warmth from the stove rushing over her. Going outside had been good for her, but now she was tired. Tomorrow would come much sooner than she wished, and the girls would arrive again, another week like the ones before. Rest now would be good.

Ella filled the stove with wood and turned the dampers. The fire would last until she awoke sometime in the night, awakened by the cold. At this moment the thought of the bed's covers felt wonderful. Their warmth would allow her mind to drift away without this pain.

Still, she wanted to do one more thing. Tomorrow morning would be rushed, and the rest of the day no better, so she desired to write in her journal tonight. Quickly Ella brought out the tablet from the dresser drawer. She turned the kerosene lamp up as far as it would go. She listened for a moment to the house around her. No human noises came from upstairs, just those steady little sounds of wood and stone when they settle down from a cold winter day.

Dear Journal,

I dared talk to Ronda tonight about Robert. Yes, I know I shouldn't have, but the words wouldn't stay inside. And I guess that started it all up. For the rest of the evening I felt like a ship tossed around on wild seas. Even my house seemed to rock along with me. Just a sign, I suppose, of how crazy I've become.

I should have been in bed a long time ago, and I feel like it — torn, weary, and heartsick. Yet I'm putting my thoughts on paper in case I need courage later. Just ride out the storm, Ella. Don't fight it. Sure, Ronda thinks Bishop Miller wouldn't try anything nasty, and perhaps she's right.

In the meantime, don't doubt Aden's love. It was real. Let no one tell you it wasn't. Even when your heart remains broken, bruised, bleeding, and crushed. Still believe. You lost love once, and you can live through it again if need be.

Cry your tears at night. Alone, where no one can see you. Be loyal to Ivan and the girls. Be strong, Ella. Be really strong. Because great love seems to come only to betray, but worse than the pain it brings is the dying you'll feel if you turn away. You can live through it again, Ella. You really can.

She closed the journal, strangely comforted, and slipped it back under the dresses in the drawer. She crawled quickly into bed and fell asleep easily, not awakening until the first touch of dawn was on the horizon. The fire in the stove had gone out hours before, and the basement windows were coated with ice inside and out.

TWENTY-TWO

Ella dressed as quickly as she could. How in the world had she managed to sleep through the night? She must start the fire at once to get the basement warm before the girls arrived. She pulled on her socks and then slippers. They would do for now. She raced across the concrete floor to the stove and pulled out the ash pan. It needed to be emptied before much of a fire could be made. She changed into her shoes — why hadn't she put them on right away? — and dashed back for the ash pan. Tossing on her coat, she went out the basement door and into a blast of cold air that struck her in the face.

It was much colder than last night when she'd gone out to look at the stars. Ella tried to push the memories of that time out of her mind. Surely she had said and thought things she shouldn't have. She had no doubt been carried away with the emotions of the day, and certainly things weren't quite as bad as she had imagined. Ivan would arrive soon, and with his arrival sanity might return.

"Good morning!" Joe called.

Startled, Ella almost lost her grip on the ash pan. The shifting pan released a small white cloud of ash. "Oh!" Ella said, gripping the handle tighter.

"Sorry," Joe said. "I didn't mean to scare you."

"It's okay," Ella said. "How's Ronda this morning?"

"She slept fine," Joe said. "It think it was all the *gut* food."

"I'm glad," Ella said, plunging through the snow. Finally having gone far enough, she heaved the contents of the tray across the snow, a billowing cloud of ash drifting in the brisk morning air.

Ella waited, watching the sight. It was beautiful in its own dark way. The cloud turned the white snow a powdery gray and left a long swath behind as it settled across the field. Here and there a bright coal, energized by fresh oxygen, burned red before blinking out.

Ella turned toward the house, only to stop in her tracks at the sight of the sunrise in front of her. She gasped at the beauty. Rays shone over the horizon, bathing the house with soft red light. The house glowed, the windows throwing back the light as if brought alive from the inside. She let the ash pan fall by her side and whispered aloud, "Aden, we built a wonderful house."

Snow fell into her shoes, the cold stinging fiercely, reminding her to move on. She ran the last few steps, moving past the red glow on the windows and down the stairs. She jerked her shoes off just inside the basement door and then leaned against the wall to dump the snow.

"There, that's taken care of. Now for the rest of the day . . ." Ella sighed deeply. This day was already a weariness to her bones. Yet strength would come; it always did. She slid the ash pan back into the oven, shaking it to tighten the airspace. Opening the stove lid she stirred the remaining ash until a few coals glowed. She dropped some kindling in, and the hungry flames rose quickly.

With heavier pieces of wood soon burning, Ella prepared breakfast. Would the girls have already eaten when they arrived? Likely, but one never knew with Ivan. She would make extra oatmeal, eggs, perhaps bacon. She would tackle the task at hand and rest later when the girls had their naps. Above her, she heard Joe enter the front door, but no sound came from the bedroom area. Ronda was apparently not up yet.

Ella thought for a moment and then made a decision. She ran quickly up the basement steps, knocked, and then opened the door at Joe's "Come in!"

"Is Ronda up yet?" she asked.

He shook his head.

"What if I bring up breakfast?"

"That would be wonderful," he said, his face lighting up. "I wasn't sure what to do, as it's hard enough for a man to pack his own lunch, much less fix a breakfast too."

Just then the bedroom door swung open. Ronda stood with her hand on the door frame, a slight smile on her face. "How about if we go down, Joe? That would make it easier on Ella."

"So you heard me," Ella said. "What about the stairs? Can you manage?"

"They will do me good. Really . . . ," Ronda squinted at the rays of sunlight through the living room window. "It's too much that you fix our breakfast. We can at least come down."

"Then we'd better hurry," Joe said. "I have to leave for work."

"I'll get right to it." Ella turned to leave.

Once downstairs, Ella put water on to boil for the oatmeal, fetched bacon from the root cellar, and slid the frying pan onto the stove. When the water boiled, she poured in the oatmeal. She had eggs in the pan when Joe appeared, supporting Ronda on his arm.

"You're lookin' well," Ella encouraged her. "Won't be long, and you'll be as good as new."

"With your cookin' I'll get better even faster," Ronda said with a laugh.

Joe pulled out a chair for Ronda and then sat down in a chair next to her.

Ella turned the kerosene lamp higher. She brought the bacon and oatmeal over, and then scooped the sizzling eggs onto a platter and set them on the table.

She sat down, and they bowed their heads. Furtively lifting her head, Ella noted that when Joe prayed silently, his lips moved. The scene was comforting. Ella held her breath and bowed her head again. She wanted the moment to stand still, to remain forever. She wanted this to be her life — surrounded by friends she loved, safe, secure.

Joe raised his head moments later as he said "Amen."

The spell was broken.

"I'm glad you could come down," Ella said, passing the eggs to Joe.

"I think we need to thank *you*," Joe said.

"For all that you're doing for us."

"I would say so," Ronda said. "We'll never be able to repay you."

"Just get better," Ella said. "And you'd better take three eggs."

"Two are enough for now," Ronda countered, holding up her hand. "If I'm still hungry I'll take more."

"It's so good to see you on your feet and hungry," Joe said, stroking Ronda's arm with his free hand.

"It's Ella's food that's the cause," Ronda said firmly.

"It's just ordinary food," Ella said. "It's eating it with *gut* people that makes it special."

"I agree with that," Ronda said.

Joe glanced around for a clock, and then gulped the last of his eggs before quickly splashing milk on his oatmeal.

"I have to be ready for work," he said, his mouth full.

"I grew up with brothers," Ella said. "Eat as fast as you want to."

"Men!" Ronda said. "They are the limit. How can food do them any good if they don't chew? Joe, it's not good for you. Slow down before you choke."

He shook his head as he wolfed down the last bite. Standing up, Joe dashed up the stairs. The two women could hear his quick steps moving out the front door. They soon heard buggy tires squeaking in the snow.

"He's a dear," Ronda said. "An absolute, precious dear."

"*Da Hah* has blessed you with Joe," Ella said. Then she looked at the clock. "Ivan will be here soon. I'm not rushing you, Ronda, I'm just saying."

"I'm almost finished. Before I go, tell me you didn't have any more nightmares about Bishop Miller last night."

"Of course not," Ella said, blowing out the kerosene lamp. "What made you ask that?"

"Well, you used to. And the way you've been talking, I thought maybe they've started up again."

"That was in the past. This is now."

"I know you're suspicious of him, but I don't think you should be. He's a *gut* man."

"Perhaps."

"You have bad memories, that's all," Ronda said. "I always thought you were a little jumpy with him. He would have made a nice husband. Of course, Ivan is okay, and with the girls and all, I can understand."

"Bishop Miller never courted you. Remember that."

"Oh, I know," Ronda said, looking at Ella.

"He's still nice. Not for me, of course, but nice."

"I guess we'll see," Ella said as she rose and started to clear the table.

"I'll help you," Ronda said, standing slowly.

"No you won't," Ella said, holding out her hand. "Just sit and talk with me. The girls will come soon enough, and I could use some adult chatter until then."

"Well," Ronda said, dropping back into the chair, "I expect Mamm will come over later to check on me. Do you want us to come down for a quick visit? Mamm would love to see the quilt in progress."

"I'd be thrilled," Ella said. "And what about your wash? Do you need help today?"

"Maybe tomorrow. Mamm might help me today."

"Holler if you need help."

"Okay, but it will be so good to be on my feet again. The time when I'm healed can't come quickly enough."

"I know."

Ronda pursed her lips and then said, "Ella, I want a child again. I want it so badly that it scares me. But will this happen twice? The doctor doesn't think so, and I asked him several times. Always he gave me the same answer, but he might just be saying so."

"I doubt that. But you don't need to rush things," Ella said.

"I know."

"I really don't think you have to worry. Things like that have a way of taking care of themselves."

Outside the snow squeaked again under buggy tires, and Ronda jumped. "That's probably Ivan. I'd best be going."

"Let me help you up the stairs. Thanks so much for the chat."

"And the same to you for the food. I owe you for that."

Ella stayed close beside Ronda until they got to the top of the stairs.

Ronda opened the door and entered her home.

Ella shut the door behind her and then rushed down the stairs, grabbed her coat, and pulled on her boots. *My, it's going to be good to see those girls again!* she thought.

TWENTY-THREE

Ivan had tied up the horse and was walking toward the house, baby Barbara in his arms. Mary ran ahead of him, her arms outstretched to Ella. Sarah was close behind . . . until she tripped and sprawled into the snow.

Ella, standing at the door watching, muffled a laugh. "Mary, go help your sister."

"I'll help her!" Ivan said, his voice carrying clearly in the still air. "Run on inside, Mary. You're cold enough already." He motioned with his hand as he bent over to help Sarah up and brush her off.

Mary needed no encouragement. She continued her dash toward Ella and then jumped into her arms. Her laughter peeled out as Ella caught her, pulling her close for a tight hug.

Ella lifted her gaze to face Ivan. He was close now, Sarah's hand in his. Ella searched his face. There were dark rings around his eyes, his beard was disheveled, the cheeks were unshaven, and his hat was sitting crookedly.

"It's *gut* to see you," Ivan said, his eyes lighting up momentarily.

"Good morning." Ella brushed the hair away from her eyes. "You look a bit troubled, Ivan. Are you okay?"

He laughed dryly, matching the morning air's coolness. He didn't seem to want to talk. Ella shivered but didn't draw back. She took baby Barbara from his hands as her compassion for Ivan stirred.

"I'll be goin' then," the widower said, turning to go.

"I take it none of you have eaten breakfast," Ella said. "Ivan, why don't you come inside? You can eat breakfast with the girls. I have plenty."

He hesitated. "Perhaps I will," he finally said with a weak attempt at a smile.

"Then come," Ella held the door open. "It's warm inside, at least."

"I have the cows milked," he said.

Ella forced herself to laugh. "Yah, I expected so. You wouldn't come over without the cows milked."

Behind her Mary bounced all over the living room before running back and grabbing Ella's arm.

"At least one member of the family is in good spirits," Ivan said, smiling wider now, seeming to relax.

He looks ready to open up about his troubles, Ella thought. *But am I ready to hear them? Yah, I have to be,* she decided. It was right that she give him her attention and an open ear if he wanted it. He might not make her heart pound, but he was the man she expected to marry.

"We're all hungry," Sarah interrupted. "Daett said we could eat here, and that's why he drove so fast."

"Really fast!" Mary exclaimed, bouncing up on a kitchen chair. "I want to eat now."

"Then we'd better get all of you some food," Ella said. "I had Joe and Ronda down for breakfast, but I made plenty extra just for you. So why don't you girls sit still, and you can eat oatmeal while I make more eggs and bacon."

"I heard about them losin' their baby," Ivan said, taking a kitchen chair as if he felt at home. "Is she okay?"

Ella nodded. "She came home from the hospital yesterday."

Ella sat Barbara in her high chair and quickly dished out oatmeal for the girls, adding sugar and milk.

If she had been alone, she would have told

the girls to start eating — that they could pray when she had the rest of breakfast ready. With Ivan here, she sat down before giving the girls their spoons and waited. He bowed his head, and the girls followed suit.

"Amen," Ivan said moments later.

His spirits must really be down for a prayer done without words. As a preacher he knows them all by heart, she thought.

He was waiting silently now, his eyes following Ella while she fried the eggs and bacon.

In an effort to comfort him, Ella smiled his way.

He blushed, fiery streaks rushing up his neck. He kept his gaze focused on the table until she was done and had taken her seat again.

"You eat the oatmeal that's left," he said. "Toast, eggs, and bacon are enough for me."

"I could squeeze some oranges. Would you like that?"

He shook his head. "I'm okay, and I have to get back to the farm."

Ella had eaten with Joe and Ronda, but she prepared another piece of toast. Despite his words, Ivan seemed in no hurry to leave. Nor did he seem ready to talk of his troubles. Perhaps the girls were what kept him silent.

When the girls were finished, Ella quickly got them down and set them playing with dolls in the bedroom area, although she hooked the curtain open so she could check on them. Their enthusiasm was fresh after being gone for the weekend.

She sat back down across the table from Ivan. Perhaps she should ask, but *nee,* it might be best not to. Ivan might only be wanting some company.

"Bishop Miller was over last night," he said, not clearing his throat or raising his voice.

"Yah, I'm not surprised."

"They're talking about the trouble I'm in." Ivan looked up, his eyes a haze of pain.

"Ivan, this is so unfair!" Ella rose from her chair, anger running through her. "Why are they doing this to you?"

Mary glanced her way, alarm on her face.

Ella quickly sat down and lowered her voice. "This is just too much. And so quickly. Why?"

"I guess to them it's serious," Ivan said, keeping his gaze down.

"This is so wrong!" Ella's eyes blazed. "So very wrong to make such a big issue out of this. I wish there was something I could do."

"Don't drag yourself into this mess with me, please. I'm just thankful now that you didn't accept my offer of marriage. That will help you with the bishop."

"Ivan, don't say that!" Ella said.

Mary looked her way again.

"You know what this means for us though?"

How different this breakfast was from when Joe and Ronda had been here. The peace was gone in less than an hour.

"I dreamed of her again last night," Ivan said, his voice a whisper.

"Lois?" she asked, already certain of the answer.

He nodded. "Sometimes I think it would be easier to just leave this world."

"Ivan, you're not serious?" Ella said, grabbing his hand. "You wouldn't?"

That evoked a small smile. "No, not by my own hand, but I would join her gladly if I could."

"Ivan, you must not speak so. Think of the girls, if nothing else. They need you."

"Ella, tell me. What do you think I should do?" His anguished eyes were questioning.

"Can't you smooth things over? Talk your way out of this? You *are* a preacher."

He laughed again, the sound hollow.

"You could try. There must be some way. Can't you see you're playing into Bishop Miller's hand?"

"Playing?" he asked, meeting her eyes.

The depth of his agony startled her.

"I'm dead serious," he said.

"I didn't mean that," Ella said, tightening her fingers on his hand. "Ivan, the truth is I think he's trying to break us up. That's what all this is really about."

Ivan laughed heartily. "How like a woman! Such imagination. In that, you remind me of Lois."

Obviously Ivan didn't believe her. "But, Ivan, at least think about it. Look at how Bishop Miller keeps going after you over such small things, such as your change in preaching style and your reading antitobacco articles. Just don't do anything, and these things might blow over quickly. The bishop can't make this more than it is. And if he does, surely the leaders ought to give you a chance to . . . repent."

"I've thought of that." He sighed. "That is, if I am willing to repent."

"But you must be. For your sake and for the girls."

Ivan smiled. "It's not in me to acquiesce, Ella. It really isn't. Let them do what they want. I am tired of the whole thing. I'm very tired."

"This must be an awful time for you in ways I can't imagine."

"I must be clear though." He paused. "About you and me, there must be no agreement of any kind until this is cleared up. I don't want you giving or deciding anything out of obligation. You are a wonderful woman, Ella, and I will not mar your life in any way."

"But Ivan . . ."

"Yah," he said, raising his hand. "That is how it will be. And if Bishop Miller asks, I will tell him so."

"It will make no difference. Not if he's doing this for the reasons I think."

Ivan smiled, his face weary. "I wouldn't imagine things, Ella. We have enough real troubles to deal with. If you continue taking care of my girls, I'm more than satisfied for now. It's the lonely hours at the house that are the worst. Even with the girls around. Your supper the other night meant so much. You have no idea how much."

"Then I will always bring you supper and eat with you," she said, stroking his arm.

His laugh caught her by surprise. "You must do no such thing. I've always been unworthy of you, and of Lois too, for that matter. This just proves it again, but . . . *nee*. I will walk the path *Da Hah* has chosen for me. Alone. That you care will be enough."

He met her eyes, the pain a whirlpool sucking in the light.

"It's just not right," Ella whispered again.

"Yet *Da Hah* allows it. Are we to question Him?"

"Don't act so defeated. We can always do something."

Ivan stood. "I really must go. Farm work awaits."

"Ivan, the farm can wait. We're not done talking yet."

Ivan continued toward the door, and Ella followed in resignation. She opened the door for him. He nodded and went up the stairs, each step heavy in the snow. Ella waited beside the door, watching through the glass until he drove out the driveway.

Twenty-Four

Ella washed the breakfast dishes slowly, giving herself time to think.

The water had grown cold, but she didn't notice. How did all this come about? Why did Ivan seem so resigned? Oh, if he would only fight — only exert himself. He is a preacher after all. And what can I do except express my outrage privately?

A new thought gripped her. *What if this is leading to excommunication for Ivan?* Nee, *how could it? Surely Ivan would repent before that could happen. Even then, the church would have to vote on it.* And her dissenting vote would be discounted because she was Ivan's intended. Would anyone else have the courage to vote against Bishop Miller and perhaps their home bishop — if it ever came to that? Excommunication damned a man's soul — at least that was what she'd always been told.

Ella shivered. *Surely Ivan wouldn't be*

excommunicated. Things couldn't really go that far over the little they had against Ivan, could they? No wonder he has dark rings under his eyes.

Would it spur Ivan to action if she persisted about her suspicions? What if she went into more detail? Yet he had already discounted her theory out of hand. And what if Ivan learned that her heart's defenses had been breached by another man — an *Englisha* man at that?

Ella took a deep breath. Was she ready to admit such a thing? That she was attracted to another man?

"There's someone here," Mary said, her voice cheerful.

"Who is it?" Ella asked. Surely it was Mamm or perhaps Dora coming to visit. She hadn't seen her parents since the funeral — and Dora and Clara longer than that. How like *Da Hah* to send someone on this dreary, sorrowful morning to bring hope her way. She wiped her wet hands on the towel, the rest of the dishes forgotten.

"It's a man," Mary sang out.

"A man?" Ella repeated. She peeked out the frosty window to catch a faint glimpse of an Amish man. Before she could open the door with a smile, she realized the identity of the visitor and recoiled backward.

She managed to open the door. "Mr. Hayes?" she said.

"Yes. You remembered."

"Why are you here?" she blurted.

He smiled from ear to ear. "Is this how an Amish woman greets a guest?" He looked as innocent as a newborn calf just weaned from its mother.

"That depends on who the guest is," Ella countered, struggling to remain calm. *He can't know Bishop Miller is using him,* she thought. *Perhaps the bishop even sent him to me today.*

"You've gone white," he said as he smiled. "But no need. I'm not a ghost, you know."

"I'm *not* scared." Ella trembled.

Behind Ella, Mary said, "She's our mamm."

"So soon?" Robert said, laughing. "Was there a wedding? Did I miss the invitation? I just saw you Sunday, didn't I? And there was no man along then."

"Are you always this obnoxious?"

"Ah, now that's a big word for an Amish lady. But Bishop Miller did say you are an intelligent woman."

The mention of the bishop unnerved her. "Exactly what do you want, Mr. Hayes?"

"Now, now, take it easy. Aren't we in Amish land, where tempers are supposedly kept low?"

She swept her eyes up and down his cloth-ing, taking in the suspenders, the shirt, the broadfall pants. They were perfect, even down to his haircut. *How in the world has he managed that? By the conniving of Bishop Miller, that's how.* Rage swept through her. "What do you want?" she repeated, spitting the words out.

He shrugged, seemingly unaffected by her foul temper. "Here I leave you just a short time ago with kind words, good intentions, and even tell you what I plan to do. You gave me the best advice I could have received — to meet with Bishop Miller — and now I return to the sound of fury and anger. My, my, how you've changed."

How did he do it? Worse, how did *she* manage to feel any sense of attraction to the man even now? He was a total mass of contradictions. Perhaps another line of at-tack would work better.

"Okay," she said, smiling slightly. "What is it that you want on this fine morning?"

"That's much better, and it becomes you more," he said.

He's a little smug, she thought. *Where does this man get his confidence?*

If he wasn't so innocent and being used by the bishop, she'd ask him to leave now, regardless of how much her heart was pounding.

"Just tell me what you want," she said again.

"Well, seeing the welcome I've gotten so far, perhaps I should leave."

She looked at him. The man was teasing, and she was sorely tempted to agree that he leave immediately, but instead she smiled. "It's cold out there. Would you like to come in for a minute?"

"That's better. Much more like the woman I remember," he said as he entered.

After closing the door, she asked, "Would you get to the point?" She hoped her voice didn't reveal her agitation.

"Well, there's this thing called Pennsylvania Dutch, which you people speak. Apparently if I wish to join, I have to learn it."

"You didn't know this before? I told you that you'd need to learn the language."

"So you did. No . . . er . . . *nee,* I'm not really surprised. But Bishop Miller says I'll learn faster with a teacher. He suggested you might be interested. For hire, of course."

"Me!"

He tilted his head. "Am I that awful that you won't teach me?"

"Nee, of course not. But . . ."

"I would like it very much if you would consent. More than you know."

"But . . . ," she said again, grasping for an excuse. Why, oh why had *Da Hah* sent her this reminder of what her feelings for Aden had been like? Was that not cruelty piled upon cruelty?

"I pay good money."

"I'm seeing Ivan Stutzman. You do know that?"

"I know." He dropped his eyes for the first time. "It's none of my business, of course. But for your comfort level, Bishop Miller informed me that since you have tenants upstairs he would personally give his blessing to this arrangement. He said it would not be inappropriate. And I go by what he says. He sounds like a pretty important bishop to me. He's sure been good to me. Taught me to drive a buggy . . . even lent me his to come over here in."

Ella managed to nod, searching desperately for her voice. "You asked the bishop about me?"

"I didn't need to ask. He mentioned you himself."

Ella's mind raced. Should she allow this — even with Bishop Miller's blessing? Of course this had his blessing, but for his own reasons. How brazen of him, to send Robert straight into her home.

"I don't know," she said, her emotions clouding her judgment.

Then clarity came suddenly, like a sunbeam breaking through the clouds. *Why not play along?* She knew the bishop would never have her hand, even with this unseemly scheme of his. Eventually, everything would be made known. Robert might feel hurt, but he was a man. He could handle it. And although she hated to admit it, she *wanted* time with him. She didn't want to evaluate or think anymore about whether he planned to stay Amish or ask a thousand other questions. She wanted to be with him. She felt guilty about it . . . even sorry, but there it was.

"Well," he said, waiting. "I can come back some other day if you need time to think about this."

"*Nee.* If Bishop Miller says it's okay, I agree to teach you."

"You people place a lot of confidence in your bishops," he commented.

"Yah. They lead the people."

"I'll have to think long and hard on that," he said. "But I expect I can keep my mouth shut, even when I doubt."

"There are those who do speak their minds — in private — myself included."

He motioned beyond her toward a chair at the kitchen table. "May I sit?"

"Yah," she said, moving into the room.

Mary and Sarah had set their dolls down and were staring at the man.

"Mary and Sarah, this is Mr. Hayes. You saw him the other day when he was here for lunch. Remember?"

A brief flash of recognition crossed Mary's face. She returned to playing with her doll, and Sarah followed her example.

"I think they like me," he said with a smile.

"I have to clean the table and get my work done first. I hope you don't mind."

"I'll help," he volunteered, getting to his feet.

"Oh, but I can't let you," she gasped, his presence looming over her.

"Something in the rules against men working in the kitchen?"

"Nee."

"Then I will help. What shall I do first?"

"Well, I guess you can clear off the table while I wash the dishes."

"Ah, with pleasure," he said.

Ella turned to the sink and said over her shoulder, "I hope you know I don't really know how to teach our language. The lessons can be free until I figure out what I'm doing."

"Fair enough. And I really don't mind a little work around here ahead of time. You can even take your shoes off if you want. Of course, it's winter. I guess I was thinking of summer — barefoot in the grass and all."

"You might as well get used to barefoot women if you plan on joining the Amish," Ella said.

"I like barefoot women," he said as he moved the last of the dishes to the counter. The table cleared, he said, "I'll go get my tablet. I didn't bring it in with me in case you threw me out."

"You know I won't throw you out," she whispered at his retreating back.

His hand on the doorknob, he paused to turn and smile at her. He had heard.

Twenty-Five

While the *Englisha* man went out to the buggy, Ella raced around the house tidying as best she could. The curtain to the bedroom area was crooked. She pulled gently, but her effort made them look worse. Another jerk and the curtain almost came tumbling down. She gave up on that. Robert would just have to think what he would.

"Why are you rushing around?" Mary asked.

"I'm trying to straighten up," Ella whispered. "Quick, take your boots — and Sarah's too — back to the stairs. They're by the front door. You do that while I sweep the kitchen."

Mary obeyed while Sarah held her dolly.

Ella grabbed the broom, hoping for even just a few sweeps under the table. With vigor she brought the broom around. She grabbed the dustpan and swept up the pile of dirt. Mary was by the front door, slowly gathering up the boots.

"Hurry!" Ella whispered.

She looked up to see Robert's tablet come past the window, heard strong steps that crunched in the snow, and the faint sounds of the doorknob being turned. With a final rush she emptied the dustpan into the fire, a brief puff of flame rising from the mini explosion. Ella shut the lid with a slam, replaced the broom, and gathered herself together.

"So you're working," Robert cooed to Mary as he entered the basement door. He bent over and removed his boots. "That's a good little girl."

"Yah," Mary said with a sweet smile, flattered by his attention.

Did Robert always have this effect on girls? He probably had tons of *Englisha* women who fell over themselves to be with him. How many girlfriends had he kissed before leaving them behind in his flight to the Amish? Perhaps that was why he was here in the first place?

"Well, now that's done," Robert said, leaving his boots neatly by the front door. He pulled out a kitchen chair again and sat down. "Now, you go on with your work. You can teach me words as you go along. Things that you are doing and so on. Would that work?"

"I guess so," Ella said. "As I said, I've never done this before."

He tilted his head, staring at her.

"How will you learn to spell the words?" she asked.

He shrugged. "Bishop Miller says your language has no official written form, but I did find a dictionary I can purchase. I ordered it, unofficial though it may be. I'll use that as my guide once it comes. In the meantime, I'll spell how the words sound. Mom didn't spend all that money on my college education without me learning something."

"You're college educated?"

"Now, now. Bishop Miller didn't think that would be a problem — from an Amish point of view. Just from mine. Things I'll have — shall we say — wasted. Does my education level bother you?"

Always Bishop Miller. Why do conversations always return to him? Oh, for a chance to be somewhere with no talk of Bishop Miller within miles.

He tilted his head again, waiting.

"Did you ask a question?"

"Yah," he said, rolling the strange word out. "I asked if my college education bothered you?"

"Of course not," she said, stacking just-washed dishes on the counter. But it did bother her. It widened the gulf between them.

"I'm glad to hear that. I was afraid it would."

She cleared her throat. "I guess there is the sense that it really makes you from another world — *their* world — and living way across the field from us."

"That's an interesting way to say it," he said, scribbling with his pen.

"Did I say something strange?" She turned to face him.

He chuckled. "A little, but that's what I want to learn. Not just your language, but the way you say things. The idioms you use. This is why a dictionary won't do the trick. I need to hear the words . . . to be around the people speaking it. Thankfully, Bishop Miller understood that and suggested you — the perfect person to work with."

Why does he continue to mention Bishop Miller? Won't he ever stop? "I'm glad," Ella said aloud, hoping she had kept her feelings out of the tone of her voice.

"So tell me some words," he said, his gaze focused on his tablet. "Say the words slowly so I can hear the syllables."

"What do I say?" she asked, her mind going blank. "I don't know how to talk to a college-educated man."

"That's nonsense," he said. "Get over it, okay? I'm like everyone else. College or no college. Now tell me what you have in your hand."

Ella glanced down at the plate. *"Della,"* she said.

"Beautiful," he muttered. "Now what do I sit at — this table?"

"Dish," she said.

He nodded and wrote it down.

"This is a *gavell*," she said, holding up a fork. When he had written that down, she held up a table knife. *"Messa."*

"Is it always the same?" he asked. "Whether it's a big knife, little knife, table knife, or pocketknife?"

"I think so," she said.

"And you are a *mann*," she said. "That's spelled with two ens." She turned her head quickly when a big grin covered his face.

"Anything else about me?" he teased.

"Well, I'm hoping you'll prove to be a *gut* man. That's *g-u-t.*"

"I'll do my best," he said.

"Just pay attention to your lesson," she snapped, regretting she had brought him up.

"Are all Amish women this free with their compliments?"

She felt his eyes on the back of her neck.

"Well, I said I *hope* you'll prove to be a *gut* man. I don't know yet," she countered, not turning around. "I'm thinking the trials ahead for you will tell the tale."

"The trials. Now there you go again. You have no faith in me. I told you I plan to join the Amish, and I'll do whatever is necessary. I've talked to Bishop Miller about baptismal classes, and he said he'll take me on in the spring, even if there are no other students. Yet still you doubt me."

"People don't just walk in and announce they will become Amish," Ella said, turning to face him, her eyes defiant. "It's not done. Unless something isn't right. Are you running from something, Robert? Perhaps a wife you left behind? A girlfriend? Children?"

"Suspicious are you?" he asked, looking at her. "Are all Amish women so outspoken? There is no wife or girlfriend or kids. But really, should you ask these things? As an Amish woman? Shouldn't such questions be asked by your good bishop?"

"Has he asked them?" She kept his gaze.

His eyes were as innocent as a baby's, disconcerting, throwing her off stride.

264

"No, come to think of it," he said. "He hasn't."

"Then perhaps he should. And what is this about Amish women? I can ask what I want to."

He laughed. "I guess if the bishop doesn't do his duty, it falls to the women. That's not just a trait of Amish women — that's true wherever people are. But I suppose I don't really blame you for being suspicious. I can see it might look kind of strange. Me just coming in out of nowhere." He laughed again.

"Is it really funny? It's not to me. I'm serious," Ella stated.

"Yah," he said, his face sober. "So am I."

She was unable to draw her eyes away from his. They seemed locked in place.

"Well . . . ," he said, breaking the silence, "perhaps we'd best end the lesson with that. The good bishop will wonder why I've been gone so long."

"Yah," she managed. "And I need to get some work done around here."

"Then one more word, and I'll be on my way," he said, standing.

"Yah?" she asked. "What's the word?"

"What is the German word for 'wonderful'?"

"Wunderbar," Ella supplied.

265

He cleared his throat. "Thanks then for this first lesson. And we're on for next time, perhaps in a week or so? I don't need a solid date, approximate is good enough."

Ella looked up. "You can just drop by when you're ready," she said. "I mean, I'll be here. There's nowhere I go. I have the girls, the house, the quilting. I don't visit much."

"All right then." The *Englisha* man turned to the two girls with their dolls and the baby nearly asleep. "Goodbye, girls. You be good!"

"Yah, we will," the two older girls said in unison.

At the door he bent over and slipped on his boots. He had his hand on the doorknob when he stopped and turned to Ella. "You are *wunderbar.*" The words flowed gently off his tongue.

Ella wouldn't have been surprised if her knees gave out and she landed flat on the kitchen floor in a crumpled heap. She had meant to walk him to the door, but it was useless. She couldn't move.

As he walked through the door, he turned to smile broadly and wave goodbye. He shut the door, and then he was gone.

Twenty-Six

Ella washed dishes furiously. Not only was she late, but now she heard Ronda's knock on the basement door above the stairs. "Come in!" she called. Footsteps came down the stairs. Ronda will want an explanation . . . and what will I say?

Ella had suddenly thought what her response would be and suddenly the ridiculousness of the situation struck her. She threw back her head in soft laughter, her hands still in the dishwater.

Seeing Ella laughing, Ronda whispered, "Ella, have you gone mad?"

"I think maybe I have," Ella said, turning toward her.

"I was just teasing, you know," Ronda said, breaking into a feeble smile.

"Yes, I know," Ella sighed. Motioning with her hand, she said, "Come, sit down. You shouldn't be standing up so long."

Ronda took a chair at the table. "Ella,

what's happened?"

Ella started to laugh again but stopped. "I'm sorry about the laughter. I suppose it's really not funny. But laughing is the only thing that makes me feel *gut* right now. That and being angry, but that doesn't make me feel *gut* for long."

"So what's this all about?" Ronda asked. "Ivan's arrival I expected, and then you had him stay for breakfast. I guess that's okay since we live upstairs. But then that *Englisha* fellow came . . ."

"I didn't ask him to come. Bishop Miller sent him over."

"Oh," Ronda said with relief.

"That doesn't mean there won't be trouble though."

"What do you mean? He didn't stay too long, and didn't you say Bishop Miller approved the visit?"

"Yah. He came for German lessons. And he'll pay me, he says."

"That's *gut*," Ronda said, relaxing in the chair and taking a deep breath. "You had me worried there."

Ella decided not to say more for the moment. No sense burdening Ronda. She had enough going on in her life with the loss of the *bobli*.

"Ella, I didn't really come down for that.

Well, maybe partly. I was curious, you know. But the more important reason is that I've been bleeding all morning. Just a little here and there. I was going to ask you earlier about it, but then you had your visitors. Do you think the bleeding is normal?"

"How much are you bleeding?" Ella asked. "Did the doctor tell you to expect some bleeding?"

"He said some spotting might be normal, but this is more than that. It's not all the time though, just off and on."

Ella's mind raced. *Is this serious or not?* She had no idea. "When is your next appointment?" she finally asked.

"Not till next week."

"I think that's too long to wait. I think you should go to the clinic. I'll take you. Can you get ready while I get the horse harnessed?"

"I'm ready, I guess," Ronda said. "I can watch the girls while you get ready."

"Sounds *gut*," Ella replied. She put on her outside clothes and left for the barn. On the way out, she gauged the weather to know how well the girls needed to be wrapped up. For Ronda, she'd take along an extra blanket. With the horse ready and tied to his stall, she went back inside and pulled the extra blanket out of her cedar chest.

"Oh, wait!" Ronda said as they were about to leave. "My mamm is supposed to come over this afternoon. I have to leave a note."

Ella grabbed paper and a pencil at her makeshift desk and handed them to Ronda.

Ronda wrote out a note, which Ella took upstairs and put on the kitchen table.

Once in the buggy, space was tight. Ronda held the baby, Ella drove with Sarah between them, and Mary sat on the floor, looking comfortable enough between their feet.

"I want to go fast!" Sarah cried, clapping her hands.

"Daett drove fast this morning," Mary explained, her small face looking up.

"There will be no fast drive this time," Ella said, shaking the lines to get Moonbeam moving.

He switched his tail, not too happy about this winter morning jaunt.

"I want to thank you again for what you did for me," Ronda said, wrapping the blanket tighter around baby Barbara. "I felt so safe with you and Joe that night. I knew he cared, but with you there, it was an added blessing."

"You would have done the same thing."

Ronda nodded. "Yah, but it's still special to feel so cared for. I was so sure the angels would soon come for me, like they did when Aden passed."

"You were not meant to pass over," Ella said. "Joe needs you."

"Yes, I suppose he does," Ronda replied.

"I think we'd better hurry," Ella said, slapping the reins. The horse protested with a jerk of his head, but he increased his speed.

"I'm okay," Ronda said. "And I'll really feel foolish about this if there is nothing wrong with me."

"I'm glad we're taking you . . . just to be safe," Ella said. "Besides it's nice to get out of the house after this morning."

Ella urged the horse on again.

Moonbeam didn't protest this time. He lifted his feet high as if he meant business. The clinic was ahead, just down the next state road.

"What are you going to do about Ivan's trouble with the bishop?" Ronda asked.

"I don't know," Ella said. "But I hope it's not too serious."

"What if he's put in the ban? I keep thinking about that. You know you won't be able to see him."

"I don't see how it can come to that, but if it does, I'll still take care of his girls," Ella replied.

"I suppose so," Ronda said, clearly worried. "I guess we're still allowed to do good to excommunicated people. No one will object to that. But you can't eat with him or take supper over like you did before."

Ella shivered. "I can take meals over and leave the food there."

"Just don't stay, Ella. I don't even think you should go inside the house. You can give him the food through the door. You don't want someone going past on the road and seeing you go inside. Bishop Miller would have you in the ban by the next Sunday."

Ronda shivered and Ella noticed.

"It won't happen. I already told you that," Ella said.

"I sure hope not," Ronda stated. "That would be too hard on my heart. If you got excommunicated, we would have to move out of your house, and I couldn't come down to quilt with you."

Ella responded with a laugh, feeling light as a feather — almost giddy. "Don't worry!" she said. "I won't get excommunicated."

"It's good to hear you say that. You're such a loyal person, and I can just see you going down with Ivan. But you shouldn't, Ella. I know you like him and the girls. But there is a limit to these things."

They had arrived at the clinic, and Ella pulled up to the hitching post. She climbed down and tied the horse to the post. She walked over and reached up to take baby Barbara from Ronda's arms. Ronda took her time stepping down, balancing carefully on the buggy step. The girls climbed out, and everyone walked slowly up the shoveled walk, keeping pace with Ronda.

Ella held the door open, and they entered the lobby area where the receptionist was waiting with a smile. When Ronda explained about the bleeding, a nurse was summoned and Ronda was taken immediately to an examination room.

Ella and the girls settled on chairs and took off their coats, but they only had a short wait before Ronda reappeared. She paid the receptionist and then walked over to Ella. After getting the children ready to go back outside, they walked out. On the way to the buggy, Ronda whispered, "The doctor said I'll be okay. He gave me something that should stop the bleeding"

"That's a relief," Ella said, lifting the two oldest girls into the buggy. Ronda handed Ella baby Barbara and managed to climb in by herself. Ella handed her the baby, un-hitched Moonbeam, climbed into the buggy, and they headed home. They said little on the way.

Arriving home, Ronda went upstairs and

then let Ella know that her mamm had left a note saying she would return for a visit tomorrow.

After she left Ella remembered Ronda's fears about Ivan being excommunicated. Was Ronda only giving in to her imaginations, or was there cause for concern? Surely not, even though the same thoughts had troubled her earlier. Bishop Miller might wish to break up their relationship, but Ivan hadn't done anything to justify such strong measures.

TWENTY-SEVEN

The morning finally arrived that Ella had been waiting for — an unseasonably warm day for winter, with a warm southern breeze and no clouds in the sky. The snow had started to melt, creating small streams of water here and there in the yard.

The change in weather offered the perfect opportunity to visit her mamm. She had much to share. There were, of course, Ivan's problems with Bishop Miller and Ronda's slow recovery from the loss of her baby. She knew she would not share her feelings about that *Englisha* man, Robert Hayes. Still, she hoped her mamm's calm voice and the steady hand her daett always supplied would help make sense out of the swirl of life around her.

A deeper reason though was Eli. She wanted to hear news about him. How was he doing in the *Englisha* world?

That her mamm and daett wouldn't approve of contact with Eli was a given, but it was disapproval without a bite. No one would punish her for contacting Eli. They might talk, but that was all. Perhaps her mamm would even agree to tell her where Eli lived in town.

She quickly cleaned up the breakfast dishes and announced to the girls, "We're going to my mamm's today. You think you're up to a little drive?"

"Yah," Mary said, her face lighting up. Beside her Sarah nodded vigorously.

"Do you think you can watch the baby while I get the horse ready?" Ella asked.

Both heads went up and down rapidly.

"We want a buggy ride!" Mary said.

"A *fast* one!" Sarah added.

"I doubt if you'll get that," Ella said with a laugh. We'll let your daett give you the fast rides. Give Barbara something to play with if she cries."

Ella went up the basement steps and out into the welcomed sunshine. She turned and walked up the porch steps to say hello to Ronda.

"Yoo hoo!" Ella called into the living room before walking in. Ronda glanced up from the kitchen sink, a weary smile on her face.

"How are you?" Ella asked.

"Okay," Ronda said, laying the washcloth

over the sink edge and sitting down at the kitchen table. "I tire faster, but that's about all."

"Are you sure?" Ella asked. "You look a bit poorly."

"Well, I haven't had any more blood loss, so I think I'm just slow getting back to normal. Joe will take the day off to drive me to my next appointment, so don't worry about that. He's such a dear. He's already talking of our next child, even in the middle of my fears."

Ella nodded, a bit envious. It must feel *gut* to have a man comfort you in the day of trouble.

"I feel so safe with him," Ronda continued. "Wrapped up in his arms at night. It makes one think the world truly will be all right again. Oh Ella, you *have* to marry quickly. I feel so bad for you, for what you're missing."

"I don't think all men are quite like what you have in Joe," Ella said with a touch of sadness. Then she brightened for Ronda's sake and said, "Well, I really have to go. I want to visit Mamm today."

Ronda must have picked up on the sadness in Ella's voice. "You mustn't be bitter," she said, taking Ella's hand. "Ivan will come out of this all right. I shouldn't have allowed my fears to run away like I did. He can take care of himself. And I think you're right to visit your mamm. Perhaps she can help. That's what mamms are for. And if you want me to take care of the girls today, I can. You've done so much for me."

Ella shook her head. "Thanks anyway. The girls need to get out of the house as much as I do. It bothers me how we've been so cooped up lately."

"They don't look the worse for wear," Ronda said, letting go of Ella's hand. "You don't give yourself near enough credit for all the good work you do with them . . . and for others."

"Well, I hope Mamm can help me." Ella sighed. "I sure feel like I could use some help. The load gets heavy at times."

Ronda smiled. "You do have a lot of male activity downstairs. They were running up and down the steps as thick as fleas the other day."

Ella burst into laughter. "I suppose that did produce quite a sight. It wasn't my fault though."

"It'll work out," Ronda said. "I'm sure it will."

"I guess we all have our troubles to bear," Ella said. "They just look worse when they're ours." She gave Ronda a quick hug

278

and turned to go to the barn. As she stepped out into the sunlight, she stopped for a moment to savor the feel of the day, then continued on into the barn where Moonbeam greeted her with a loud snort.

"You're a good boy," Ella told him, stroking his nose as he worked his jaws and anticipated some oats.

"Not now." She slipped his bridle on. "Perhaps you can have some oats when we come back. If you're a good boy."

It would be nice if men were like this. A little oats dumped in their feed box — and contentment was the result. Instead men were mostly uncontrollable. She shivered, longing for warm arms to wrap around her tightly, for strength that exceeded her own, for love that never died. Was such a thing to be found?

"You wouldn't know," she said, when the horse nuzzled her, breaking in on her thoughts. "Now get ready for a good long run. We're going to visit Mamm today."

The horse stood patiently while Ella threw the harness on. She led him outside. When she had secured the buggy tugs, she tied him to the hitching post and went inside for the girls.

"You were gone a long time," Mary said when Ella came through the basement door.

"I talked to Ronda too," Ella said. "And then I got the horse ready. Now you girls get your coats. It's warm out, but not warm enough for no coats." She got baby Barbara ready. They went outside, Mary and Sarah running ahead of her and the baby.

"Careful!" Ella called. "The melting snow makes things slippery." She held her breath as the two raced for the buggy. She could see one or both sprawling on the wet snow, breaking a leg or an arm, all because she hadn't thought to walk them to the buggy.

She sure was jittery, but then there were reasons for it. Still, she needed to be careful that she allowed the girls their fun. Perhaps they would have to come outside more often, especially if the weather cooperated.

When the two arrived safely at the buggy, she sighed with relief and made her way carefully to the buggy step. She lifted baby Barbara inside, and turned to help Mary and Sarah. Grabbing Mary's hand, she pulled upward while Mary stretched her legs and then jumped off the step, giggling as she landed inside.

"I want to do that!" Sarah insisted.

"Not yet," Ella said. "You're still a little small."

"But I *want* to."

"We can't always do what we want," Ella

replied, lifting Sarah by the armpits and set-tling her inside.

Ella climbed in, slapped the reins against Moonbeam's back, and said, "We're off!"

"We're off!" Mary echoed.

"Off!" Sarah agreed, smiling from ear to ear.

Twenty-Eight

Ella drove south, allowing the horse its head. There was no need to urge him on this morning. He apparently wanted to stretch his legs. The girls sat quietly, enjoying the ride. Even baby Barbara seemed content to watch the passing countryside. Ella drove on, looking forward to the comfort of her mamm and the gentle smile and wisdom of her daett. So often she had taken these things for granted while growing up, but now she saw through different eyes.

At the stop sign, Ella turned right, driving down through the creek. Nothing looked quite the same, and she was glad. Last spring the pain of Aden's passing had still been with her. Hopefully this year the wounds would have healed more. Still, this was where they had often come. It would always hold memories of the warm air and being in Aden's arms, of his hand in hers, of the smell of fresh flowers, of the sound of the rippling water. These would forever touch a tender spot in her memory. Here she and Aden had spent some of their happiest hours together.

The road soon diverged up and out of the riverbed. The view of the world opened up before her. The great stretch was white with snow but still beautiful. Here one could see the sweep of the valley below Seager Hill rising up and up until it reached the houses along the ridge. Ella drew in her breath sharply at the sight.

"Are you sad?" Mary asked, noticing the tears on Ella's check. The girl's face turned up to her from her seat on the buggy floor.

Ella wiped away the tears. "*Nee,* just happy. Sometimes tears are from being happy, not sad. Don't worry, dumpling."

Mary looked at her as if wondering if such a thing were possible.

Ella laughed, surprised at how easily the sound bubbled up inside her. Oh yes, this would be a good day. The closer she got to home, the more distant her problems seemed.

Moonbeam walked up the last few hundred feet of the long grade, and Ella didn't urge him on. Not only wasn't she in a hurry, but the schoolhouse lay on her left, bringing back school-day memories. She gazed into the yard. The children were inside at the moment, the little school door shut securely.

"You'll be going to school soon," she said to Mary.

"What's school?" Mary asked, looking up.

"There," Ella said, pointing. "The place with the bell on top. That's where they teach you to read and write."

"I will come here?" Mary asked, craning her neck to see.

"No," Ella said. "Not to this school. There's one closer to where you live, and you'll go there."

"Is it fun?"

"Most of the time," Ella said, remembering. "The teachers are nice, but you have to learn a lot of things . . . like numbers, words in books, and how to spell."

"I like books," Mary said. Sarah nodded from her place on the buggy seat.

"You'll both do well, I'm sure. You're smart little girls."

Mary glowed.

"Will I go with Mary?" Sarah asked.

"Nee," Ella said.

Sarah's face clouded over.

"You have to be six to go to school," Ella explained.

"Then I want to be six."

"You'll be six someday," Ella said, stroking her hair back from her face.

Ella pulled on the reins, turning Moonbeam left into the driveway and up the lane. When she reached the hitching rack, Ella climbed down and tied up the horse. Then she helped Mary and Sarah down. Behind her she heard the front door burst open. She looked toward the house to see Clara come out at a run.

Ella met her sister with open arms. They clung to each other for many moments. "It's so good to see you," Ella finally whispered. "It seems so long."

"Yah!" Clara sniffled.

"Are Mamm and Dora here?"

"They're inside," Clara said. "But I wanted to see you first."

There was something in Clara's voice that concerned Ella. She reached into the buggy for the baby and, hoping she was wrong, asked, "Anything wrong, Clara?"

Clara stared at the ground. "I can't do any more drawing."

"You can't do what? No drawing? Who said so?"

"Mamm and Daett said so earlier this week. I still have five drawings for you to see that I've already done, but I can't do any more."

Ella pulled Clara tightly against her. "How has this happened?" Thoughts raced through her mind. *Did one of the ministers in their district cause the problem? Has someone complained? Perhaps Clara's schoolteacher, Katie, has spoken against the drawings.*

"They won't tell me why," Clara said, tears running down her cheeks.

What has gotten into Mamm and Daett, Ella wondered. She was almost afraid to know the answer, but she said, "I'll talk to them. Perhaps there's something that can be done."

"I don't think so," Clara said, blowing her nose. "They have their minds made up." She tried to smile through her tears as she took Mary and Sarah by the hand.

They all started toward the house.

Surely this is all just a simple misunderstanding, Ella thought.

When they entered the house, Dora met Ella with a quick hug and took baby Barbara from her. Nothing was said, but Dora didn't need to. Her look said serious discussions were going on.

With care Ella approached the familiar kitchen door. A thousand times she had passed here in her childhood. Through this door had come news of Aden's death. Ella trembled now with the sudden conviction that dire news once again lay on the other side.

"Hi, Mamm," she said as she entered the kitchen.

"Hi, Ella!" As if reading her daughter's mind, Lizzie continued, "I thought it best if Clara told you about the drawing issue. It has been a hard decision for all of us."

Ella sat down at the kitchen table. She could hear Dora and Clara entertaining the three girls in the living room.

"What happened?" Ella ventured.

"It might be best if your daett told you," Mamm said. "He'll be comin' in about now. We were hoping to see you soon. If you hadn't come over today, we might have visited you on Sunday."

Ella nodded and looked up when her daett came in. Her heart felt as heavy as lead. There was clearly more coming than a discussion of Clara's drawings.

Noah nodded when he entered, glancing at his wife and then holding out his hand toward Ella.

Ella was sure she would burst into tears. *Why is my own daett wanting to shake my hand? Am I a stranger now who needs to be greeted with formality?* His grip was firm, but nonetheless seemed cool.

"I'm glad you came today." Noah pulled

out his chair. He rested his elbows on the table, his long familiar beard almost brushing the top of his arms.

Ella waited, her eyes on her daett's face.

"We've heard about Ivan's troubles," Noah said, his eyes meeting hers. "We are very sorry about the news."

"What have you heard?" Ella asked, her voice strained. *Is this Bishop Miller's doing? Has he reached my own parents and turned them against my future husband?*

"The news has come from your district's bishop," Noah said, his voice low. "Bishop Hochstetler made a trip over to see us last week. He thought it best that way. He was hesitant to approach you directly."

"This is not right! Ivan told me the reasons Bishop Miller approached him. Ivan has questions about tobacco use due to some Amish articles he's read. Why is that so much cause for alarm?"

"It's more than that, Ella. I guess it's normal in these types of cases, I s'pose," Noah said, his voice losing none of its seriousness, "that the guilty one does not confess everything. It sorrows my heart that Ivan didn't tell you all. I always thought highly of the man, but the bishop said Ivan has never been the same since Lois died. Some men are like that; they take death very hard. But even so, that's no excuse for his actions — actions that may lead to excommunication."

Excommunication! So it has come to that? Should I ask the reason? Even as she debated whether she should ask the words came out: "What did Ivan do that warrants possible excommunication and threatens damnation of his soul?" She knew her voice sounded angry — and rightfully so. The situation was so unfair.

"You must not speak in such a tone," Noah said, his voice a gentle reprimand. "I know you are not promised to him — or so we expect. You must withdraw yourself from the man. And this is not damnation. It is *correction* of the soul. Sometimes a man can only be reached by that method, and you know the Lord Himself has so ordained it."

"What did Ivan do? That's all I want to know. All I've heard are a bunch of trumped-up charges to break the two of us up."

"I hoped you wouldn't take this so hard," Noah said. "I was afraid you would though. I do believe, Ella, there is cause enough that you must cut off contact with Ivan. I wish I weren't the one telling you this, but the truth is that Ivan has been seen entering the Baptist church in town — accompanied by an *Englisha* woman."

"Ivan confessed to this?" Ella was barely able to get the words out.

"*Nee,* and that is the sad part. He refuses to speak of the matter. He refuses to repent or give a reason why he would do this. This grieves us all greatly."

"And is this in any way related to Clara's drawings?"

Noah's voice was heavy. "In times like this, when one of our own ministers falls so deeply into sin as Ivan has, we must be extra careful. It causes us to examine our hearts and all our actions. Clara's drawings were always a little in question, and I feel now like no chances should be taken."

"Oh, this is all Bishop Miller's fault!" Ella exclaimed.

"You may not think highly of the man right now," Noah said, speaking slowly. "But perhaps after this you can see that you made a mistake in your judgment of him. He would be a much, much better choice for a husband than Ivan, Ella. That has become obvious. And after this is all over, I believe there would still be time to make things right with him. If you like, I would be willing to speak to him on the matter."

"Did Bishop Miller tell you to give me that message?"

Her mamm quickly placed her hand on Ella's shoulder. "You must not be bitter with the bishop."

"Then he did?"

Noah shook his head. "No, it's only my idea and suggestion. I have always respected the man, as you know. I am speaking as your daett."

Ella lifted her face toward the ceiling before burying her head in her hands. Great sobs racked her body. The day — and the whole world — had fallen around her with a mighty crash.

TWENTY-NINE

"I don't believe it!" Ella whispered through her mamm's soaked handkerchief.

"You've always been a faithful soul," Noah said, his voice gentle. "But this time you must not let your loyalty blind your eyes."

"When Ivan tells me, perhaps then I'll believe it." Ella raised her tear-stained face to look at her daett. She glanced nervously toward the living room. No sound was coming from there, so hopefully Dora and Clara had taken the girls upstairs. She felt the tears burn again and allowed them to flow freely.

"Then one would hope Ivan tells you the truth," Noah said. "He has not been honest so far. Bishop Hochstetler told us so. Ivan would not bare his soul when he was approached."

"Perhaps it's because of his pain," Ella said, meeting her daett's eyes. "Has anyone thought of that? He loved his wife greatly, and now he has to go on without her. I know a little bit about that myself. I can understand the pain."

"Yet he has asked you to be his wife . . . hasn't he?" Noah questioned, trying to be gentle but anger was in his voice.

"Yah," Ella said. "And I've been thinking about saying yes. Is there a sin in that? Is that a reason for Bishop Miller to persecute him in this way?"

Lizzie brushed her daughter's forehead.

"I think you have seriously misjudged the bishop," Noah said. "Bishop Miller has done none of this out of spite or revenge. I see you think so, and that is why your heart is so set against him. But I pray that you see your mistake. Bishop Miller is a man of God, one like we haven't had in my time. He would make a great husband for you."

"I know you think so," Ella said, swallowing hard. "Yet it is I who would have to wed him . . . and I cannot. Not even if my relationship with Ivan were to be broken."

"It *will* be broken if Ivan is excommunicated." Noah rose to his feet. He paused and put his hand on Ella's shoulder. "You must consider the evidence, Ella, before you give your answer to Ivan. Such a mistake would be too costly."

As he turned to go he said, "The chores

beckon me. There is much extra work to do since Eli is gone. The pain from his choice has hurt us all. I cannot lose another child to the world. Surely you would not consider following Ivan in his fallen ways?"

Ella met his eyes, seeing the depth of his concern and the burden he had already suffered, and pressed back her tears. "I have no plans to join the *Englisha* nor does Ivan. I wish you would believe that."

"Yah, we know you believe so," Lizzie said, stroking Ella's forehead again and offering a fresh handkerchief.

"Then my heart is some lighter." Noah sighed. "At least about you. Ivan . . . I will leave him to the leaders to address. I trust their judgment more than I do even your opinion, Ella. You are too close to see clearly. You must also trust our leaders more than your own mind. *Da Hah* works in these ways. As the Good Book says, it was Eve who got herself deceived in the garden."

Ella felt the anger rising again, but their love had disarmed her. "I will not marry Bishop Miller," she said weakly. "Not if I must remain single all my life."

"No man can change a woman's heart, I suppose," Noah said, sighing again. "I wish I could, but we must live with what happens. If you do not join the *Englisha,* then I will be satisfied."

"I won't," Ella said.

What would her daett think if he knew about Robert Hayes and her troublesome feelings for him? His heart — and Mamm's — would surely break to pieces if they knew hers had gone after an *Englisha* man. Fear gripped her, even as her father looked at her with relief on his face.

"I see the fear of *Da Hah* is still with you," he said, reaching for her hand, a slight smile on his face.

"I will try," Ella whispered. She almost cried when he smiled.

"I know you will," Noah replied, touching her shoulder gently. "You bring joy to my heart."

When the outside door shut behind Noah, Lizzie said, "Eli has broken his heart. It would simply be too much if another of his children followed the world."

Fear came again as Ella remembered afresh the look of Robert's face. She knew she had no control over her emotions. They were what they were. *Nee,* she would never follow him into the world — even if Ivan was taken from her. That she could control, if not the wild beating of her heart.

"Come now. We must speak of other things," Lizzie said, trying to smile.

Ella wiped her eyes. Perhaps the storm was over for now. "But Clara," she said, remembering. "Can she still do the drawings? Now that you have spoken with me?"

Lizzie shook her head, "Noah will not allow it. Not with things as unsettled as they are."

"But you can persuade him! Tell him it's not Clara's fault. Speak to him."

Lizzie lowered her eyes. "You must not blame your daett. I also question the wisdom of allowing Clara this diversion. We have lost one child, and we cannot afford to lose another."

"But Clara has taken this so hard," Ella said. "I saw the look on her face."

"We cannot shield Clara from all of life's pains," Lizzie said. "Only some of them. And this one, Clara must learn to live with."

"Perhaps, then, she can at least come home with me today. Get away from things for a while. I would love that, and it's been so long since I've seen her."

"How will she come back tomorrow?" Lizzie asked.

"I can bring her back."

Lizzie considered for a moment. "I know a better way. Yah, you can take her with you, but I'll come for her tomorrow after I've helped Dora with the first chores. I've so wanted to see your place again. So why don't we tell Clara?" Lizzie walked into the living room to holler up the stairs and ask the girls to come down. Quick steps followed her request.

"Oh, Mamm, that's a good idea," Ella said as she followed her mamm.

Dora appeared first, baby Barbara in her arms. She glanced cautiously through the stair door, smiling when she saw Ella.

"The storm is over then?" Dora asked, coming down the steps. Clara followed with Mary and Sarah.

"Clara, how would you like to spend the night at Ella's?" Lizzie asked.

Clara's eyes got big. "To Ella's place? I would love to!"

"Then run up and pack," Lizzie said, motioning with her hand. "Ella hasn't got all day."

"Oh, Mamm!" Clara shrieked, disappearing up the stairs to Mary and Sarah's astonished looks.

"They must not be used to seeing women who dash around like Clara does," Lizzie said with a laugh.

As soon as her mamm was gone, Dora approached Ella and whispered, "So what happened?"

"Let's go upstairs to talk," Ella said.

Dora nodded.

"Mamm, we're going up to my old room until Clara's ready," Ella yelled toward the kitchen.

"Then leave the girls down here," Lizzie said. "I'll watch them."

"We'll be back soon," Ella said to Mary and Sarah. She set baby Barbara on the floor. They looked contented and fascinated enough with the new surroundings to stay quiet for a few more minutes.

Ella's old bedroom looked much the same, though Dora had moved in and made some changes. The dresser had a new doily and a different patterned quilt covered the bed.

"Let's sit on the bed," Dora said. "It'll be just like old times."

Ella sat down, remembering the years she had spent here. It seemed like ages ago . . . back in Aden's time . . . in a world she would never inhabit again.

"So what's up?" Dora asked, her face full of questions.

"A whole bunch of rumors about Ivan," Ella said and then gave the details, along with her opinion.

"Do you think he'll get excommunicated?" Dora asked with a frown.

"He will unless someone stops Bishop Miller."

Dora laughed, "You don't really think he's doin' this just to break you two up, do you?"

"Yah," Ella said, "I do."

"You sound like me," Dora said. "I'm the one who would think such dark things."

"Well, this time it's me," Ella retorted.

Should she tell Dora about Robert? *Nee,* she would not. There was too great a chance Dora would tell Mamm. Robert would be gone soon enough, and there was no sense adding extra worry to her parents' already burdened minds.

"So what do you think will happen?" Dora asked.

"Ivan will figure some way out of this," Ella said. "He won't be excommunicated. And if it comes to that, I'll help him any way I can."

Dora laughed. "You take too much on yourself, Ella. You always have. But this time I think you're whipped. Especially if Ivan really did go to the Baptist church in town. With or without a woman . . ."

"I don't believe it for a minute!"

"My, you are so sure," Dora said with raised eyebrows.

"Now, let's talk about something else," Ella said. "Tell me about Norman. Is the wedding still on for next year?"

"Yah," Dora said. "It seems so."

"You sure are cheerful about it," Ella said wryly.

"I guess love does me *gut,*" Dora said with a short laugh. "I never thought I would say that."

"I always knew it would happen some-time," Ella said.

"I wish it would happen to you again," her sister asserted.

"Dora . . ." Ella's eyes suddenly brimmed with tears. Perhaps her feelings for the *Englisha* man would come out after all.

But then Dora spoke again. "I know you haven't found it yet. Not like what you had with Aden."

"Perhaps real love comes only once in a lifetime," Ella whispered.

Dora hugged Ella. "Oh my, how I wish it would happen for you again. You so deserve it, Ella."

"I don't," Ella said, her voice catching. "You don't know everything about me."

"I know all I need to know," Dora said, letting her go slowly. "Don't let anyone tell you otherwise."

"I'm ready to go!" Clara called loudly from outside the bedroom door. "You two old chickens can cackle later."

Ella gave Dora one last hug, and they walked out together.

"Why are you two crying?" Clara asked. "I'm the one who can't draw anymore."

"You'll cry someday over bigger things than pictures," Dora said dryly.

"Ella, hurry. Please get me out of this place of darkness, at least for a while," Clara said as she raced down the stairs with her suitcase.

Ella followed, laughing; Dora behind them grumbling all the way.

THIRTY

The early afternoon air had chilled. Ella pulled the buggy blanket up around the little girls' chests before pulling out onto the lane. Mary piped up from her seat on the floor. "I'm glad you could come with us, Clara. I can show you my doll."

"I have one too," Sarah echoed.

Clara laughed. "I'd like to see them very much," she said, exchanging smiles with Ella.

"I'm glad you're coming too," Ella said. "It's been so long."

"Yah," Clara said. "And the change of scenery will do me good."

Just ahead Ella saw the wooden pay phone shack standing in stark relief against the white snow. She'd been watching for it. She pulled to a stop and said, "I'm going to call Eli, Clara."

Clara gave her a questioning look but said nothing. She took the reins as Ella stepped down.

Finding several quarters in her pocketbook and hoping they would be enough, Ella picked up the phone book. She noted the date on the phone book and realized it was too old. Eli's number wouldn't be listed in it. Hopefully information would have the number.

"Yes," the operator said in response to her query. "There is an Eli Yoder in Randolph. That's the only one we have."

"That must be it," Ella said, grabbing the pencil that hung by a string on the wall. She scribbled quickly on a scrap of paper as the operator intoned the number.

Taking a deep breath, Ella dropped in more quarters and dialed. The phone rang several times. She was ready to hang up when a sleepy voice finally answered.

"Hello," she said, finding her voice. "Eli?"

"Yah," he said. "Who is this?"

"It's Ella." She waited for his response.

"It's nice to hear from you, Ella. Is something wrong? Is it Daett or Mamm?"

"No, Daett is fine. So is Mamm. It's about something else. Can you come out to my house sometime when it suits you? I'd so love to see you."

"Does it have to do with me returning to the Amish?" His voice had an edge.

"No, Eli. I miss you."

"Then perhaps I can come," Eli said, his voice relaxing.

"This afternoon?" Ella asked.

"I'll be there," Eli said. "It will do me good to see someone from the old life."

"You'll see Clara too. She's visiting."

"Great!" Eli said. "I'll be by later then."

Ella hung up and returned to the buggy. She climbed in and took the reins from Clara.

"Did you get ahold of him?" Clara asked.

Ella nodded. "He's coming by this afternoon. Does he ever come out to the farm?"

"Sometimes, but not often. Daett always comes in from the barn when he visits. He doesn't want Mamm to be alone with him. They sit at the kitchen table talking."

"It will be *gut* to see him," Ella said as she drove the buggy back out on the road.

"Just don't give him anything to eat," Clara said.

"Why shouldn't I offer him food?"

"I just wouldn't," Clara said, shaking her head. "I don't know how it all works, but if Daett finds out you've had Eli over and had him in to eat, well, I wouldn't want to be around then. You might never be allowed back home."

"Really, Clara. I think you're exaggerating. But okay, we won't offer him any food."

"Don't say *we*," Clara said. "Keep me out of it. It's bad enough that I can't make my drawings anymore. I wish people would stop getting themselves in trouble with the bishops."

"You can say that again!" Ella said, her voice tinged with bitterness.

The creek bottom was cold, and Ella drove fast, anxious to get home. She slapped the lines as they turned up Chapman Road and approached the white house.

Clara gasped when it came into full view. "Ever since the first night I spent here, I've loved this place."

"So have I," Ella said, allowing herself to get caught up in the moment. "So have I." She turned into the driveway and parked by the barn. Giving Clara the reins, she jumped down to help the little girls. She and Clara unhitched together, and then Clara held Barbara and waited with the two girls while Ella led Moonbeam into the barn. She urged him on, "Remember, oats lie straight ahead."

He neighed as if his faith in womankind had been restored and increased his pace. After she pulled the harness off and put him in the stall, she gave him a large bucket of oats. He chomped greedily.

"Mind your manners!" she said with a laugh as she left. She shut the barn door tightly behind her. From the looks of things, the wind might be wild tonight, and the barn was cold enough without the door springing open.

Ella pulled Clara's suitcase from the back of the buggy, and they headed for the basement.

"I'm in the mood to do something," Clara said, once the girls were settled down to play.

"I want to check on Ronda first," Ella said. "It shouldn't take long. Then we'll figure out what to do for supper."

Ella knocked twice on Ronda's door and then stepped in. "Ronda, I'm home with Clara. Are you all right?"

"I'm fine," Ronda called from the bedroom. "I'm feeling much better, and I think I will actually get some work done later."

"Did I wake you?" Ella asked.

"No, I was already up," Ronda said, coming to the bedroom door in her work clothes. "I had my nap earlier and I was cleaning the bedroom."

"You let me know if you need anything," Ella said firmly.

"You've done plenty already, Ella."

Ella turned to go. Reaching the bottom of

the stairs, she took the last two steps in a single bound. Why, she didn't know. It just felt *gut.*

"We'll make bread and soup for supper," Ella announced.

Clara raised her eyebrows. "Yah. Well then, let's do it."

Ella stoked the nearly expired embers in the oven and then added wood. The fire was soon roaring, and the soup and bread preparations were started. Clara was kneading the bread dough while Ella gathered the soup ingredients from the root cellar and began slicing vegetables. They worked quickly, chatting as sisters do, but keeping their minds on their work. Ella glanced over to check on the girls occasionally. At one point she stopped and put baby Barbara down for a nap. By late afternoon, Clara was setting the table as Ella hovered over the soup pot, stirring occasionally. The sun dipped below the horizon. Ella lit the gas lantern as Clara took the brown loaves of bread from the oven and set them on the counter. She began rubbing them with butter.

"I bet these are just like the loaves Jesus multiplied for the crowd," Clara said as Ella ladled soup into a large serving dish.

"Well, I doubt they had butter," Ella said.

"And Jesus didn't have to make His bread with an oven."

"Mamm says *Da Hah* doesn't make things easy for us because we need hard times."

"Are you interested in theology now?" Ella teased.

Before Clara could answer, they heard the crunch of *Englisha* car wheels in the driveway. They both raced to the door and stepped out.

A man emerged from the car, and Ella realized it was Eli — mainly by his bearing. Otherwise she wouldn't have known him in the dusky twilight. He was wearing *Englisha* clothes — his pants were store-bought and a shiny belt hugged his waist. She could see the glitter of silver things on it all the way across the driveway.

"Eli!" she gasped, unable to keep the joy out of her voice.

The distance between them melted away as Eli ran toward her with quick steps across the snow, wrapping his arms around first her and then Clara.

"It's so good to see you, Ella!" he said, his voice catching.

"Oh, Eli!" she said, holding him at arm's length. "How could you do this? You are an *Englisha* man now."

"I'm still Eli," he said.

She saw the tears in his eyes.

"See? Don't I look the same?" His voice was pleading.

"Not exactly," she said. "But I doubt you'd listen to anything I have to say on the matter since Daett said you wouldn't listen to Bishop Miller."

"Is that why you asked me to come after all?" he asked, his eyes flashing, his mouth set in a stubborn line.

"Nee," she said. "I promise."

"Okay, then. You know, I can stay all evening — even for supper," he hinted hopefully.

Clara gave Ella a look of warning and then said, "I'll go inside and keep an eye on the girls. I'll get the baby up."

Ella nodded and turned back to Eli. "I wish you could stay, Eli, but it would be best if you didn't. I'm sorry."

Eli laughed, but his expression showed his pain. He cleared his throat and asked, "Is this true what I hear about my dear sister? That she is hanging around with an *Englisha* man, giving him German lessons?"

Ella gasped. "How have you heard of such things?"

"So it *is* true?" He smiled again. "Remember, I know you, Ella. You are my best sister."

Ella's heart melted and she touched his arm. How *gut* it felt to have someone care about Robert and her, but she must not allow Eli to see her feelings. She took a deep breath and turned the question back on him. "Eli, won't you go back to the farm? Daett needs you so much."

He didn't say a word, but he shook his head.

"Why not, Eli?"

"I love Pam," he said quietly.

"Yah," she said, touching his arm again. "So we will leave that alone. I had to ask though."

Eli nodded. "So what about this *Englisha* man, Ella? I want to know what he's up to with my sister."

Ella tried to read Eli's eyes, "Has he done a crime or something?"

"I hope not. But tell me about him."

Ella looked away. "His name is Robert Hayes. He arrived here in the community not long ago with plans to join the Amish. Bishop Miller has taken him under his wing. As to his past, I don't know anything more than what he's told me. And I see no reason to doubt him."

Eli rolled his eyes. "And you're not looking for dark secrets?"

Ella shook her head.

"Well you should be, Ella. Believe me. I've been out in their world for awhile, and there are always secrets."

"We really shouldn't talk about this Eli, please. I called you so I could see you, not to talk about my problems."

"Well, your problems are important to me," Eli insisted. "I want to look into this man's history for you. Things like his past life, his girlfriends, wives, children. Any secrets he may be hiding, that sort of thing. All I need is some basic information to start with."

"Please," Ella pleaded. "I don't think Robert is the problem at all. Bishop Miller is, but that's another matter. You can't do much about him."

Eli laughed, "I suppose not, but humor me. I'm your little brother and I worry about you."

"Not so little," Ella managed a smile, finally relenting. "Okay. Robert's mother's name is Marie Hayes, and she's from Cumberland, Maryland."

"Thanks." He smiled then turned to go.

Ella walked to the car with him. "Eli, please know you are loved . . . and missed." She gave him another hug.

Again he said nothing, but Ella noticed more tears forming in his eyes. And then he was gone, the headlights of his car cutting into the dark sky as he bounced down the driveway.

"I thought he might ask again to stay," Clara said after Ella had come inside.

"He understands why he can't," she replied.

"I wish he could." Clara helped Sarah into her chair. "He's still my brother."

"I know. He's mine too."

They took their seats at the table and bowed their heads together in silent prayer. Above them the faint sound of the front door opened, and they could hear Ronda's muffled words of welcome for Joe.

"At least someone's happy," Ella said after saying amen.

Clara nodded soberly.

THIRTY-ONE

The next morning Clara helped Ella with the girls and then settled in to work on a quilt. "I can almost do the smallest stitches," Clara said, flexing her fingers.

"I've noticed," Ella said. "You're getting good at this."

"But not as *gut* as I am at drawing," Clara countered.

Ella had no answer to that. There was nothing either of them could do about it.

Over in the corner, Mary and Sarah played at their own make-believe washday. Baby Barbara watched them, fascinated as they dipped their doll clothes into a small dish of soapy water, scrubbed them by hand, and then wrung them dry before hanging them on a little string stretched between the rocker and a kitchen table leg.

"Mamm should come here before long, don't you think?" Clara asked.

"Likely, but both of you can stay as long

as you want. All day if you please. I suppose Mamm already knows that."

"She does, but I'm sure there's work at home for us to do."

"With Eli gone and me gone, I guess it's the same amount of work but fewer hands to do it. I'm sorry about that, Clara."

"It's not your fault. We make do. But it doesn't leave us much time for anything else."

"Like . . . boys?" Ella asked with a smile.

Clara grinned. "Well if there *were* a boy, I'd make time for that."

Ella pressed on. "Whatever happened with Paul, the boy from your school days? I think you liked him quite a bit. Is that still true?"

Clara gave her a look with narrowed eyes.

Ella laughed.

"He's got his eyes on a few other girls now," Clara said.

"Are you sure? You're the best lookin' one around."

"Oh, Ella, don't tease me," Clara said. "Apparently not to Paul. And I wouldn't be surprised if he asked Katie Troyer home soon."

"It goes that way sometimes. I thought for sure Aden would never look twice at me."

"They're not all like Aden. You once said that to Dora."

"I didn't know you were listening."

"That's what comes from discussing things around little sisters."

"Yah, that's true!" Ella replied, laughing. "Well, if not Paul, is there anyone else? I'm sure you have lots of boys who would take you home — I mean sometime — when you're older."

"Not that I'd consider them," Clara said, keeping her eyes on her needle.

"Aren't they as handsome as Paul?"

"Looks aren't everything, you know."

"I agree," Ella said. "A good man makes his own good looks."

"Then what would you say if I let Ezra take me home?" Clara asked, glancing up.

"Ezra?" Ella said, the surprise in her voice evident.

"See, there you go. What's wrong with Ezra?"

"I'm sorry," Ella said. "I thought Paul was the one you had your eye on since your school days."

"Why don't you like Ezra? Is it because he lives at the bottom of the hill, and his father doesn't own a big farm? You think he's not good enough, don't you?"

"I didn't say that."

"But you thought it."

"Well, Ezra is a solid boy, I guess. At least

what I know of him."

Clara laughed, "*Solid.* I like that. You make him sound like a rock or a piece of dirt. I haven't dared tell Mamm yet, even though I think Ezra may ask me home soon."

"What makes you think so?"

Clara blushed and admitted, "Because I encourage him. So there! I like him. Ever since the day in school when I saw how much I meant to him. A boy like that would go around the world for a girl — he really would, Ella. I know it's hard to see what the boy is made of, hidden as it is under all his fears. But I don't intend to make him run through a bunch of barnyard mud to get to me. I won't make him think I'm so far above him that he has to be so much better than he is before he can have me. It's not his fault he doesn't live on top of the hill or that his daett doesn't own a hundred acres.

"That boy has a heart of gold. He can make a horse do almost anything without a whip or a bridle. I saw him do it, Ella. Ezra can have my heart, and all of it, whenever he wants it. And I don't care what anyone says."

"Well," Ella said, "that was quite a speech. And you expect me to disagree?"

"I don't know," Clara said, breathing hard. "But it felt *gut* to say it."

316

Ella shrugged. "I don't think either Mamm or Daett will object, and I certainly won't."

"It's better than what Eli did," Clara said. "At least Ezra's not *Englisha.*"

"Don't measure your life by Eli's."

"I know . . . it's just always there, hanging in the air."

"We will have to live above it somehow," Ella said, thinking of her own feelings for a certain *Englisha* man. Thankfully Clara didn't know about him.

Behind them footsteps came down the concrete steps. After a quick knock the basement door burst open, bringing in a blast of cold air.

"Mamm!" Ella and Clara said together as they bounced to their feet.

"Good morning!" Lizzie took off her shawl and bonnet. "If you can't even hear your own mamm driving in, you must be having quite the sisterly talk."

"Yah . . . guilty," Ella admitted. "Why didn't you yell for us? We would have come out to help you."

"Because all I had to do was tie up and throw the blanket on the horse. I can't stay long. There is a ton of work to do at home."

Clara groaned.

"Before you complain too much, I have

317

something for you," Lizzie said. "Your daett and I had a long talk last night and we decided something. Now do you want to run out to the buggy and see what I brought?"

"What is it?" Clara asked.

"Just go," Lizzie said, waving her hand. "Quick now, and bring them all in with you."

"Did you bring anything for me?" Ella asked teasingly as Clara pulled on her coat and dashed out the door.

"No," Lizzie said. "Daett and I talked about Clara, but not about you. I'm afraid your situation with Ivan is in the ministers' hands. They will make the correct decisions, I'm sure."

Ella was silent. Out the basement window she saw Clara racing back down the snowy stairs, risking life and limb in her haste.

"Clara!" Lizzie said when the door opened. "Slow down, child. You'll fall and break something."

Clara was dancing around the living room floor. "Ella, my pictures!"

"Yes, yes! Now calm down," Lizzie said. "You will overwork yourself and be useless for the rest of the day."

"Oh, Ella!" Clara squealed, waving the pictures around. "Just look!"

"Now just a minute," Lizzie said. "We thought Ella might be able to sell what you've done, but you can't draw anymore. Is that understood?"

"Oh, yes! Thank you," Clara cried. "There is hope left in the world."

"There is *always* hope, dear," Lizzie said, hugging her tightly when Clara flew into her arms. "Your daett wants to be reasonable. But no more drawing for now — remember that."

Ella took the pictures tenderly from Clara and carried them to the spare bed she used for a quilt display. "I will hang them on the wall as soon as the weather breaks. That way they'll stay nice."

Mary and Sarah got up to see the pictures everyone was excited about. They cooed over the drawings.

"They're to look at, not to touch," Ella warned.

Clara had calmed down. She turned to her mother and said, "Now might be the best time to tell you something you might not like."

"Oh?" Lizzie said, glancing at Ella.

"Mamm, the sisterly talk you walked in on was about Ezra. Ella doesn't think you'll object if I tell you that if he asks me home, I'm going to say yes. I know he doesn't have a big farm and lives at the bottom of the hill. Is Ella right? You won't object?"

"Ezra?" Lizzie said. "Oh, Clara, I've known you've been interested in Ezra for quite some time. A mamm knows these things. You had me worried. I thought you were going to tell me something really awful."

"So then you don't mind?" Clara asked, studying her mamm's face.

"Ezra's a fine boy. I don't object. Is that what you want to hear?"

Clara's face broke into a smile.

"There now," Lizzie said. "That's settled. Now, really, we must get on the road."

Ella hesitated, but since the day seemed to be one of confessions, she said, "Mamm, I should tell you that Eli stopped by last night. I spoke with him for a little while."

"Eli?" Lizzie said, turning toward Ella. "Does he do this often?"

"No, Mamm," Ella said. "I asked him to come by so I could speak with him."

"He has stopped in at home a few times," Lizzie said. "I suppose your daett won't say too much, but do be careful with Eli — even if he is your brother."

"Yah," Ella said. "And I could have invited him in for supper, but I didn't."

"I know it's hard," Lizzie said. "We hope

and pray he comes to his senses soon." She turned to Clara. "And now, we really must be going."

Ella watched from the doorway as they went up the stairs. At the top, her mamm turned and said, "Be careful with Ivan too."

Ella nodded and closed the door as her mamm and Clara walked to the buggy.

Sarah wanted to watch them leave, so Ella held her up to the window as the two women drove down the driveway, vanishing from sight when they turned onto the main road.

"I wish I could go with them," Sarah said.

"You can't, darling. But your daett will come for you tonight. You'll be going to your own home for the weekend."

Sarah looked at her, eyes brimming with tears.

Ella glanced away. *Ivan needs to resolve the girls' fate before too long. Yet how will he do it? Certainly we can't wed, even if I were agreeable. Not if there is a chance he might be excommunicated. And what of the* Englisha *woman he was seen with? Perhaps when he arrives for the girls we can talk about it.*

With Clara gone, the afternoon passed slowly. Ella played with the girls between short shifts working on the quilt. Sometime after three she gathered the girls' things, and for the second time in the day was surprised by the sudden sound of footsteps coming down the stairs. When she opened the door, Ivan stood there, looking rather pathetic she thought. His hat was lowered almost to his eyebrows, as if to hide as much of his face as possible. When he took it off, his hair was unkempt. His trousers looked unchanged for the entire week and had straw and little pieces of silage hanging on them.

"Ivan," she said, holding the door open.

Mary and Sarah squealed together and ran into his arms as he stepped inside and squatted to receive their hugs.

"I'm a little early," he said, glancing up from the floor. He stood slowly with Sarah in his arms.

"I've just started to get the girls' clothes ready. I'm afraid you'll have to wait while I finish. It shouldn't take long."

"That's fine," he said, sitting in the rocker in the living room, little pieces of straw dropping to the floor.

Ella finished packing the girls' things and then said what was on her mind. "Ivan, I need to ask you something."

"I know. It's about excommunication. The answer is that the bishop is going to call for it."

"Oh, Ivan! How can it have come to that? Is it true then what they're saying?"

"What are they saying?" he asked.

"That you attended the Baptist church in Randolph? That you attended with an *Englisha* woman?"

He looked to the floor and cleared his throat.

"It's partly true," he said, glancing up at her face.

Ella pulled a chair out from the kitchen table and sat down.

"Partly?" she whispered. "And which part would that be?"

"Ella, please," he said, rising to his feet. "Are you going to join their side?"

"Ivan," she said, meeting his eyes, "it's not about joining sides. I need to know the truth . . . from you. You can't go on like this. You know what's right and what's wrong. You are Preacher Stutzman. Does that mean nothing to you anymore?"

He turned to stare out the window.

Ella glanced at Mary, but thankfully she seemed uninterested in the adult conversation.

"Ella, I don't know what to believe anymore."

"My daett says you won't speak with the ministers about this. Is that true? Yet you speak with me, but you have not told me the entire truth either."

"I have not spoken with them because I have not decided yet what I'm going to do."

"You told me none of this the last time we spoke. I deserve to know what's going on. Is this why you might be excommunicated?"

"If I don't repent of it, yah," he said.

"What is wrong with you?" she asked, standing to her feet, whispering. "Don't you know you are playing right into Bishop Miller's hands?"

"I'm not sure that's so," he said. "Ella, like all of us, I'm just trying to find my way through life — the life left to me with its sorrow. Things look so different to me now than when Lois was alive. Surely you know all about that?"

"Of course I do. But do you realize how this will affect all of us?" she asked, waving her hands toward the girls. "Don't you *care?*"

"Of course I care!" he said. "I care more than you know! Yet I can't seem to help myself. If you want to know the truth, I didn't plan on this. None of it. I was in Randolph the other night, and I happened to drive past the church just as they were singing a hymn. It was such a beautiful sound. I just felt like walking in and listening — so I did. I didn't stay for long. But as I stood in the back listening, it was almost as if I heard Lois's voice among them. You should have heard it, Ella. It was so beautiful. Now, you tell me that if you heard such beautiful music and you thought you heard Aden's voice among them, you wouldn't have been as moved as I was. What was I to do? What am I to do now? You tell me."

Ella took a deep breath. Weighing her words, she said, "You can tell the ministers just what you told me. That you heard the music; that it overcame you. That you went inside to listen to the music and then left. Everyone can understand such a temptation. We are not people with hearts of stone, Ivan. But then you should tell them you're sorry, and you won't return to such a place."

"*Nee,* I can't promise to never return," he said. "I heard Lois's voice, and if I hear such a thing again I must go in . . . even if it comes from an *Englisha* church."

"And thus they will excommunicate you," she said. "You know what this will do to us? And to the girls?"

"I think they will still let you care for my girls. That will be enough for me."

"But this can't go on forever," she said, raising her voice and causing Mary to glance up.

"I wish I knew the answer," he said, standing. "I hope you can find it in your heart to forgive me." He turned to his daughters. "Girls, time to go!"

He gathered the two older girls by their hands and headed outside. Ella slipped on her coat and boots and carried baby Barbara and the suitcase out to his buggy.

When the girls were settled, Ivan held out his hand to Ella.

She shook her head and said nothing.

He climbed into the buggy and said, "I will see you Monday then."

"Yah," was all she could muster.

The buggy rattled out of the snowy driveway. Ella didn't stay to watch it leave. She turned and headed toward the basement.

THIRTY-TWO

Ella awoke with a headache, stemming, no doubt, from her exasperating conversation with Ivan. How could the man have gotten himself into such a mess? Worse — he apparently had no intention of getting himself out of it. The morning chores did nothing to reduce her headache, and when Ronda appeared in her doorway, she hoped her visit would be brief.

No sooner had she entered than Ronda said, "Who beat you up?"

"Do I look that bad?" Ella asked, trying to laugh but the sound stuck in her throat.

"Well, to be honest, yes," Ronda said. "What can I do to help?"

Ella rubbed her forehead, smiling weakly. The help she really needed, Ronda could hardly give.

"Do you want to quilt this afternoon?" Ella asked. "We're behind on our orders."

"I suppose we should, but it's Saturday

and I've got work to do upstairs. And don't you dare set foot up there to help me. You've done enough already. Instead, why don't you take a day off and just do nothing? You sure deserve it."

"I think I'd feel a little guilty," Ella said, pulling a chair out from the kitchen table. "I don't usually take days off."

"Then I'll take all your guilt away," Ronda said, grabbing a hand full of air between them and throwing it toward the window. "There! It's all gone now."

"Oh my . . ." Ella leaned back in her chair in mock relief. "That feels so much better."

"See? And it was so easy."

Ella had to laugh. Ronda was the perfect friend for a day like this.

"So take the rest of the day off then," Ronda said. "Agreed?"

"Agreed," Ella replied, only half believing it.

"Then I'm going back to my own chores." Ronda shook her finger at Ella. "Now don't you dare come up and offer your help. I've got everything under control."

Watching Ronda go up the basement steps, Ella considered her advice. It seemed like ages since she had taken any time off. In the old days a good book on a Saturday afternoon being read while curled up on her bed was not uncommon. That was before Aden, and love, and duties, and all the rest. Perhaps she did need a day off. That wouldn't change anything though. Everything would still be the same with Ivan, the bishop, Robert, and Clara. But it would still be there if she worked too. Well, maybe just a bit more cleaning and then she would relax. She would forget about her troubles for a while.

Out of curiosity, Ella opened the basement door to check on the temperature. Still chilly, but not as cold as she'd expected. She gathered up several area rugs and took them out to shake and hang on the wash line to air out while she cleaned.

She quickly swept the basement floor and then went out to beat the rugs thoroughly before bringing them back in.

Ronda chose just that moment to call out the kitchen window, "Stop working!" with another shake of her finger for good measure. They both laughed.

Ella left the rugs to air some more and went back inside. The kitchen clock said it was a little past three. The afternoon suddenly looked long with nothing to do on this "day off." She needed a book to read. A good one, but from where? The ones from her youth were at her parents' house.

Perhaps Ronda might have some. Ella raced upstairs, taking two steps at a time.

Ronda met her at the door with, "No, you may *not* help me!"

"I just want to borrow a book to read," Ella explained, catching her breath.

"Oh, well then, come on in. The few books I have are over there," she said, pointing to a small bookshelf by the couch.

Ella walked over, wishing this were the public library in Randolph. At the moment she wanted something wild to read — perhaps even a love story with a happy ending. She was sure Ronda wouldn't have such a thing. She looked over the few titles and finally said, "I'll take this, *The Pilgrim's Progress.* I haven't read this in years."

"I read it not too long ago," Ronda said. "I didn't quite understand it all though."

"I don't suppose anyone does," Ella said. "Unless maybe Bishop Miller."

"Bishop Miller," Ronda said, laughing. "Are you thinking of him again?"

"*Nee,*" Ella said. "And I don't want to either." Turning to go, she added, "Thanks for the book. I'll bring it back up when I'm finished."

"I'm not worried," Ronda said. "Take your time."

Ella took the steps two at a time again.

Back in the basement, she settled on the couch, taking a minute to relax by listening to the silence of the house. Only an occasional squeak came from Ronda's soft patter of footsteps upstairs. She opened the pages of the book and was soon lost in Christian's journey toward the narrow gate.

When the pilgrim reached the Slough of Despond, Ella felt sympathy for the man's travails. It was not unlike her life — lost in a swamp. But she had no evangelist to pull her out.

Christian soon found his way through the narrow gate — a familiar point that preachers frequently stressed. The text read on, past "*the way* that was always straight, with no turns or byways in it."

She laid the book aside. Her headache was gone, and her head felt a little clearer. Perhaps she could think rationally now. How muddled had all this become? Her anger over Bishop Miller, her attempts to help Ivan, her talk with Eli. She felt tears threatening to overflow. She went over to the basement window and looked out. The snow still lay thick on the ground. Would there ever be another spring? Would her heart ever become alive again? Had she perhaps strayed down a path that was a byway? Had she, unlike Christian who usually picked the right way, chosen wrongly?

The question was troubling. Gone was the idea of rest — a day off. She paced the floor. She should have left the book alone when she thought of it in conjunction with Bishop Miller. That should have shown her how it would affect her. Now her troubling thoughts had the best of her. Of immediate concern was her anger at Ivan. Yes, she finally admitted it. She was angry, even if she shouldn't be. How could the man go to an *Englisha* church for help? And then there was her anger at Bishop Miller, at the whole situation. No doubt, she had strayed off the right path somewhere, and little good would come of anything until she found her way back.

Yet *how?* Ella went back to the kitchen and set some leftover soup on to warm for supper. Dusk was falling, so she lit a kerosene lamp. *What if I'm wrong about Bishop Miller? Could I possibly be? So many other people seem to think only* gut *of him. My parents and Ronda. And even Ivan seems to take the responsibility for his situation on himself.*

What if they were right, and she was wrong? And what if Robert really wasn't what he professed to be — an *Englisha* person who had honest intentions? But that was not possible. Her knuckles got white as her fingers dug into her hands. Did she fear love? What if she really were free to love Robert — with passion, with abandon, as she had done with Aden?

"*Nee*, it can't be," she whispered. "Love cannot come twice. There can't be another man as good as Aden. I can't believe it." She wept openly at the thought, her soup forgotten. She buried her head in her hands to muffle the sobs lest Ronda hear her and come racing down to help. With great effort she brought the outburst under control. She ate her soup slowly, still struggling to hold back the tears.

After the soup was finished, she took the kerosene lamp in hand and retrieved her journal. She sat at the kitchen table to write.

Mr. Journal,

I say that because I feel like addressing you in a formal way, with words we never use for our own people. Mr. Journal seems like that to me. Like a stranger that I have never spoken with, and yet you know my thoughts because I have written them down.

I am faced with a terrible realization. Terrible in its implications, and terrible in that it cannot be true. I love a man again. For a long time I have tried to deny it because I supposed it never could come to anything. Yet the matter must be faced. I do love, and I wish I didn't. The risk of pain is simply too much.

Such a love was taken from me once — and probably will be again. How can it be otherwise? And then too, there is the matter of the girls. How can I live with myself if I walk away from them?

They are connected to Ivan, as they should be — as am I now. But as he is surely cutting our relationship with his probable excommunication, so too will he be cutting my ties with the girls. There seems little chance of his repentance anytime soon, not with his actions at the Baptist church and attitude toward our leaders.

What if he does join the Englisha? But how can he? It is simply too large a question for me. But if he does, and the girls go with him out into the world where they will be lost from our people forever, then would I be free? Yet free at what price? I shudder to think. Those three dear sweet girls lost into the great mouth of the Englisha world. I would never see them again.

Dora would say I am like her now — thinking such dark thoughts — and perhaps I am, but my heart is very bitter about this. I'm tired of tears, and yet I can't stop them. Nor can I walk away from what I love. Not the girls or Robert . . . until I know more about him. I hardly know whether to wish he has a sordid past or no past at all.

Is there something wrong with me? Worse yet, is there something wrong with a God who creates such impossible conditions of the heart? I tremble at the question. As the dark has fallen outside my house, it makes me fear for my very soul.

I can do little right now but cry. I so hope the straight and narrow road will become clear to me again. Somewhere I must have taken an awful turn away from the right path and there is no Evangelist to instruct me as there was for Christian.

May the great Da Hah who made the heavens and the earth, and all that dwells in it, have mercy on my soul. I know of nothing else to ask. I am sick of love and all it has done to me. I wish that Da Hah had never made such an emotion.

Ella took the journal and stepped outside. The night was clear, a brisk wind coming in from the north. It would soon be even colder. She held the journal open in both hands and stretched her arms heavenward.

"See, Lord," she whispered. "I have written my thoughts, and now do to me what You wish. I cannot tear love out of my heart, and if You do so — if You must — I will try not to complain, regardless of the pain."

She shivered, holding her arms aloft until they stung, her eyes on the stars. She almost expected a streak of light to fall, burning up the pages on which she had written the awful words, but nothing moved in the sky. It was as if the stars themselves held perfectly still, daring to twinkle in the face of such great human folly.

A long moment later Ella dropped her arms, numb from cold and feeling weak. Back inside, she tucked the journal away in its hiding place and prepared for bed, though it was still early. She slipped quietly under the covers and fell into a dreamless sleep.

THIRTY-THREE

Ella awoke well before dawn, but from what she wasn't certain. The alarm clock still showed twenty minutes until it should go off. When she reached over to push the button in, it hadn't even been set. This was Sunday — an off Sunday — so that must be why she hadn't set the alarm last night. Her headache was gone, but everything else seemed hazy and distant. Even with her body rested, the turmoil of last night had left its mark.

She considered trying to go back to sleep, but the more she tried, the more she tossed and turned. No, more sleep was out of the question, so with her blanket wrapped around her, she found a match and kindling and lit the fire in the stove. The coals had died out, leaving only the faint glow of cinders at the bottom of the ashes.

Ella fanned the little pile of kindling and then carefully added a larger piece of wood.

The flame seemed sluggish, but then it reached out, wrapping around the edge of the new piece of wood, flaring on the barked edges. Ella watched in fascination. As the flame grew hungry, eager for more, she added another piece. The smoke wanted to come out the lid, and she waved it back inside and up the chimney. She closed the lid. A soft roar started, and she shut the damper to quiet the fire and force the heat into the room.

She really needed some quiet time, needed to find inner peace. She considered that a walk might be good for her. Hunger stirred, but she wanted something else first. Was it too cold to go outside? A quick check out the door convinced her it wasn't.

She quickly dressed and put on her thickest coat and gloves, wishing she had one of Eli's or Monroe's stocking caps to wear. That was one of the benefits of males in the house — they could be borrowed from. Convinced no one would see her, she found a large piece of discarded quilting fabric and wrapped it around her head in a makeshift covering. It was heavier than any scarf she had and splendid for the moment — as long as she didn't have to see how she looked in it.

The first rays of the sun had not yet lit

the horizon, the sky was clear, and the stars a great swath of brightness across the heavens. To the north, the big dipper hung upside down, as if to quickly pour out the final drops of milk before the sun could rise. She must get out of sight of the house in case Joe or Ronda were up early. There were no lights on yet, and since this was an off Sunday, the coast should be clear.

With confidence she crossed the driveway and opened the gate into the pasture. She was briefly startled when Moonbeam came up at a run. He appeared like a ghostly specter against the eastern sky, great puffs of steam coming from his nostrils. She drew in her breath and laughed, the sound rising into the morning air.

"Good morning!" she greeted him as he skidded to a halt. Knowingly she added, "No oats yet, old boy. I'm just out on a walk."

He dropped his head and followed behind her as if he were her shadow. The soft crunch of his heavy hoofs on the snow supplied her with welcome company from a world less troubled than hers. Did God make animals to show humans how simply life could be lived? Yet how was she to live like that? She wasn't an animal. She was human — very human.

She stood and gazed around her for a while, letting the peacefulness sink into her soul. She again lifted her heart to God and waited. The words that came to mind were just a whispered, "Trust Me," to which she could only whisper back, "Thank You." The cold soon sunk in past her coat and bulky head scarf. Ella patted Moonbeam on the nose.

"I'm going back inside now," she announced. He followed her to the gate, standing with his head slung over it while she walked across the driveway.

At the top of the basement steps she turned for one last look to the east. The sun's rays lit up the horizon, the soft glow warming her heart.

As Ella went down the steps she could hear Joe and Ronda stirring in the house above. Quietly she entered her basement home and made her breakfast. As she sat at the table to eat, she noticed Joe and Ronda's buggy drive out the lane — apparently off to visit someone.

With nothing planned, Ella turned to her book and was soon engrossed in the progress of Pilgrim. At noon, she barely stopped to fix a sandwich and was still reading when Joe and Ronda returned sometime after four. She heard Ronda's steps coming down the basement stairs and glanced up with a sheepish look.

"You've been here by yourself all day?" Ronda asked as she came in.

"Yah," Ella said. "I enjoyed it."

"Well, too much quiet isn't good for you. You have to come for supper."

Ella laid the book aside. "Only if I can come up and help get it ready."

"It's already done," Ronda said. "Will you come at five thirty?"

"You're going to spoil me."

Ronda smiled and disappeared up the stairs.

Ella picked up her book and returned to Christian's journey, now in the middle of the Land of Beulah where he was given a glimpse of the Celestial City. By the time of the crossing of the river, the clock showed five twenty. She didn't want to get into the middle of what couldn't be finished, so with a piece of paper she marked the book and went upstairs.

Joe was in his rocker, absorbed in a farm magazine.

"So where did you go today?" Ella asked Ronda, who was standing at the kitchen counter.

"We visited Joe's parents."

"That's *gut.* Anything I can do to help?"

Ella asked.

"No, sit down," Ronda said. "We serve you tonight."

Ella obeyed and Ronda joined her, bringing the last dish to the table. Joe sat down and they bowed their heads for prayer. They began eating, the meal passing quickly. Ella stayed to help wash the dishes, and Ronda didn't protest.

"Joe wants a farm someday," Ronda said quietly, her hands deep in soap suds.

Ella brought the last of the dishes from the table. "Any prospects?"

"No, but if nothing turns up, do you think we'll be able to stay here until next summer?"

"I think so," Ella said. "I just don't know what's going to happen. Ivan is convinced he faces excommunication and that means there will be no wedding."

"I know," Ronda said in sympathy. "I've heard the talk going around. It does leave a lot of uncertainty for all of us — you especially."

"We just have to live with it, I suppose."

"That's all? Just live with it?" Ronda said. "You don't seem particularly upset about it."

"I guess I'm learning that getting upset doesn't do any good. It just results in headaches. Now I'm going to try to let *Da Hah* handle things and not worry so much. It's out of my hands, really."

"I can understand that. I can't imagine what you're facing. And you're a much better person than I am."

"Don't say that," Ella said. "I'm no better than anyone else."

The two worked quietly on the dishes and finished a few minutes later. Ella thanked Ronda for supper and said goodnight to Joe.

He nodded, glancing up briefly to smile at her.

Back in the basement, Ella picked up her book again and continued to read. Christian soon crossed over the dark River of Death, arriving safely on the other side. Ella got to her feet and stretched. Somehow the story had given her renewed confidence in *Da Hah*. She felt tired even though it had been a day of rest. Another good night's rest would be just the ticket.

Ivan arrived with the girls a little after seven. She met him at the top of the steps, and took baby Barbara from his arms. He looked better than he had on Friday — almost rested.

"Do you want to come inside?" she asked.

He hesitated, seeming to search for words.

She persisted. "Ivan, I really need to speak with you."

He nodded, apprehension crossing his face.

"Sit," she said, once they were inside.

"You don't have to say anything," he said, taking a seat on the couch.

"Yah," she said, sitting down beside him, "I do."

Was there any way to reach this man? He seemed so distant, so lost. How had the great Preacher Stutzman fallen so far? It was beyond her, yet she could try.

He looked at her, his eyes narrowed.

"Ivan, there must be a way for you to straighten this out with Bishop Miller. Apologize for going in the Baptist church. It was wrong. How many times have you preached about the world and its temptations? You could never be happy in a Baptist church. How could you be?" She touched his hand, running her fingers slowly along his arm.

Ivan didn't move.

"Can't you see that? For the girls' sake, if nothing else? If you don't repent, we can't marry."

"You would marry me if I'm not excommunicated?"

She met his eyes, allowing him to look as

344

long as he wished.

Finally convinced, he looked toward the window.

"Ivan, it might be the best either of us can make out of this mess of our lives. But you must repent of what you have done."

He looked back at her. "You deserve better than marrying me. It's not right."

"Not right? Why? Is not love offered for the better of the other always holy?"

"Perhaps," he said. "But this has always been more one-sided than anything else. You know that. The love you would give me is sincere, but it's a love of convenience. You deserve more than that. You don't love me the way you will some other man. The kind of man you deserve."

"You are a *gut* man," she said. "Please don't let this destroy you."

"I won't." He smiled weakly. "It might make me a better man."

"Excommunication?"

"I don't know," he sighed. "I can only hope so."

"Can't you come back . . . from where you've gone?"

"You are a great woman. As wonderful as Lois," he admitted, touching her face. "But no, Ella, I don't believe I can."

"Then what will happen?"

"I don't know," he said. "But one thing I do know is that you are now free of me forever."

Ella's shock was evident. For a moment she found no words. "Ivan, are you sure?"

"Yah," he said. He stood and put on his hat and turned for the door.

Ella remained on the couch and heard the latch click softly behind him. Emotions she couldn't identify roiled in her heart. Should she have not spoken up this way? Had she made matters worse by driving Ivan away from her?

"We had breakfast," Sarah said, coming to stand quietly beside her.

"I'm glad," Ella whispered, stroking Sarah's hair back from her face. She had almost forgotten the girls in their quietness.

Ivan's voice played in her mind: *You are now free.* Was she really? Did she dare to be free? What about the girls? One answer gained seemed to beget more questions. Ella sighed and hugged Sarah before getting up. There was work to do, and work usually made things better . . . didn't it?

THIRTY-FOUR

As the week unfolded, Ella's emotions became a seesaw as she wondered each day if this would be the morning Robert would return for his German lesson. She was surprised at how eager she was to see him again. Was it Ivan's words that released her to love another? She had not heard from Eli, but that was surely a good sign. If Eli turned up something bad, he would have reported it to her quickly. Each day without Eli pulling in the lane was a good day.

Even Ella's feelings toward Bishop Miller softened. After all, hadn't Ivan himself said that his troubles were of his own making? And what of the *Englisha* woman who was reportedly seen with Ivan? Had Ivan lied to her about that? Was there a reason for his deception?

The hardest thing to bear was that now she would surely lose the girls. When that realization struck her on Thursday, she gathered Mary and Sarah on the couch along with baby Barbara and hugged them all hard. Mary and Sarah stared at Ella, puzzled by her sudden show of affection. Ella did well to hide the tears gathering in her heart.

Shortly after ten o'clock that morning, the girls were on the couch with Mary pretending to read to Sarah. Ella smiled at Mary's inventiveness in coming up with words that matched the pictures on the pages. She looked up suddenly from her quilting when the sound of a buggy could be heard coming up the drive. She knew at once that it was Robert. It was all she could do not to race outside and meet him at the top of the basement steps. Such a display would be inappropriate and out of character, so she merely headed to the door to open it.

"Robert's come for his lesson," she told the girls.

Mary and Sarah both looked at her with blank faces.

"Robert?" Mary asked.

"Yes," Ella said. "Do you remember? The man I'm teaching German."

Mary's face brightened. "Oh now I remember!" she said. Sarah nodded.

Ella waited, her heart racing. She felt like a house with all the windows and doors open to bring in the summer breeze.

"Hello!" she said as she opened the door for him.

"Good morning," he said, tilting his head slightly. "What is the lovely Amish maiden up to this morning? Does she have time for a reforming *Englisha* like me?"

"Perhaps," she said, laughing, joy flooding her heart.

"Then may I come inside?" he asked, raising his eyebrows.

"Oh, yah! Do come in," she said stepping back. "I'm afraid the house is in a mess."

"Hah," he said with a broad smile. "That's something I've noticed about Amish women. You always think the house is a mess, when actually you could eat off the floor with a spoon."

"Oh? And do you see a lot of Amish women?" she asked primly, shutting the door behind him and not daring to look into his face.

"A few," he said. "Being the house guest of a bishop does result in a few supper invitations. But I can't say they're without intent. I think I am a little of a novelty."

"Yah, indeed you are." Surely he meant *married* women were fixing these meals for him.

"So you're busy," he said. "So many things

to do — the quilting, the children, the house, the renters upstairs. A busy, busy woman, and now German lessons to teach."

"Is there something wrong with being busy?"

"No, not at all. In fact, I like it. It's one of the reasons I'm joining the Amish. I like their hard work, honest toil, *and* their solid womenfolk."

"You make us sound like rather joyless creatures."

"Not at all. What more could a man wish for?"

"Yah," she said. "Tell me, what could he wish for?"

"Well," Robert said, spreading his arms, "the Amish man has the world by the tail. He works, he has children — lots of them — and he loves his wife. That's enough I think. More than enough, wouldn't you say?"

"I don't know." She turned away so he couldn't see her face. "I haven't been married."

"Which is a good thing," he said with a sweet smile. "I mean, it gives you something to look forward to."

"Perhaps we should start the lesson," she said, keeping her eyes on the kitchen table. "I am, as you said, busy."

"That's another thing about Amish women — or perhaps you, Ella. At first you're warm and welcoming, and the next minute it's down to business. You women change like the weather."

"Perhaps marriage settles us down," she said, surprised at his frank appraisal of her. Is that what he thought? "I'm not used to such a frank discussion of a girl's temperament, and that right in front of her."

He laughed, a heartfelt bellow that echoed through the basement. "My, my, this is interesting. Perhaps I need more than German lessons from you. Perhaps lessons in Amish women. Shall I take notes?"

"Is that what I am to you — a dispenser of Amish information — and emotions? Perhaps just an experiment, the results of which you can store in that fancy college brain of yours? Robert, we Amish women — and men too for that matter — aren't monkeys in a zoo to be observed."

"I'm sorry," he said. "Bishop Miller said I might run into this when he told me I could come here for lessons."

"Run into *what?*" she asked, holding his gaze, her hands now inexplicably shaking.

"Well, you are a dating woman — or were. I'm not sure of your customs."

"What do you mean *were?*"

"Your beloved — if that is what he is . . . isn't he about to be excommunicated?"

"And how do you know this?"

"Bishop Miller told me, of course."

"When did he tell you about Ivan possibly being excommunicated?"

He regarded her for a long moment.

"Tell me the truth," she said.

"I don't know what this is all about," he said. "But I sense a trap under my foot."

"And why should there be a trap under your foot?" she asked, feeling tears sting her eyes. "I'm sorry, I know it's not your fault."

"What makes you think . . ."

"Robert, answer the question."

"Before I answer, let me say this," he said, uneasily. "My mother told me about the kind of woman you are, Ella. But in person, it's different. Even better. When I saw you that first day I was here, when you asked me to stay for dinner, I can't explain how that felt, how at home it made me feel. All my life I've wanted that feeling, Ella. No, I've wanted more than just the feeling. I've wanted someone like you. Yet you were seeing someone. You told me so yourself. But you never said if you loved the man. I don't know, perhaps you do. But where I come from, a man can tell how a woman feels about the man she's seeing.

"Now, this man you were seeing is in a lot of trouble. And so I have to wonder that if that's true, does it change anything between us? Would I have a chance with you, once I'm baptized and all that? Please, just consider it, Ella. I'm not trying to pull any tricks. Really I'm not."

Ella hardly knew how to react. She felt a familiar pain on the inside, but before she could answer his question, she had to know the answer to her question. "I want you to answer my question, Robert. When did Bishop Miller tell you Ivan might be excommunicated?"

He sighed. "One of the first nights I came. We talked about Amish life, and naturally he asked me why I was interested in becoming Amish. I told him that I was attracted to the life — and, forgive me, Ella — I confided in him that I was attracted to you too. As we talked, he told me about excommunication among the Amish. He told me there might soon be a case in point. He told me it involved you."

Ella trembled with anger. "Robert, you have no idea what you're involved in," she cried, placing both hands on the kitchen table.

She caught sight of the girls watching the two of them.

She calmed her voice and said, "Please just go back to the big wide world where you came from, Robert. You are a babe lost in the woods. You will get over this, but it will not be here among us. Please leave, Robert. Leave now."

"But I love you," he said, his hand touching her arm.

"Don't," she said, pulling back, her voice now cold. "It's no use. Just go."

"Was I out of place — with what I said about the two of us? Do you not speak of these things before baptism?"

"Robert, I'm seeing that it's really true that we come from different worlds. Two worlds that can never be joined together."

"Bishop Miller is allowing me to come over."

She stared at him, refusing to answer. There were many things she was, but a betrayer of her people she was not. Never would a word cross her lips that this man from the *Englisha* could take back with him and shame her people.

"I will be baptized," he said, his voice firm. "I start the class in the spring, and I will become part of your world. How can you hold it against me, the fact that I was born in what you call 'the world'?"

"Robert," she said hearing her voice

choke. "I cannot tell you . . . what needs to be said, and you must not make me. You will soon see things happen here among us. Watch them carefully, and perhaps you will see it in time. I hope that you do, long before you are made bitter and hard. I pray you're spared, because, yah, Robert, the truth is that I do love you, but it cannot be."

"But why not?" he asked, gripping her arm until she pulled away in pain.

"It is just best that you do not ask . . . and that you do not come back here anymore."

He paced the floor rapidly. "But surely there is hope for the two of us?"

"You will have to speak with *Da Hah* about that."

"The Lord," he said, as if this were part of his German lesson. "God, give me patience to understand these people," he asked.

"It would be easier if you didn't try."

"I suppose it would be," he said with a bitter taste in his mouth.

She waited, saying nothing.

Finally Robert pulled his hat on top of his head and opened the front door. He disappeared up the basement steps.

She waited for the tears to come, but none

did even as she listened to his buggy drive
down the lane.

THIRTY-FIVE

With a heavy heart Ella arose and got ready for church. This was the Sunday a decision would be made about Ivan's future. After barely touching her breakfast, Ella hitched her horse to the buggy. She returned to the house to change into better clothes. In truth, she wanted desperately to crawl back under the covers and never come out again. But like a bad dream from which she couldn't awaken, today and its events would have to be endured.

Church was to be held at Albert Stoll's place, the announcement having been made two weeks in advance. Where the deed was done didn't matter. One place would serve as well as another. She simply needed to know in which direction to drive, like the French prisoners she had studied in grade school who were led to the guillotine.

Ella left her house late on purpose. She didn't want to face Joe and Ronda, so it was sometime after they left that Ella turned Moonbeam north at the end of her driveway and pulled out onto Chapman Road. Few buggies were on the road anymore, even when she approached the Stoll driveway. The long line of men and boys still stood in the barn yard, but already they were moving toward the house. Ella drove past the walks where the women were dropped off and parked beside the last buggy. Its owner had his horse unhitched and was pulling on the horse's bridle, directing him toward the barn.

Ella's cousin James appeared around the back of the buggy, along with a boy she didn't know.

"Why are you so late?" he asked, as if the answer mattered.

"Just one of those mornings," she said, trying to smile beneath her bonnet.

James shrugged and unhitched Ella's horse and led him forward at a trot. His companion threw the tugs up over the horse.

"I'll help you get the horse out after church." James tossed the words over his shoulder as he headed toward the barn with Moonbeam.

Behind her, the line of black-suited men was already at the house door, with the young Bishop Miller in the lead. He was here on official business, his suit clean and brushed. Behind him followed the home bishop, Bishop Mast, walking with his head bowed. Behind him came the other ministers, and then the men forming a long line across the yard. They entered slowly, filing through the house and into the living room to sit on the benches, the ministers in front.

Ella was still in the washroom, her bonnet strings knotted, when she heard the women begin moving into the main part of the house. If she hadn't been late, other women would have been around and noticed her plight. Someone would have helped her untangle the mess. With great frustration, Ella considered a quick jerk, which would have surely resulted in tearing the cloth.

Instead she tugged as hard as she could and finally moved the knot out past her chin where she could see it with her eyes turned painfully downward. A sharp tug and the tie loosened, the bonnet quickly joining the others on the stacked pile. The shawl went into another pile. She rushed into the kitchen. Faint smiles played on several of the young girls' faces. They parted as a group, stepping back so she could at least get in line with the last of the girls her own age.

The ministry filed out at the start of the

second line of the first song, Bishop Miller in the lead again. Ivan walked with them in his usual place. He might even sit on the minister's bench for the entire service. There was little middle ground in this world. You were, and then you were not.

What would Robert think of this? Surely he wasn't here — she had checked the row of unmarried boys. Hopefully he had taken her advice and returned to his own world.

The men's benches squeaked as the second song started. A few of the boys' chins went down on their palms, faces sleepy. They perked up when Bishop Miller's black shoes appeared at the top of the stairs just before the next song was announced. What this early return meant was uncertain, but Ivan now brought up the rear of the line — out of place.

The change had already begun. He looked weary, his face lined with sadness.

Bishop Mast had the first sermon, and then Bishop Miller stood for the main sermon. Ella felt bitterness rising in her heart, but she had to give the man credit. On this day it must be hard to preach. Bishop Miller could have assigned the task to another minister, but he had chosen to shoulder the burden himself.

Ella had already decided to forgive the

man. It was the way of her people. You laid your burden at the feet of *Da Hah,* allowing the pain to come, and then walked away from it. Vengeance belonged to Another, and you prayed that He would be merciful with His judgment, even as you yourself needed mercy.

This might have started with impure motives from the bishop — desiring to come between her and Ivan — but even Ivan had come to realize that he had done himself in. And now she could expect a visit from Bishop Miller sometime in the weeks ahead. The man had loved her, professed his great admiration for her, so perhaps he could be excused for using what means lay in his hands to win her heart.

Still, she would smile, and tell him *nee.* There was no harm he could do to her or to her family. The worst had already been done. Joe and Ronda could have the house for all she cared — or her daett could decide the matter. She was worn out, her heart in shambles. She would gladly move back home. That was where an old maid belonged anyway.

The only unsettled matter, really, were Ivan's girls. Ella would care for them as long as Ivan wanted — but likely that wouldn't be long. Usually those who left for the *En-*

glisha world didn't do it halfway. Ivan would quickly pull the girls along with him.

As for Robert — wherever he was now — he could take care of himself. He was a man. Ella hoped that the ray of faith he held had not been destroyed. Surely he hadn't thought Amish people were saints. If so, that illusion had probably been shattered.

Bishop Miller closed his sermon, his eyes moving around the room one last time before settling on three men who would give testimony. Two of them came from the minister's bench, and the other from the audience. All three took their time, since it was still early. No one had found any errors in the sermon, and the final song came to a close. The clock on the living room wall showed exactly twelve o'clock.

"Will all those who are members please stay in," Bishop Miller said, now on his feet again. A rustle of whispers went through the congregation as children were given final instruction for their time outside without adult supervision.

Even though Ella knew what lay ahead, her spirit sank as low as it had been yet. This was not a dream. It was very real.

"We have the labor of the church before us," Bishop Miller said, still standing. To his credit, he didn't seem to be enjoying this

362

duty. "The work of *Da Hah* is necessary work, just as the work on our farms is necessary. We must tend to it or things fail — the cows don't give milk and the crops don't grow." He cleared his throat.

The men's benches didn't squeak at all.

"Our brother Ivan Stutzman has allowed himself to be drawn into a clever trap of the enemy. A trap from the one who is the enemy of all our souls, who seeks to destroy us. This matter first came to our attention some time ago, and we have spoken often with Ivan since that time.

"Ivan Stutzman has, in our opinion, allowed the sorrows of his wife's death to cloud his judgment. He has grieved for her beyond what is fitting for any man or woman and has not placed the matter fully into *Da Hah*'s hands. Others may have different opinions on the matter — about how this has happened. We do not argue with them or say they are wrong.

"What we can all agree on — first as the ministry and then hopefully today as a congregation — is that our concerns have been for a reason. That these concerns could have been solved in a reasonable manner was always possible. Concerns about Ivan's change in his preaching style, which I am sure all of you have noticed. Ivan also began to read articles, written by Amish people, yah, but they are against our beliefs. This we could still have worked with, but now in addition to these concerns, it has been confirmed with Ivan that he attended a Baptist church in Randolph. Once when we first spoke with him, and twice since then, including this very morning. He has also told us that of this indiscretion, he is unwilling to repent.

"There were also reports brought to us that Ivan has been seen at the Baptist church with an *Englisha* woman. Ivan has assured us this is not true, that he attended alone. We accept that explanation, but still warn him of the enticements from the many *Englisha* women, no doubt, who would accept his hand in marriage.

"I will now ask the other ministers to express themselves," Bishop Miller concluded. He sat down. Bishop Mast spoke first, and then the other minister. Neither had anything new to add. Each expressed their support for excommunication since Ivan had been given warning and plenty of time to repent.

Bishop Miller rose again and addressed Ivan. "Will our beloved brother now leave, so that the council of the church can be taken on this matter?" He waited as Ivan left the room.

Ella couldn't take her eyes off Ivan's face, even when she tried. His pain cut her deeply. How she wished he wouldn't be so stubborn. They could still make something of their life together. Why couldn't Ivan see that?

"The ministry will now ask for the voice of the church," Bishop Miller said, sitting down.

With a soft rustle, the deacon stood first, soon joined by two of the ministers. They moved between the tight benches, bending over to listen to each member whisper in their ear. There was little to say, since no one would desire or dare to object.

When the deacon reached her, Ella had planned to only shrug her shoulders and the deacon would move on. He knew her connection to Ivan and would understand. Instead she whispered, "My heart is very heavy today, but I cannot see what else could have been done."

The deacon nodded, moving on. He bent toward the girls beside her, waiting, then moved on to the next person. Bishop Miller got to his feet when the reports had been brought back and given to him in quiet whispers. Someone went out to bring Ivan back in.

"In this case," Bishop Miller said, turning to face Ivan who sat on the front bench, hanging his head, "I now, with the full support of the church, will hold Ivan Stutzman to be in a fallen state, both before *Da Hah* and man, until such time as he comes to repentance. We have nothing more to say about the matter."

The older boys who had stayed in the meeting now left, followed by the men. The girls' side began to move toward the kitchen, where they began the food preparation in an obviously subdued mood. Ella joined in. She wanted something to do. She needed to feel the presence of others around her. Soon enough the dreaded time would come when the aloneness of the basement would surround and haunt her.

Prayer was announced, spoken, and slowly the usual hum of voices filled the house. These were men and women who worked every day around death and disaster on their farms. A man's soul had been dealt with today, but even then they quickly returned to the faith that *Da Hah* worked all things out for the best.

Ivan could have left for home, if he'd wished, and no one would have blamed him. Instead he stayed, and someone gave him a place at the first round of tables. Only it was in a little bench off to the side. No one could eat with him now. He sat there, his head bowed, his face haunted. A little bowl of peanut butter, two pieces of bread, butter, and some pickles sat before him. He was offered coffee and shook his head.

Ella watched him as he slowly spread his bread. As he took his first bite, little Mary broke out of the crowd and climbed on the bench beside him. She whispered something, and Ivan attempted a smile for her and stroked her face, tucking in the stray hairs under her covering as she snuggled up beside him. Ella wondered if Jesus had looked anything like this when He had left His beautiful heaven to taste of earthly sorrows. Such a thing seemed very possible.

"It is a sad day," Ronda whispered in her ear.

Ella nodded, wiped her eyes, but said nothing. Beside her a few women noticed and made sure she got on the next table to eat. She didn't feel like food would go down, but accepted their offer of comfort. It was all they knew how to give, and she was thankful she could still eat with them.

THIRTY-SIX

The *Englisha* Christmas decorations were out, wreaths hanging on the doors, Christmas trees sparkling in the living room windows, but Ella barely noticed. Her routine with Ivan hadn't changed despite his new status in the community. Every Monday morning he showed up with the girls, and every Friday he picked them up on schedule. Little was said between the two, and it was best that way.

He waited for the girls outside the door, making no attempt to come inside, and Ella didn't ask him in. His clothes were still Amish, and he looked the same as always. Ronda said that he was attending the Baptist church in Randolph on Wednesday nights . . . or so she had heard.

For now, he still came to the regular Amish church services every two weeks. He stayed home on the Sundays in between. For some reason Ella didn't know about,

Ivan had not yet told the girls about his departure from the faith.

Ella's heart felt as frozen as the winter snow that continued to fall day after day. A severe storm off the lake had blown in, closing the back roads for a day. After the plows came through, a group of *Englisha* carolers stopped by, all wrapped up in mufflers and overcoats.

The little children's cheerful red faces were the only reason Ella allowed them to stay long enough for two songs. That and the memory of Aden and his love for *Englisha* people's Christmas carols.

Ronda called out of the first floor window once they were gone, "I can't believe you let them sing, Ella. Do they stop here every year?"

"I don't know," Ella said. "This is my first winter in this house."

Every so often Ella wondered about Robert. Nothing had been said about him, but he had not returned. She didn't dare ask questions of anyone. When buggy wheels turned into the driveway at odd times, she half expected it would be Bishop Miller, come to stake his claim to her again. Her speech was prepared for his arrival. She would be as nice as possible, smile, but her answer was *nee.*

Lately Ella felt compelled to teach Ivan's girls while she still could. She had visions of what might lay ahead for them in an *Englisha* world — the change in clothes, the automobile, the use of the modern things the *Englisha* women had. She knew anything she might say about the dangers of the world would be of little benefit to them, but surely the basics of the faith would stand them in good stead. Did not the *Englisha* people believe many of the same things?

The day she had hoped to begin her instruction baby Barbara came down with the flu. Ella sat up in the rocker with her for most of two nights. When the baby recovered, Ella began reading Bible stories to the girls after supper. She didn't own a fancy children's Bible storybook like the one she had seen in the library at Randolph. Nor did she have an inclination to borrow one. Instead she read straight from the biblical text, using the English words and adding her own as they occurred to her.

She read chapter after chapter to them, stories of Abraham, Joseph, David, and his son Solomon. She expected Mary and Sarah to tire, but the stories held their interest, and the next evening they seemed to look forward to more stories.

Joe and Ronda left for Ronda's parents'

place the evening before Old Christmas. Before they left, Ronda came down. "You're not going anywhere? Isn't it time you got out?"

"I guess I could go to Mamm and Daett's," Ella said, offering a weak smile. "It's not that I don't want to. I'm just tired."

"Will they come over here then? Surely you need to see your family."

"I don't know. It's a ways over there, and with all the stuff that's gone on . . ."

"They don't blame you for Ivan's excommunication, do they? That's not your fault at all."

"I don't think they do, and no one else seems to either. At least from what I've picked up on Sundays."

"I'd hope not," Ronda said. "And how are you doing?"

"To tell you the truth, I feel frozen. I feel scared . . . mostly for the girls and what will happen to them."

"All the more reason to drive over to your parents. You can get the horse ready or Joe can, if that would help. Just spend the day with your family. Really, Ella, you ought to."

"This will be a hard time for Mamm and Daett. It's the first Old Christmas since Eli left. I'm not sure a visit would be all that helpful . . . for me or for them. We'd all be thinking about Eli, even if nothing is said."

"I feel so sorry for you," Ronda said. "Is there anything Joe and I can do?"

"I'm afraid not," Ella said. "Life will have to heal itself."

And that was how it would go. Life would slowly heal itself, and she would settle into her role of being an old maid.

With Joe and Ronda gone for the evening, Ella read her usual Bible story to Mary and Sarah, with baby Barbara on the floor in front of them. When bedtime arrived, she decided to do something unusual — perhaps memorable for the three girls. Baby Barbara might not remember, but hopefully Mary and Sarah would.

"Would you like to go out to the barn to hear the Christmas story?" she asked the girls.

Mary thought for a while and then nodded. Sarah quickly nodded after she did.

"Then get your coats and boots," Ella said, "I'll see how cold it is outside."

Ella opened the basement door and took a deep breath. Her lungs didn't burn and her face didn't sting.

"Let's go!" she said with a laugh. "Tonight I'll tell you the best story of all . . . right close to where it really happened."

Bundled up, Ella picked up the kerosene

lamp in one hand and baby Barbara in the other. She led the other two girls out. Keeping the lamp lighted proved hard. The first gust of wind blew out the flame, so she had the girls wait on the steps while she went back for matches. Once they finally made it into the barn, Ella set the lamp on a bale of straw and gathered the girls around her.

Baby Barbara wanted down, and since the straw was clean, Ella let her. After all, what was the worst the child could do? Chew on straw? Something Ella had done many times in her growing up years.

Moonbeam neighed, sticking his head over the stall wall as far as he could. Ella laughed at him, sure they made a strange sight in the flickering light of the kerosene lamp. A woman with three girls all wrapped in coats and scarves, seated in the straw on the barn floor.

"There was once a night, so very long ago," she began, "when the world had grown old and weary, where men killed each other in wars, and woman and children were kept despised and suffering. Cripples lined the streets, begging for bread, and *Da Hah* seemed to have forgotten His people.

"The people had stories of the old days when King David ruled the land, and when his son Solomon built the most beautiful temple the land of Israel had ever known. The people then had plenty, they said, and the walls of the cities had been secure and the babies were born free. But now Rome ruled the land. Cruel Rome, they said in whispers, and wished to be free.

"The temple rulers read the Scriptures on the Sabbath, but the words seemed to mean little. And with each year that passed, the words meant less. Words about a Savior who would come and save His people from their sins. Sin, they knew about, but 'saving' meant nothing to them.

"Then one night, out of nowhere, with no warning except to a few people, a young woman and the man who was to become her husband rode into the town of Bethlehem on a donkey. They didn't want to be there, hadn't planned to give birth in this town. But all the inns were full, and Joseph couldn't find a place to spend the night. They walked all over town looking for a place because Mary knew she would soon have her baby.

"Her husband, Joseph, finally found the only place left in town to stay — a barn. There among the sheep, the goats, and the horses, baby Jesus was born in a manger, and all He had to lay in was straw and some swaddling clothes."

"What's swaddling clothes?" Mary asked.

"Something like strips of blankets. See, Joseph and Mary were very poor and very far from home."

"Was it like this?" Mary asked, motioning around the barn.

In the flickering light of the lamp, Ella said, "Yah." It seemed very possible.

"I would have wanted to be there," Mary said.

"They say the animals talked with the Savior that night, right after He was born," Ella said.

"Even the horse?" Mary turned around to stare toward Moonbeam.

"I think so," Ella laughed. "But that's just what they said. We don't know for sure."

"I believe it!" Mary said, still not turned around. "Will the animals ever talk again?"

"Perhaps when the Savior comes back," Ella said. What Preacher Stutzman would think about such an idea, Ella wasn't sure.

"I want to hear a horse talk," Mary said, and Sarah nodded in agreement.

"We do know one thing," Ella said. "There were angels that night who appeared in the sky, out where the shepherds watched their sheep in the fields. They sang wonderful songs, filling the heavens with the joyful sound. They said the Savior had been born in Bethlehem, that peace had come to the earth, that goodwill was given to mankind because *Da Hah* would take away their sins."

Ella paused, caught up in her story. She glanced over Mary's and Sarah's heads to Moonbeam. He blinked in the dim light, looking very much like he wanted to talk. Ella smiled and then said, "And that's the story of Christmas. The birth of the One who would save people from their sins . . . Jesus Christ."

Mary yawned as Ella gathered baby Barbara in her arms and led the girls to the barn door. The moon would be enough light, so Ella blew out the kerosene lamp. They headed to the house.

On the walk back they paused to look at the stars. There was not a cloud in the sky; the air was crystal clear. Ella could easily imagine bands of angels suddenly appearing and singing beautiful songs. What she couldn't understand was why peace and goodwill hadn't come. *Da Hah*'s ways were strange sometimes and hard to understand.

"I want to see angels!" Mary said, waving her hands at the heavens.

"Yah, that would be nice," Ella agreed. "Now, let's get you girls inside before you freeze."

"I like the barn," Sarah said. "Can we do

this again?"

"Christmas only comes once a year," Ella said.

"Then we can do it again next year," Mary said.

"I hope so," Ella whispered. "I really hope so."

THIRTY-SEVEN

Old Christmas Day dawned dreary, the clouds hanging heavily on the horizon. Ella had planned to sleep in and hadn't set the alarm, but she now stood by the basement window, the girls still asleep in the bed behind her. She felt groggy and weary, having awakened before she planned to. This was her people's day to celebrate the Savior's birth, but the truth was that celebrating was far from her mind.

Still it *was* Old Christmas and something should be done. Memories of last night with the girls in the barn cheered her thoughts a bit. What could she do that might make the day more memorable? Should she make a late attempt to visit her parents?

Nee. With Eli gone, this first Old Christmas at her parents' place wouldn't be a very cheerful affair. Was that then a good reason to go? To cheer up her parents? But what had she to give them? Very little in the state she was in.

To *give.* The thought gripped her. After last night with the girls and the story of the Savior's birth, this was what she should do — what she *wanted* to do. The memory of Ivan's face rose before her. Could she give to *him?* Did she dare?

With a steady gaze at the low, heavy clouds, she pondered the question. The world seemed such a cruel place, with what men did to each other and with what life did to them. Were actions made holy because they were called holy? What would happen to her if she dared to do the unspeakable — take a meal to Ivan? A knee confession at most, if she was caught. But so what? If it came to that, she could bend her knees and say the necessary words.

The years stretched out in front of her. Years to be lived in the faith, keeping free from the dangers of the world. Those years seemed bleak indeed if she drew back from this moment. In the frozen landscape of her heart, this last token must be given to love. Before the death of all desire came, she would *give* and value the consequences less than the gift. Yah, on this Old Christmas Day she would go to Ivan. She would take him supper — the best she could make. Furthermore, she would eat with him, sitting at the same table.

Ella felt no fear at the thought. Her heart was stirred. If she could never love a man like she had loved Aden, then perhaps she could love one like the Savior would.

With purpose Ella returned to the kitchen. Only the best would do. She took the flour out and began to make bread, even though two loaves already sat on the kitchen counter. Ivan loved freshly made bread.

With the fire hot in the stove, the basement warmed up quickly. Ella smiled when she had to crack the window by the door. The action seemed to fit the day now, the window to her heart would also remain open for a little time.

Mary and Sarah awoke, apparently from her bustling in the kitchen.

Ella quickly helped the two girls up and then made them breakfast. As they ate, she returned to the bread dough.

"Why are you still cooking?" Mary asked as she finished her egg.

"I'm making a special meal for this special day. We're going to take the meal to your daett's place. And then," Ella concluded with satisfaction, "we are going to eat with him."

"But it's not Friday," Mary said.

"It doesn't matter," Ella said. "It's Old

Christmas Day, and it's a special day. We'll come back here afterward, and you'll stay until Friday like usual."

"Why can't we stay at Daett's?" Mary asked. "Like you did once a long time ago."

"Because we're not married," she finally said.

Mary looked at her but didn't say anything.

"Perhaps your daett will marry again soon," Ella said, trying to put hope in her voice. "Then you can all be together in the same house. And you will have a real mamm to care for you."

"You're our mamm," Mary said.

"I try to be," Ella said. "But you know I'm really not."

"I know," Mary said. "But I wish you were."

"Dear heart," Ella said, pausing to draw her into a tight hug, "I wish so too."

"Can we help?" Sarah asked, pulling on Ella's sleeve.

"Of course, dear," Ella said, letting Mary go. She gave them each a little dough to knead as she peeled potatoes, remembering her mamm's instructions to keep the peelings thin. Ella felt a lump in her throat at the thought that the girls might never receive such instructions.

"Do it like this," Mary said, demonstrating her technique to Sarah, who watched carefully, and then tried to imitate.

Ella watched, caught up in their efforts. *Does Ivan fully understand what his decisions mean for those of us around him?* She placed more wood on the fire. She needed to get her mind on more cheerful thoughts. What good would her efforts be if she arrived long-faced? That really wouldn't do.

"Tell us the story again," Mary said, forming a small loaf with her dough.

"Me too," Sarah said, nodding rapidly.

"You mean the story of the Christ's birth?"

"Yah," Sarah said. "The one about sheep and goats that can talk."

"It really wasn't about that," Ella replied, smiling. "But I can tell you the real story again."

They waited with expectant faces, but the story was interrupted by baby Barbara's cry from behind the curtain. When she had been changed and seated in the high chair with breakfast in front of her, Ella tried again. Even the baby seemed to listen as Ella spoke, her hands busy helping Barbara eat. When the babe was full, Ella moved to the counter and worked with the bread dough and on the meat for the main dish.

"That's a good story," Sarah said when it was over. "I want to hear it again."

"You can hear it next year," Mary said in a big sister voice.

They worked on, taking time for a brief lunch at noon, and by late afternoon — after the girls had taken their naps, the food was ready. Ella got the girls up and dressed warmly. She left Mary and Sarah to watch the baby while she harnessed the horse. With Moonbeam in the buggy shafts, she tied him to the hitching post and brought the girls out and then returned inside for the food.

She carried out two old quilts, one to wrap around the casserole and the other around the bread and rolls. Ella squeezed them in carefully in the back of the buggy, satisfied the casserole wouldn't tip over during the trip. The blankets made huge lumps, and would keep some of the warmth in the food on this wintry day.

The girls said little on the drive over. They were wrapped up in the buggy blankets. Perhaps their spirits were affected by the weather or by the undercurrent of seriousness in the journey.

Before long Ella pulled in the Stutzman driveway. "Here we are!" she said as the girls leaned forward and looked for their daett.

The yard looked cleared of snow — at least between the house and barn. Otherwise the place looked deserted. Was her errand to be rendered useless by Ivan's absence? It was a possibility she hadn't considered. Perhaps Ivan was in town — or somewhere else.

"I don't see anyone," Mary said, pulling the buggy blanket down from her chin.

"Well, we'll get out and look," Ella said.

If Ivan wasn't home, surely Susanna would be there with their father. She could leave the food with them if necessary.

Ella climbed down from the buggy and headed for the barn door. Once inside, she looked for signs of Ivan, but found none. "Hello!" she called, her voice echoing in the silence. Through the window to the barnyard, she could see the cows and hear their mooing, indicating they were waiting to be milked. Ivan had to be around somewhere then. The cows increased their soft bellows with more hope and urgency.

Just as Ella was ready to go back out, the door to the silo opened and Ivan appeared, a pitchfork in his hand. Silage covered his hat, and he seemed embarrassed at the sight of her. He took off his hat and knocked it against his leg.

"I wasn't expecting you," he said, offering

a tentative smile.

Ella looked him over for any signs of *Englisha* influence. He hadn't looked any different when he dropped off or picked up the girls, but he might around his own place. From what she could see, all his clothes were the usual Amish garb.

"It was kind of sudden," she said. When he didn't answer, she said, "Well, I don't see signs of *Englisha* clothes on you."

"Would you leave again if you did?" he asked.

"Perhaps," she said.

"So?" he said, letting the word hang. "You are here."

"Yah . . . I brought supper. I thought it might be a good idea, being that it's Old Christmas and all. The day of *Da Hah*'s birth."

"That's nice," he said, smiling. "It's been kind of lonely."

"I suppose so. I see you haven't done all your chores yet."

"Yah, I do need to finish," he said. "But I am thankful for the food you brought."

"Why don't I help with the rest of the choring?" she offered. "First, I'll take the food inside to keep it warm in the oven. I don't know what we can do with the girls though. Is Susanna home?"

He shook his head. "Daett and Susanna are gone. And you don't have to stay. Really."

"But I want to. I want to help."

"Okay," he shrugged. "I guess they won't excommunicate you for that."

"Then what do we do with the girls?"

"I have a stall cleaned out over here where I let them play sometimes." He motioned with his beard, looking embarrassed again.

"Oh, well why not? I'll bring them in and then take the food to the house."

"Yah," he said. He watched her leave and then returned to his work.

The girls giggled when Ella told them the plan as she took them inside the barn. She then went out to wrap a horse blanket over Moonbeam. She would stay for supper, but not too late.

Her food took two trips and the fire in the stove took a little while to catch. Ivan didn't keep things handy or where she expected them to be. The lack of a woman in the house was obvious.

Afraid the fire would stay too warm during the time it would take to do the chores, Ella set the casserole on the stovetop instead of in the oven. If it was cold when they came in, that could be remedied. Burnt food couldn't. The bread and rolls she also left on the stove shelf. What heat could reach them would have to do for now.

Outside, dusk had begun to fall. Ella made her way quickly to the barn. Inside the girls went to the stall where their daett had set aside an area for them to play in. Baby Barbara was able to sit on a hay bale with Mary and Sarah on each side of her, holding her up.

Ivan came back in from the silo, this time holding something in his hand that he gave to Mary. Ella peered past Ivan to see it was a kitten, its little meows drawing giggles from the girls.

"You have a cat now?" Ella said.

"It just came by last week," Ivan said.

"But I thought . . ." Ella started to say something . . . and then stopped.

"I know," Ivan said, smiling. "I don't know why either. I guess it was time."

"I like the kitty," Sarah said, stroking the fur gently before setting it on the floor.

"Let Barbara pet it too," Mary said.

"Let me show you something that's fun," Ella said. She took down one of the three legged stools from the wall, picked up a milk bucket and sat down beside the nearest cow. Carefully she got the cow comfortable so she'd let down her milk, and she then squirted a stream of milk across the concrete floor toward the kitten.

"Bring the kitten closer, so he sees the milk," Ella said.

The girls came over with the kitten in hand. Baby Barbara carefully toddled across the straw.

As Ella continued to squirt the milk from the cow toward the kit ten, Mary asked, "Why are you doing that?"

"When the kitten gets big, it will catch milk sprayed into its mouth. It's really fun. For now, we just need to let him get the idea."

"I want to see it then," Mary said.

"The kitten has to be bigger," Ella said, sending another small squirt across the floor toward the kitten, who seemed only mildly interested.

Both girls laughed.

"It'll be funner when the kitten gets bigger," Mary said to Sarah who giggled in agreement.

Ella hid her face in the side of the cow. That was something she would not get to see herself. When Ivan joined the *Englisha,* she wouldn't be around.

The girls took the kitten back to their play area, and for the next half hour Ivan did his chores with some help from Ella. Finally Ivan said, "You can go get the supper ready.

I'll be done in just a few minutes."

"Okay," she said with a warm smile. Then turning to the girls, she said, "Are you ready to go in for supper?"

The older girls nodded, and Ella picked up baby Barbara. "You girls did great out here waiting so patiently."

"I think they're more patient with you here," Ivan said.

Ella glanced away. Ivan shouldn't be saying things like that.

"Why don't you eat first," he said. "I'll be in soon, and then you and the girls can leave."

"*Nee,* I'm planning to stay, for supper," she said.

"I appreciate that," he said. "But I won't have you waiting in the living room while I eat."

"*Nee,*" she said again, this time meeting his eyes. "We will eat *with* you."

"Ella, I appreciate the thought, but you can't eat with me."

She touched his arm. "I'm not leaving, Ivan. I want to eat together as a family. It's Old Christmas Day. The girls deserve it, and yah, it will do you *gut* too."

He swallowed hard. "I can't allow it, Ella. You know the rules. They will do awful things to you."

"I don't care," she said, her eyes still looking into his. "We will eat together tonight."
With Mary and Sarah beside her, the baby
in her arms, Ella returned to the house. She
would leave him to think this through on
his own and perhaps it would be easier
when he arrived in the house.

Ivan was left staring blankly at the barn
wall.

Ella settled the girls down in the living
room, leaving baby Barbara with Mary and
Sarah. Soon she had the fire roaring in the
stove and the food cooking.

"Ella, I can't do this," Ivan repeated, suddenly appearing at the kitchen door.

Ella had the table spread, the bread warm,
the butter platter out, and the casserole
steaming in the center of the table. She'd
just seated the girls in their proper places.

"Sit down," she said. "And don't talk."

"But you . . ."

"I want to do this," she said. "It's Old
Christmas, and the Savior was born on this
day."

"So our people believe," he said, taking
the chair, and slowly sitting down. "But,
Ella, knowing what this means, are you
sure?"

"I'm quite sure," she said, waiting with
her hands folded.

Ivan struggled with the idea.

Ella waited.

He looked to his girls and then back at Ella. He bowed his head, and the German words came. Words he had known for so many years, spoken to others, for others, but now Ella thought they must be spoken for himself. Never had she heard such a heartfelt prayer from the lips of this man. Not even in his prime, when he thundered in his Sunday sermons.

She had tears in her eyes when he was done, and she was certain he did also. Not wanting to draw attention to either of them, she looked away, measuring out the food for the girls. When she was done, Ivan still sat there, as if frozen to his seat, his hands on his lap.

"You can eat," she said, catching the look in his eye and the pain roiling inside of him. An idea came to her, and she simply responded. As she had done for the girls, she dished out his food for him, filling his plate with steaming casserole and then taking a piece of bread and buttering it for him.

"Which jam?" she asked.

He pointed and she spread blackberry jam liberally on the bread. She laid it beside his plate.

"Ivan, if you don't eat, I'll feed you," she

said as he sat silent, unsure of what to do. She saw the tears forming in his eyes.

"This is too much, way too much, Ella. You shouldn't do this for me."

"Let me worry about that," she said, filling her own plate.

"Are you trying to win me back to the faith?"

"Nee," she said. "That's not my place. I told you — it's because it's Old Christmas."

He nodded and, taking up his spoon, began to eat. If someone should look through the window from the road and see them eating together, it would just have to be so.

After the meal, Ella washed the dishes over his protests and put away the leftover food, which he was to keep. Finally, when it was time to go, Ivan hitched Moonbeam to the buggy and then helped her carry the girls out and lifted them inside.

"You'll never know what this means to me," he said, his hand on the side of the buggy. "I thank you from the bottom of my heart."

"I can't come again," she said. "But I hope you decide soon what you're going to do — for the girls' sake as well as your own. It's not *gut* to go on this way."

He nodded in the darkness, his face barely

visible. "May *Da Hah* keep you safe and bless you greatly."

"Thank you," she said. She slapped the reins and they took off. Only when she was on the road did she realize she had thanked an excommunicated man for his blessing. That was strange. It had felt like a real blessing.

THIRTY-EIGHT

By the last week in January winter still showed no signs of breaking. Ella had decided to take a chance on a washday. If the weather turned too cold to dry clothes on the line, the basement would serve as a last resort. Drying laundry inside made a mess, with water dripping all over the concrete floor, but it was better than frozen wash.

Everything else in Ella's life seemed frozen in place too. Each week the regular routine came and went. Ivan dropped his girls off on Monday and picked them up on Friday.

Robert Hayes had not been heard from, nor had Eli shown up with any news about the man. The *Englisha* man would best be forgotten, even if Ella felt the occasional pang remembering his presence right here in her living room. As for Bishop Miller, he had made no move yet, but Ella figured it would come when she least expected it.

As it turned out, the day would allow her to hang the laundry on the line after all. And so she hurriedly did the wash and took it out to hang on the line. After a few minutes, her fingers were cold and red from the wet wash, and she welcomed a greeting from behind her as Ronda opened the kitchen window and called, "Good morning, Ella!"

Ella turned and waved. At least Joe and Ronda seemed to love each other. It was *gut* to have such an example close at hand. Perhaps it would rub off on her. Ella laughed bitterly at the thought. Love for her seemed utterly out of the question.

No sooner had Ella turned her attention back to the laundry than from out on the road came the sound of horses' hooves, the driver arriving at a great pace. When he slowed down, Ella turned to see who it was but couldn't tell from this distance. Surely of all things this wasn't Bishop Miller coming to see her this morning. Not on laundry day. She turned and slowly pulled the final wet dress from the hamper, shook it carefully, and pinned it to the wire. She made no attempt to approach the buggy.

Steps sounded behind her. It sounded like a man was approaching. She would have to face him after all. From behind her a voice came.

"Ella?"

Startled, she turned. It was not the deep voice of Bishop Miller; it was someone else . . . someone unfamiliar. "Yah," she said, turning around to see one of Ivan's nephews walking quickly toward her. What was his name? She searched her memory. Lucas?

"You must come!" he said, his young voice urgent.

"Come?" she asked, her red hands dropping to her side. "Come where?"

"It's Ivan!" he said. "There may not be much time."

"What?" she asked, suddenly feeling cold all over. *Has Ivan lost his mind? Burned down his house? With the pressure on him, anything seems possible.*

"I'll tell you on the way," he said, seeming ready to grab her hand if she didn't respond.

"I must tell Ronda and ask her to take care of the girls," Ella said, picking up her clothes hamper. It felt like her body was moving in slow motion.

"Then you must hurry!" he urged, following close behind her.

At the front door she didn't knock but simply walked in, the young man following.

"Ronda!" she called.

"Yah?" Ronda answered from the kitchen.

"Can you watch the girls? I have to go with . . . Lucas. Something has happened with Ivan."

"Oh!" Ronda said. "Of course I will. You go. I'll bring the girls upstairs. Don't worry — just go!"

Ella allowed herself to be led out the front door, and then she shook off the young man's hand. "I'll come," she said.

"Then *run!*" he commanded, and they ran together toward his buggy.

Her coat was much too thin for a buggy ride on a cold morning, but she didn't say anything. There obviously was no time for such things.

In the buggy she pulled the blanket up to her chin, but it did little to cut the bite of the wind. She hadn't been driven so fast since Joe's night drive to the clinic. Still, Lucas urged the horse on with sharp slaps of the reins. Snow flew up from the buggy wheels as it slid sideways at turns. Lucas hardly slowed at the stop signs.

"You have not told me yet," she said, her teeth chattering.

"Ivan was cleaning off snow with the shovel — the big one they pull with the horses. He was using the colt hitched with his older horse and something happened. I don't know what, but the horse got away from him."

"Did anyone see it happen?" Ella asked, trying to pull the blanket up higher.

"Daett saw it when he was already being dragged," he said, his voice dropping. "We live pretty far down the road, so you can't see a lot. When I got there, he looked like he had been under the shovel for a ways. The lines were all tangled up under his arm. It's hard to tell what all happened, but Daett and Susanna are with him now."

"Why am I needed?" she asked, glancing at him.

"Ivan asked me to bring you," he said. "In case . . ."

"But why wasn't he taken to the clinic?"

"Ivan wouldn't let Daett call for the ambulance or load him onto the spring wagon. Ivan only wants to speak with you."

"But they didn't have to listen to him," she said. "I can't do anything for him."

"I don't think anyone can," he said. "And I don't think it would have done much good to move him. It might have made things worse from the way it looks."

Ella shook her head.

"He might want to make things right with you," he said. "That's what Daett was thinkin'. And Daett sent for the bishop too."

formation. Positive ions produced are generally MH^+; cation attachment also occurs if alkali salts are present. Negative ions are also formed, generally $(M - H)^-$. Single-fission events are detected using a time-of-flight analyzer with channel plate detector. Accumulation of data is quite slow, often requiring several hours, and resolution is quite poor using the TOF system. Nevertheless, some very impressive results have been obtained by PD-MS on numerous biomolecules with molecular weights up to several thousand.

To date only a couple of reports have been issued describing the PD-MS analysis of synthetic polymers (22–23). Analysis of some poly(ethylene glycol) (PEG) samples yielded quasi-molecular ions (MH^+, MLi^+, MNa^+) for various oligomers (22). The distributions of quasi-molecular ions were reported to be indicative of the average molecular weights of the polymers, but no actual comparisons of molecular weight averages determined from PD-MS data with those determined by classical methods were given (22). It is evident that PD-MS deposits a great deal of energy into desorbed ions and neutrals. Thus it is likely to experience the same problems in polymer molecular weight analysis as the rapid heating techniques described in the preceding section. Its utility for determining polymer molecular weight distributions has not yet been assessed in any detail, however.

ELECTROSPRAY

Attempts to obtain mass spectra of high polymers ($MW > 10^4$) have thus far met with very limited success. The difficulties associated with getting stable, charged macromolecules of several thousand molecular weight into the vapor phase are indeed formidable. Without doubt the most ambitious project in this respect has been the work of Dole and coworkers over the past 20 years or so with electrospray mass spectrometry (ES-MS) (24–28). The concept is to spray very dilute solutions of macromolecules into a gas-filled chamber. The solution is forced through a syringe held at high potential (a few kiloelectron-volts), and the resulting aerosol droplets are charged. In theory, the droplets should break down, losing solvent and charge, so that eventually singly charged macromolecular ions will result. Earlier experiments using a time-of-flight mass analyzer had limited success because of difficulties in introducing the macroions into the mass spectrometer and in detecting the ions with the normal secondary electron multiplier (25). Later experiments used a plasma chromatography (or ion drift spectrometer) for mass analysis (26). This instrument has the advantages of atmospheric pressure operation and ion detection via a Faraday cage–vibrating reed electrometer system. The results

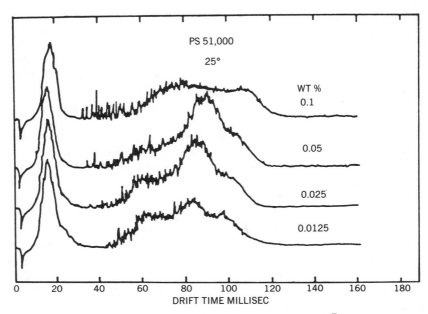

Figure 4. Electrospray ion signal versus drift time for polystyrene ($\bar{M}_n$ 51,000) in plasma chromatograph. (Reprinted with permission from Ref. 26.)

with this instrument were also disappointing, since it was not possible to clearly distinguish between polystyrene samples that differed widely in average molecular weight. This deficit was apparently due to cluster formation and multiply charged species.

In Figure 4, the signal intensity of polystyrene ($\bar{M}_n$ 51,000) is plotted against drift time in the plasma chromatograph (26). The ions observed at ~40–120 ms were believed to be rather large multiply charged aggregates of solvent and solute molecules. Dole has abandoned work on ES-MS and has concluded that accurate molecular weight averages of polymers cannot be determined using this technique (27). It is unfortunate that a method with so much potential has succumbed, at least temporarily, to the numerous experimental difficulties involved. It is encouraging that other workers are now experimenting with electrospray sources (29).

SECONDARY ION/FAST ATOM BOMBARDMENT

Secondary ion mass spectrometry (SIMS) has historically been used mainly for atomic (elemental) analysis of surfaces. Recently however, "organic" (or more generally "molecular") SIMS has found use as an analytical technique (30–35). The organic material is deposited as a thin film on a metal foil, sometimes with the addition of a salt. The sample is then bombarded with a primary ion beam, and secondary ions are sputtered from the surface and analyzed, usually with a quadrupole mass filter. Ions characteristic of molecular weight can form via several processes (32–35). If the molecule is already ionic, intact cations and/or anions can be produced by direct sputtering. Polar organics tend to form ions via cation attachment. Nonpolar organics can form odd-electron molecular ions ($M^{+\cdot}$ or $M^{-\cdot}$) via electron transfer, although ion attachment also occurs to some extent. So far SIMS spectra for molecular organic species have been obtained only on relatively low molecular weight materials (up to a few hundred amu). This is partially because the quadrupole mass filters normally used have a rather low mass range (< 1000 amu), but also because the SIMS process is relatively high in energy. Thus, thermal damage (pyrolysis) ensues, particularly with higher mass materials, and ions due to fragmentation–decomposition processes are prominent. SIMS has been used to study pyrolysis of high polymers (36, 37), and the new technique of time-of-flight SIMS (35) shows considerable facility for obtaining spectra of high mass polymer fragments. So far no reports have appeared describing the direct analysis of low molecular weight synthetic polymers, but SIMS may have some potential applications in this area.

The fast atom bombardment (FAB-MS) technique, introduced in 1981 (38), has become a very popular ionization technique for nonvolatile molecules. FAB is conceptually rather simple and is closely related (essentially identical) to organic SIMS. The sample, either a solid or a viscous liquid, is mixed with glycerol or other suitable matrix and placed on a flat metal probe. The probe is inserted into the ion source where it is bombarded with a stream of argon or xenon atoms (2–8 keV) from a gun. Both positive and negative ions are produced. Although very similar in concept to organic SIMS, FAB has certain advantages that make it more useful for analysis of large organic molecules. First, since the viscous matrix constantly resupplies fresh sample to the surface, spectra are intense and long-lasting. Second, since the primary beam consists of atoms rather than ions, ion source charging is reduced and essentially eliminated. Third, double focusing analyzers can easily be used, which extends the mass range and makes high resolution and metastable ion analysis possible. Fourth, the sample matrix (solvent) can be varied, with a view to extending the technique to include numerous classes of compounds. Finally, having the ion source at ambient temperature may provide an advantage over other techniques that rely, to a greater or lesser extent, on more direct thermal processes to effect vaporization.

Ions are formed in FAB primarily by proton attachment or abstraction; that is, for most organics, MH^+ is seen in positive ion mode and $(M - H)^-$ in

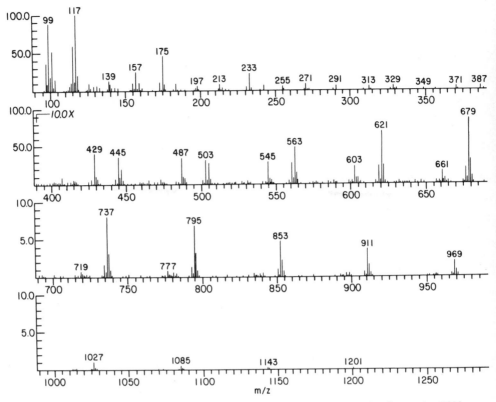

Figure 5. Fast atom bombardment mass spectrum of poly(propylene glycol) sample 41993. (Reprinted with permission from Ref. 39.)

negative mode. Cation attachment is also often observed. FAB seems to work best for highly polar organics, and as with other desorption ionization techniques, it has been used primarily for the analysis of large biomolecules. The FAB spectrum of a poly(propylene glycol) (PPG) with added NaBr salt is shown in Figure 5 (39). This sample gave high abundances of MNa^+ ions, among other species. Fragmentation was extensive, however, giving rise to intense low mass ions. Nevertheless, the spectra were easily interpretable in terms of protonated and cationized oligomers. FAB results for polyglycols (39) and poly(ethylene imine) (PEI) (40) show that oligomer quasi-molecular ion distributions can give approximate indications of molecular weight averages for the polymers. The molecular weight distributions are not quantitative in comparison with results determined by other methods, however. More

Ella knelt beside the girl. "Not yet, but someday. Only *Da Hah* can take us to heaven — when He is ready for us."

"Will you be our mamm now?" Mary asked, her face upturned.

"Yah," she said, tears stinging her eyes. "I am your mamm now."

Mary shivered in the cold but drew close to Ella. Ella drew Mary and Sarah tightly to her. Baby Barbara rested in her arms.

"Come, girls," she said. "We'd best go inside."

Mary and Sarah followed her without a backward glance.

The girls are mine now, Ella realized, the reality of it drawing ever nearer, crashing upon her senses. *Forever mine.*

THIRTY-NINE

Ella stayed inside with the girls as people began to arrive. There was little to do but wait for the body to be returned.

"I need to go back to the house and make sure everything is okay. I also need to pick up a few things," Ella told Susanna. "May I borrow your buggy? It shouldn't take too long."

"*Nee*, you should stay here with the girls. We'll send someone," Susanna said. "That's what people are here for — to help."

Ella reluctantly gave in and gave instructions to the girl who would be in charge. "I have wash lying around yet and some in the basket. Just fold it and lay it on the kitchen table. I can take care of it after the funeral. And tell Ronda upstairs to keep some fire in the stove. She'll know how much."

The girl nodded and left with two other girls who would help.

The hearse returned late in the afternoon,

and Ivan's body was brought into the main bedroom. Ella waited until the *Englisha* men were gone and Susanna had left the room before she took the girls in. She wanted to be alone with them the first time they saw their daett's body.

She held baby Barbara tightly against her shoulder, and had Mary and Sarah on either side of her.

"Why doesn't Daett move?" Mary asked.

"That's just his body," Ella explained. "He's really in heaven now."

"I didn't want him to go," Mary said. "Will I have another daett now?"

"I don't know," Ella said, pulling the girl tightly against her with her free hand. "But come, let's go now. There are other people wanting to come in."

Ella tried to smile when Susanna met them in the living room. At least her life had purpose now, with three people depending on her. It would be hard, but they would make it somehow. People would tell her that now more than ever she should marry the bishop, but now more than ever she knew she couldn't. Besides, he likely wouldn't want a woman with three girls anyway. Girls who weren't even her own by birth.

"You don't have to take the girls," Susanna whispered, when she sat down. "I know how it was between you and Ivan, and I know it never would have worked out."

"Don't you want me to have them?" Ella asked. *Is Susanna trying to interfere? If the family is going to make a fuss about this, I'd best fight their decision early. I'm going to abide by Ivan's request.*

"I just wanted to be sure you weren't feeling pressured," Susanna said.

"But you heard what Ivan said," Ella whispered.

Susanna nodded. "I'm not asking that Ivan's wish be changed. We owe him that much, and the family will not object. If there is any problem, I will see to it myself. But I want to make sure you're okay with the arrangement. It's a huge responsibility."

"I can love them as my own," Ella said. "And it is in my heart to do so."

"Then we will help with income," Susanna said. "It would be more than fair since Ivan has most of the farm paid off. You might even consider moving here."

Ella sat still for long minutes, thinking. Should she leave the house on Chapman Road? It might be a wise move. The girls could grow up on their parents' old place. On the other hand, it was also the farm where both had died.

"Nee," Ella said, shaking her head. "I will

keep them where we are. As far as help, hopefully I can support them myself."

Susanna nodded. "Well, if you change your mind, let me know. If you won't live here, I'll likely rent it out. Daett will not be with us much longer anyway."

Ella nodded.

The family soon gathered, the brothers and sisters of Ivan — most of whom Ella knew. They stood in the kitchen speaking mainly in whispers, most likely about the funeral plans. Supper was served by the neighborhood Amish women, after which a long line formed for the viewing that evening. The decision was made around nine o'clock that the funeral would be the next day.

People came and went till late that night, the bench wagon not arriving till after midnight. Ella stayed upstairs with the girls, getting them to drop off even with the noise downstairs.

She walked to the window and looked out at the sky, now heavy with low-hanging clouds. Ivan had found love again — and in such an unexpected way. What must it have been like for him to see the face of Lois? From his last expression she could only imagine the depth of his joy. How strange — and yet beautiful — this ending to his

life. And now there was the funeral tomorrow.

Ella turned back to the bed and slipped in
beside the two older girls. She quickly
dropped off to a fitful sleep. She awoke
before daylight and for a moment had to
remember where she was. When it all come
back, she went downstairs to find breakfast
already on the table.

One of the women in the kitchen came up
to her and whispered, "With all the people
coming and going, everyone is to eat when
they want to."

"Thank you," Ella said. She prepared her
plate and ate quickly. She returned upstairs
so she could get the girls up.

She checked through the suitcase the girls
had brought last night, finding everything
she needed until she was ready to change
her clothes. No one had thought to bring
her black dress, and she had forgotten to
ask for it.

Was there still time to send for it? *Nee,*
and she certainly didn't fit into Susanna's
clothes. She had worn Lois's dress once, so
why not again?

The girls were still asleep, and Ella decided they should get all the rest they
wanted, so she went downstairs. She whispered to Susanna, "Do you think there

would be one of Lois's black dresses in the bedroom? Would it be all right for me to borrow it? Otherwise I'll have to send someone for my own."

"I don't know why not," Susanna said. "There's no one in the bedroom, so you can go ahead and check."

Ella opened the door carefully, remembering the other times she had been here. But everything was different now. She paused at the casket, and then went to the closet. She found a dress and took it upstairs. Mary and Sarah had just awakened and stared sleepy eyed at her.

"Are we home?" Mary asked.

"Yah. Do you remember what happened yesterday?"

Mary nodded, staring out the window.

"Well, today is the funeral," Ella said. "Do you want to go down for breakfast? Are you hungry?"

Mary nodded.

"I'll get dressed and then we'll get you dressed." Soon Ella helped Mary and Sarah out of bed. The girls slipped on their dresses, but there was no way she would dress the baby before breakfast. Barbara made much too big a mess at the table. Taking the baby in her nightgown, the four made their way downstairs.

By the time they were through eating, the yard had filled with buggies. Men came in and moved the living room furniture to the side and filled every available place with benches. Ella took Barbara upstairs and changed her. When she returned downstairs, Mary and Sarah were standing by the front window, watching the activity outside.

"Come," she whispered loud enough for them to hear. "Take your seats with me. It's almost time."

A few minutes later, Susanna came out of the kitchen and sat down beside them. The benches had filled up as people came in for the funeral. When the room was nearly full, four men slowly brought the casket from the bedroom, setting it on benches by the front window.

Bishop Miller led the line of ministers in at eight-thirty, and Ella looked away. Hopefully, after all that had happened, he wouldn't have enough nerve to preach today.

As many as possible were seated in the house, the windows cracked open for fresh air, cold puffs of steam circling in and hanging close to the ceiling. Several of the older women glanced up and gathered their shawls tighter around themselves.

One of them motioned an usher over and

whispered in his ear. He stood, looking around, breathing deeply as if to test the air, then shook his head. A decision had been made, and the windows would stay open.

Ella jerked upright as Bishop Miller slowly got to his feet. Against her will, she couldn't seem to pull her eyes from his face as he spoke. She was astonished to see streams of tears flooding down his face. He stood for over an hour, speaking of Ivan's life, telling the stories of how greatly his ministry had touched others, of how much he had admired Ivan.

Ella listened, hardly daring to move. She couldn't believe this and wanted to push it away, but the man's sincerity was too obvious. How was it possible with what she knew he had done? If it hadn't been for Bishop Miller, Ivan would not have been excommunicated. The bishop must have repented of his feelings toward Ivan.

As if he could read her thoughts, Bishop Miller lowered his eyes to the floor and spoke of his own sorrow and reluctance for the severe action that had to be taken. He regretted if some people thought this had been unnecessary. It was with the opinion of several ministers, including Bishop Mast himself, that they had come to their conclusion.

Bishop Mast sat on the end of the preacher's bench nodding. Bishop Miller continued by reminding the mourners that the action had accomplished its intended goal in that before Ivan died he had repented and asked for forgiveness. And so they, as men, must now follow the forgiveness of *Da Hah.* If Ivan had asked for forgiveness and *Da Hah* had forgiven him, then they must also. As of this morning the excommunication was lifted because it had been removed yesterday in the eyes of *Da Hah.*

Again Bishop Mast solemnly nodded. Beside her, Susanna was wiping the tears from her cheeks. Other family members did the same. The great burden of excommunication had hung heavily on all of their shoulders.

As Bishop Miller sat down, other ministers stood to speak, concluding with the same point — that Ivan had been accepted back into the fold of *Da Hah* and man before he passed over the river.

When the last minister had finished, a line formed to move past the coffin. Ella sat and looked at the bishop. Perhaps if he could change, he was a better man than she had thought him to be. But even so, she still wouldn't marry him. There was simply no way.

The young men were coming through the line, and Ella glanced up, nearly gasping out loud at the sight of Robert Hayes. He was dressed in Amish clothes as before, his eyes on the floor. Not far behind him came Eli, also in Amish clothes. She watched, her heart pounding. How was this possible that Robert could still be here? Eli was no surprise, even with his Amish clothes. He would know enough to show up properly dressed.

Please, O God. Ella groaned without a sound. *Please help me.*

Robert moved slowly up to the casket and paused for a long moment as Ella watched. How could a man so forbidden create such a storm of emotion in her heart? And he did so without knowledge of his power, and right here, in a funeral, at the most sober and sacred of times.

With shame she bowed her head, forcing her eyes to look away. If anyone saw her, they would think the tears were caused by Ivan's departure, her soul overcome with his loss. To think that she was thinking of another man would add insult to injury. Ella squeezed back the tears and thanked *Da Hah* that man cannot read the thoughts of others.

When the last person had filed through, the family stood. Ella led the girls through the line. One last time she lifted each girl up so they could see. Mary's face was white; Sarah clutched Ella's arm. Baby Barbara couldn't have known fully what this meant, but she clung to Ella's shoulder.

Susanna had the buggy ready for the ride to the cemetery and made sure Ella knew she was welcome to ride with her. Ella accepted with a weary smile. Susanna got down to help the girls up. They drove the long miles to the graveyard.

When will this all end? Will one dark day simply follow the other, days of death and dying, stripped of all love? Ella wondered.

The buggies had to wait to cross the state road due to heavy traffic. At the graveside, Bishop Miller waited patiently until everyone had gathered around. He spoke a few more words over the grave and, after he concluded with a prayer, the young boys began to cover the casket with dirt.

Ella was stirred again by Bishop Miller's show of emotions. She had never known the bishop to be so touched by anything. Tears continued to roll down his face, even as he took his turn at a shovel.

With the mound rising gently out of the ground, the last boy stopped shoveling and the crowd slowly began breaking up. Eli caught up with her beside Susanna's buggy.

"Can I stop by this evening?" he asked. "I have something to tell you."

Ella nodded. It would not go well for her if they spoke at length in public. Even so, her heart sank at Eli's words. She wished now she had never consented to this look into Robert's past.

Across the road she saw her parents and waved. With the girls in the buggy, Ella waited as her mamm walked carefully across the snowy road.

"I hoped I'd have a chance to say hello," she said, smiling slightly at the girls. "They told us the news about Ivan's last request. Ella, are you sure you want to take on this responsibility?"

"I do," Ella said. "I love the girls very much."

"Well, I know how attached you are to them," she said. "But remember what your daett said. You really need a man in that house of yours."

"Yes, I remember," Ella said quietly. She looked down at the girls. Mary was all ears. "Little pitchers have big ears," Ella said, knowing her mamm would get the hint.

"Perhaps I speak too plainly," Lizzie said, looking down to Mary. "But I didn't know when I would see you next. Why don't you come home to visit sometime? We all miss you a lot."

"I'll try, when I can," Ella said. "And you can come visit us."

"When the winter breaks, perhaps we'll try," Lizzie said. "I know Clara wants to come to see you again. Ella, let us know if you need anything. And don't go taking more work on than you can handle. It's not *gut* for you. You know we care a lot about you."

"I know you do," Ella replied. "And thank you."

Around them the buggies were pulling out, the horses impatient to stretch their legs after the long wait in the cold. Susanna was by her buggy, obviously waiting for Ella and the girls.

Her mamm gave Ella a hug and returned across the road. Ella made her way to the buggy with the girls.

They had no sooner crossed onto the road than Mary said, "What is 'a man in the house'?"

Susanna glanced up in surprise. "Where did the girl hear that?" she asked.

"Mamm was talkin'," Ella said through

tight lips. Hopefully Susanna didn't think more was said than what actually was.

"What is it?" Mary asked again.

"It's when you marry," Ella said, running her hand over Mary's forehead. "That's when a man lives in the house with you like Joe does with Ronda."

"Will you marry someday?" Mary asked.

"I don't know," Ella said, her voice strange in her ears. "We can't know what's in the future."

"Well, I know I'm going to," Mary said. "As soon as I can."

"Sounds like the girl has it all figured out," Susanna said with a quiet laugh.

"I wish it were that easy," Ella said.

FORTY

Eli sat at Ella's kitchen table waiting for his promised supper. He had shed his Amish clothes somewhere, and now his *Englisha* car was parked in her driveway. Dusk had fallen outside, but Joe and Ronda had likely seen him come into the house. Well, it would just have to be. He was her brother even if he drove an *Englisha* car and dressed in a way that unnerved her.

"I've put the girls to bed," she said. "We can talk in private."

"No rush. I mean, your cooking is well worth the wait."

Quickly Ella sliced the bread, put out the butter and jam, and set two places at the table.

"Supper may not be what you think it is," she teased. "I just had time to make vegetable soup."

He gazed at the pot on the stove and said, "Whatever it is, it suits me just fine."

"At least the bread is fairly fresh, as I made it the day before the accident." She brought the serving dish to the table and sat down. "We still pray around here before we eat," she reminded him.

"What do you think I am, a heathen?" he asked.

"I don't know, but let's pray anyway."

"I *always* pray," he said as they bowed their heads in silence.

When they were finished, she dished out the soup and said, "Okay, now tell me what you found out about Robert. You can speak freely."

"You like this guy a lot, don't you?"

"Eli, don't tease me. This situation is bad enough as it is. Just make it easy and quick."

"Yep. I would say you have it pretty bad," Eli said, eyeing the soup and then glancing up to see her frightened look. He burst into laughter.

"Eli, what have you got to say?"

"Really?" Eli said, savoring his bite of soup and reaching for a piece of bread. "Let's see . . . about Robert. Hmmm . . . my but your home cooking is just awesome."

Eli always was a tease, but this was beyond Ella's limit. "Eli!" She muffled her frustrating cry, lest the girls wake up and hear.

Her brother laughed and buttered his

bread. "This is such fun," he said.

"You won't think it's fun when I pound your head. Now start talking."

"Well, I searched his town, and found his mom and dad's place. They are big business people in town — insurance. It's a big office and looks prosperous. I heard they own other things too, so he's not poor, Ella."

"That's *not* what I want to know," she said, hardly daring to breathe.

"Just a point," he said. "But I found nothing wrong about him. In fact, the whole family sounds quite upright from what I could tell."

"How are you sure?"

"I talked with his mother."

Ella stared at him. "Why would she talk with you?"

"I told her who I was. That I was your brother."

"Oh, Eli . . . you did not!"

"Sure I did. Are we not honest people?"

"Of course we are — but that's not the point."

"It doesn't matter," he said, pausing long enough to swallow a large spoonful of soup. "I got the impression she wasn't surprised at my visit."

"Oh great. So now there was nothing to your fears, and Robert's mom thinks I'm after him."

"Well, aren't you?"

"Okay, Eli, that's it! It doesn't matter anyway. There will never be anything between Robert and me."

"Well, at least I did my part. Don't you want to at least hear how hard I worked? Pam told me all about how it's done, and I followed her instructions completely."

Ella tried to smile. "And what would that be?"

"I went to his old high school and asked around. The principal was quite willing to speak with me. I even saw Robert's picture on the wall. He won a trophy for track or something. The principal said he never knew Robert to date. So there you go."

"Everyone dates, Eli."

Eli laughed. "I don't think so. I even went to a lawyer like Pam told me to. Paid him a fee and all that. I got the letter last week."

"You spent money? But you don't have that much money."

"Enough to settle the love life of my big sister," Eli teased.

"Quit saying that," she snapped.

"Anyway . . ." He paused to butter another piece of bread.

"So you did find something? Eli, speak right now."

"There never was a marriage, and there is no ex-wife or child in sight. The man's clean as a whistle."

"Don't tease me, Eli."

"I'm not," he said. "It's the truth. You ought to just give up and take him to be what he says he is."

"But he stays with Bishop Miller."

"Like that's a sin. Really, Ella. Why can't you just believe he might be *Da Hah*'s gift to you?"

"Eli, don't."

"Good things *do* happen to Amish people, you know."

"Yah, then why don't you come back to the Amish? You know how Daett and Mamm are hurt by your situation."

"Ella, I can't live my life by their wishes," Eli said, now serious. "I love Pam, and we will get married. It's just like that."

"You always were stubborn."

"And you aren't?"

"Not like you."

"Look how you're acting now. I do all this work for you, and still you want to throw it all away."

"Can I pay you for the lawyer or for your time? Because I do appreciate this."

"You're changing the subject, Ella. But since you mention it, yah, supper once in a while would be a nice payment. And if I could bring Pam?"

"Perhaps," she said. "I'll have to think about that."

"When you marry that Robert fellow, I can come all the time. He'll understand me."

"You're a bad, bad boy, Eli. You should go before I chase you out the door."

"Not until I have another bowl of soup," he said as he ladled out another helping.

Ella thought about this news as Eli finished his meal in silence.

When he finally got ready to leave, Eli turned at the door and said, "Thanks for supper then. I will be back."

"You had better give me some notice," Ella said. "Especially if Pam comes along."

"I will," he said. "And don't worry so much." He waved and was out the door.

Ella listened to his *Englisha* car starting up, the sound dying away as he drove off.

So Robert is who he says he is. She got up and paced the floor, considering the ramifications.

The clock said nine o'clock, and Ella was tired, but she retrieved her journal to write a short note. The day seemed to merit it: The day Ivan had been buried and life already was moving on at a dizzying pace.

Dear Journal,

The funeral of Ivan Stutzman was today, his death a day ago totally unexpected. I was called to his side to receive his last request — that his girls stay with me. I am as surprised as anyone, but certainly have no regrets. It is not how I would have chosen to receive them, but I have learned the hard way that Da Hah usually has His own plans.

Eli was here with the news that Robert is apparently who he says he is. I'm too tired right now to know what all that will mean, if anything. Things always seem to run off in the direction I least expect. I told Robert to stay away from me, so I suppose it really doesn't matter. What man would come back after such a send-off?

I can easily think of myself as an old maid — growing old alone with the girls. It is a life not unfulfilling in the least. I could watch them grow up, leave for school, join the young folks, and eventually marry. I cannot imagine any other end for all three of them. They are the sweetest little things, but who knows what will happen next? With as many plans and thoughts as I've had, life still does what it wishes.

What if I could find real love again . . . like Aden and I had? Not the kind that might lie somewhere in the future, but the kind that stares me in the face and leaves me breathless with its wonder and warmth.

I laugh at the thought of it. I know I'm cynical, but I think I have some right to be. Things haven't been easy for me. Not that I want to complain, but there, I said it anyway. There doesn't seem much good in life that doesn't get beaten to death or taken away.

It would be just like life to starve me in this house of mine, with three girls to take care of, forcing me to take the next hand of marriage that's offered me. Even if he's some old geezer on his last legs!

See, I told you I'm cynical, but at least I can still laugh at myself. I laugh and I am tired of it all. I don't want to think anymore. I don't want to plan anymore. I just want to spend time with the girls and work till I'm too tired to move. I think my heart will just have to get used to it.

Ella smiled and closed the tablet carefully. She carried the kerosene lamp behind the curtain and set it down on the dresser. She put the journal in its place and then looked at the three girls as they slept. How sweet they were . . . and now they were hers to raise. Her heart swelled at the thought.

With one last look, Ella blew out the lamp and undressed in the darkness. She slipped into the bed and drew the covers up to her chin. "Protect us, *Da Hah,*" she whispered. "Keep us safe, as we need You now more than ever."

FORTY-ONE

It was the middle of February. Ella stood by the barn watching the blaze of orange and red left by the setting sun. It meant another day tomorrow of cold, clear weather, dashing her hopes for signs of spring.

"What a beautiful sunset," Ronda called from the front door.

"Yah," Ella said.

"Spring is coming soon."

"I sure haven't seen any signs of it."

"You have to believe it's coming," Ronda said. "You ought to bring your girls out so they can enjoy the view. It's really special tonight."

As if on cue, the basement door creaked open, and Mary's and Sarah's heads popped over the edge of the steps.

"I guess they heard us talking," Ella said. "Come over here, girls."

"What is it?" Mary asked.

"It's a beautiful sunset," Ella said, motioning to the west.

The two girls ran past the house and looked toward the sky.

"It's beautiful," Mary said.

"Yah," little Sarah managed to say.

"*Da Hah* is good," Ronda said.

Ella nodded. That was true, regardless of her mixed feelings at present.

They stood together for long moments as the color deepened and then began to fade.

"I guess nothing lasts forever," Ronda said.

That's true," Ella said, her spirits sinking further.

"Looks like you have visitors," Ronda said, glancing toward Chapman Road.

Ella pulled her eyes from the sky and followed Ronda's gaze.

"I'm not expecting anyone," Ella said. "Do you know something I don't?"

"*Nee,*" Ronda said. "I don't know anything but that buggy's comin' this way, and I'd best be gettin' into the house."

"You can stay. I really don't care."

"*Nee,*" Ronda said over her shoulder. "I think not."

The door closed behind Ronda, and Ella turned with a sigh as buggy wheels rattled into the driveway. The buggy door was closed on her side, so she couldn't see who it was, but what did it matter? No one arriving could change anything. *Da Hah* might paint His glory in the skies, but on earth He used an awfully rough brush.

Out of the buggy a man's legs came, his feet hitting the ground. For a few seconds they didn't move.

He must be searching for his tie rope under the seat, Ella thought. *It's likely some incompetent poor farmer from the north who can't even find his own rope in his own buggy. This serves me about right. I've turned down some of the best men in the community, and this is all that's left for me.*

The rope dangled out from under the buggy just before the man finally moved, his voice speaking softly to his horse.

Ella turned to the girls and said, "Girls, why don't you run back inside where it's warm and watch baby Barbara. I'll be down soon."

Mary nodded and grabbed Sarah's hand. They scurried off.

Turning back to the buggy, she nearly let out a cry as she saw that Robert Hayes was walking toward her.

"From your reaction, I must be a ghost," he said, smiling gently. "Does the good woman of the house accept callers this time of the evening?"

"Why are you here?" she whispered.

"What a greeting!" he said. "I remember you told me not to come back. Shall I leave then?"

"Robert!" she said, pressing her hands against her face. "I think you know I don't want you to leave. I'm so sorry about everything."

"What is there to be sorry about?" he asked, coming closer.

"Everything."

"But it wasn't your fault."

"Why are you still here among us? I thought you would have left a long time ago."

"Why do you keep asking that question?"

"Because I still don't know the answer."

He smiled. "May I come in?"

"Looks like you plan to anyway," she said, meeting his eyes.

"Oh, I can get in my buggy and drive away if you want me to, but first I hope to understand some things about the two of us."

"I would like nothing better," she said. "But the girls aren't in bed yet."

"Then can we talk here on the steps?" he asked.

"If Ronda doesn't get it into her head to

listen," Ella said, taking a seat atop the first step.

Robert glanced up. "I don't think she is. The window looks empty."

Ella launched in. "There were things going on, and I thought they would drive you away."

"But I am still here among your people, and I have come back to see you. Does that tell you something?"

"Yes, but it seems almost too much to believe."

"So let's start over," he said with a smile. "Why did you send me away this winter? Why did you say it's all impossible between us . . . and then your brother shows up at my mother's, apparently to investigate me?"

"That was not my idea," she said.

"And did your brother find out what he wanted?" he asked, his eyes locked on hers.

Ella nodded, feeling as if nothing else on her body worked at the moment.

"And?"

"My brother said you are who you say you are. You're from a good family. And that you have no girlfriends or ex-wives or children."

He laughed as if highly amused.

"It's not funny, Robert."

"And you expected there would be a bevy of ex-wives and girlfriends and kids?"

"Not really. But Eli did raise my doubts."

"Well, I'm sorry to disappoint you," he said with a grin. "But on my part, Mom was impressed that your family would go to such effort. Especially after she learned Eli was your brother. But she had told me from the get-go what an exceptional woman you are."

"Don't say things like that, Robert, please. You're going to have me crying."

"I'm sorry," he said, touching her arm. "I have a message for you."

"A message? From whom?"

"Bishop Miller told me to tell you something. He said he's sorry for everything. He said that he's dating someone. You are, of course, supposed to tell no one."

Ella felt the blood leave her face, certain she would have fallen down the steps if Robert hadn't grabbed her.

"I'd say that must be some important news," he said, his face now close to hers. "Do I need to get you some cold water?"

"Nee!" she said, gasping and struggling to stand.

"Perhaps you'd better pass out more often. Of course, I don't know where to find such news every day. What exactly does it mean to you?"

"It means that everything changes," she said, her voice weak. "About Bishop Miller . . . and about you."

"I'm not sure I understand."

"I'm not sure I can explain," she said. "Perhaps it would be best to leave it unexplained for now. I don't want to disappoint you with the revelation of the whole tale."

"Come on, try me, Ella. I want to know."

She began slowly. "I thought in some way Bishop Miller was using you to break up my relationship with Ivan Stutzman. And then he would turn on you after the deed was done. Then you would be gone, *psst*, like that, without his support in the church."

"And he told you this?"

"Of course not."

He smiled. "Wow. And I thought I was leaving the world of the soap opera."

"What's that?"

"Don't worry. It doesn't matter. I'm surprised you didn't think I could handle myself."

"Are you angry with me . . . with us?" she asked, daring to touch his hand.

"Oh, I'm steaming mad," he said.

She studied his face for a long moment, "*Nee,* you're not. You're teasing."

"So may I court you now?"

"Court me?"

"Yah. Don't you know what that means?"

"I don't," she said, shaking her head. "I

have no idea what it means."

"Yah, you do," he said, gathering her in his arms. "I think you know exactly what it means. Now you're teasing me."

"Oh, Robert," she said, her voice muffled on his chest, "I have no idea what to say."

"Then say nothing," he said. "Just don't chase me away again."

"I will never chase you away again — not as long as I live."

"Is that a promise?"

"Yah, a very solemn promise."

"Will you love me? Love me dearly?"

"You know I will."

"I'm making sure, that's all."

"Will you be a *gut* daett to the girls?" she asked, pulling away to see his face.

"As if they were my own," he said, pulling her back against him. "Do I get German lessons again?"

"All the German lessons you want," she said, suddenly laughing, amazed at the feeling of joy coursing through her.

"You are a strange people," he said. "*Now* may I come inside?"

"You had best not," she said. "I mean, I would want you to. But it's too late for German lessons."

"Okay," he said. "That's fair. But you

know I won't tolerate this situation for long."

Her heart beat furiously. "You know you have to be baptized first?"

"Yah. And will you come to my first baptismal instruction class in two weeks?"

"Robert," she gasped. "You're really going to go through with it then?"

He threw his hands in the air. "When will you stop doubting me?"

"It's just too *gut* to be true, that's all," she said, nestling on his chest again.

"It's nice of Bishop Miller to fix this up for us," he said. "You people do take care of each other."

"It would have been nice if he hadn't messed it up in the first place," she snapped.

"Let's just be happy for what we have," he said. "This is much more than I ever imagined, Ella. I hope you know that, and I hope it continues."

"Does Mr. Confidence doubt his powers to make it continue?"

"Perhaps," he said. "You make a man doubt if he ever could — as beautiful as you are. *Wunderbar.*"

"Stop it!" she said. "Now go before I chase you away again."

He pulled her into a tight hug and kissed her on the cheek. Then with quick steps he

435

returned to his buggy.

Ella watched until his buggy lights moved out of the driveway and disappeared in the distance.

The window above her opened softly and Ronda's voice called down, "So it was Robert. What did he want?"

"German lessons," Ella said with a straight face. "But not tonight."

Ronda's face broke into a broad smile, "Ah, so you two have patched things up. Well, that's just wonderful. You are so perfect for each other."

"Ronda, not a word of this to anyone!" Ella said.

"Oh, how can I stand it? This is such delightful news," Ronda said, her voice breathless.

"You can find some way," Ella said. "Now, good night."

But Ronda had already disappeared.

The stars twinkled brightly as Ella listened for any lingering sound of horse hooves in the distance. Had she dreamed the whole evening? Had it really happened?

"*Nee,* I didn't dream," she whispered. "Robert was here, and he's coming back."

She walked down the stairs and opened the basement door to find the girls playing happily on the floor.

"We're hungry," Mary said.

"Yes, dears," Ella said. "I'll get supper started right away, but it's just going to be warmed over food from last night."

"I don't care," Mary said.

"Can you set the table?" Ella asked. "You're a big girl now."

Mary glowed as she got up from the floor to find the plates and silverware. With Ella watching she completed the task with some success, the forks and spoons lying at cross angles with the plates.

"That's *gut,*" Ella told her. "You'll soon be very *gut* at it."

When the food was warmed, she brought it to the table and helped the girls into their seats. They bowed in prayer and then began to eat.

Later, with the meal done and the dishes washed, Ella tucked the girls into bed. Walking to the basement window, she looked out at the starry sweep of the sky.

"I love you, Robert," she whispered. "I love you so very much."

FORTY-TWO

During the first week of March, spring made its first attempt at a return. Ella brought the girls outside to see the signs of the coming transformation. "Spring!" she said, with a wave of her hand. "Feel it firsthand, girls! Experience the warmth of the sun while you're still surrounded by chilly air. Hear the soft sound of melting snow as it runs down the basement steps. Feel the temptation to take such deep breaths that it burns the lungs. Yes, it's spring, girls."

"Stop acting silly, Mamm," Mary said, even as she followed Ella's gaze.

"It's time to be silly," Ella said. "The snow will be gone soon, and the birds will be singing."

Mary dashed down the driveway, and Sarah ran after her.

"You can't play on the grass just yet," Ella hollered after them, leaning over to kiss baby Barbara cooing in her arms and kicking her legs.

"Do you want down?" Ella asked as she lowered the baby to the ground, clutching her by the armpits.

Baby Barbara toddled wildly for a few seconds, laughed, and then cried, wanting to be lifted up again. Ella picked her up and held her until she calmed down again.

How like herself Barbara was. She too ran — and yet soon wanted to be held again, comforted from her fears. Today Robert would come for his German lesson. Perhaps that too was part of her joy this morning. But it still seemed so impossible that she was going to have happiness after all. Especially now that she had never wanted it more.

She saw Robert in her mind — how fresh and cheerful he looked the other Sunday. Bishop Miller must have told him who among the Amish women was the best seamstress because his new black suit coat was perfect.

How could Bishop Miller have interfered like he did? The question was painful. Yet she supposed he had to be forgiven. And at least the bishop's poor judgment had brought no reproach on anyone. She had been the one who was nearly harmed — and Robert, but

Da Hah had been with them.

Could she leave all the turmoil behind? Robert looked as if he had. The Sunday of his first baptismal class he had led the way upstairs since he was the oldest. Perhaps he thought it an honor. He sure held his head high. That was a matter she would have to instruct him on. People would expect him to show some humility, lowering his head during church matters.

Yet Robert *was* a very humble man, otherwise he never would have stuck it out this long. And in six months he would be baptized, and they could date officially. Her heart raced at the thought. What would that be like? To have a man she truly loved, one who gripped her heart, her mind, and her imagination? Six months was a long time, and so much could happen.

She had to trust, as hard as that was. One simply couldn't go through life and always expect bad things to happen. That had been Dora's way, not hers. It would embitter her in ways she didn't want if she let it continue.

"Time to go inside!" she called to Mary and Sarah. "We have work to do."

They ran toward her, and Ella watched with concern lest they fall and skin their knees. She sighed with relief when both girls got to her safely, still on their feet. Already she was a worried mother hen fussing over her children.

Carefully Ella helped Sarah down the first wet basement step, though she insisted she could make it on her own. Ella let go of her hand, and she did indeed arrive at the bottom unharmed, a proud smile on her face.

"You did it!" Ella said. Sarah soaked up the encouragement.

For lunch, Ella made sandwiches and sat down to eat with the girls. By one o'clock she had the kitchen table cleaned and the girls down for their naps. A knock on the basement door came without warning. She jumped and turned toward the door.

When she walked over and opened it, Robert was standing there. She held out her hands, and he gently took them in his.

"Robert," she said.

"Now, now," he said, releasing her hands. "We can't be acting like this all the time. I'm not even baptized yet."

"I guess you're right," she said. "How did you drive in without me hearin' you?"

"I'm just that way," he said with a smile. "But if you want to see, the buggy is right up there."

She walked past him, went up a step or two and saw the horse tied to the hitching post.

"Still don't trust me?" he asked.

"I do," she said. "I just had to look."

"Are the girls down for their naps?"

"Yah," she said. "We can talk quietly, and they won't wake up."

"That's good," he said. "How would I take German lessons without talking? But I can't stay long today, and I want to talk about us, if you don't mind."

"Oh . . ." Ella sighed. "Something has come up, I guess?"

"No," he said, his eyes on her face. "Relax, Ella. Nothing like that. It's just that Bishop Miller told me about Aden, about all that you have lost already. I'd heard of your love for Aden, but not as Bishop Miller told it. I can't imagine what you've gone through. I wanted to tell you I know about how hurt you were by his death."

"When did he tell you?" she asked.

"Only yesterday," he said without hesitation. "Always the questions, yah?"

"I suppose it will take a while for me to not worry so."

"Aden must have been a very good man."

"He was," she said.

"I'm sorry I never got to meet him."

"Our people believe that in all things, *Da Hah* knows what He's doing. We must live that way, even in the midst of great pain."

"He has led us together, and for that I am glad," Robert said, sitting down at the kitchen table.

"I am glad also," she whispered, taking the chair beside him.

For long moments they sat in silence. Then he reached for her hand, gently running his fingers over hers.

"How soon can I marry you?" he asked.

"Marry me? Don't the *Englisha* usually ask first?"

He laughed. "Yes, but I mean by the rules of the church."

"As soon as you're baptized."

"That's not too long then," he said.

"You still have to ask," she said.

He smiled. "And can a person ask before he's baptized?"

Ella nodded, not daring to meet his eyes and not wanting tears to come. She felt his fingers touch her chin and lift her face upward until her eyes met his.

"Then will you marry me, Ella Yoder — fiery Amish woman and the hope of all my dreams?"

"You must have met someone else," she whispered. "That's not me."

"I have never met anyone else," he said. "Just answer the question."

"It is yah," she said, pressing back the

tears, holding the moment in her heart.

He didn't answer aloud but brought his face closer to hers, his hands on both sides of her face, pulling her toward him.

She closed her eyes, waiting for his lips, but they never came. She opened her eyes as his cheek brushed hers.

"I think I'd better get baptized first," he said, chuckling softly.

"Perhaps," she whispered, drinking in every line of his face, tracing them with her fingers.

"I think I'll change my name to Bontrager," he said.

"No! I like Hayes," she said, pushing him away.

"But it's not Amish," he said. "Is name changing against the rules?"

"No, but you mustn't."

"Aren't Amish wives submissive? If I say so, then it will be so."

She laughed.

"And we will, of course, live here."

"So that's what you've been after all along. You're marrying me for the house."

"Ella, I really only want you." He took her into his arms, holding her against his chest.

The embrace lasted until Ella regained herself and said, "So, are there to be German lessons today?"

"I don't think so," he said, getting to this feet. "I promised to help Bishop Miller with some work on the farm. And there will be plenty of time for German lessons yet. My whole life, yah?"

"*Our* whole life," Ella corrected. "If *Da Hah* wills it."

"Yah," he said, smiling. "And may He will it." Then he was gone, as silently as he had come.

Ella walked to the basement window to watch him go, stepping outside to catch the last glimpse of his buggy over the top of the stairs as he drove north.

The afternoon air had already begun to chill, and soon nighttime would drop the temperature even lower. Had this all been a dream? She felt the racing of her heart drop to a slow beat. She would believe it, impossible as it was. *Da Hah* had really sent someone for her, and they would live here, in this place, raising a family and growing old together.

FORTY-THREE

Ella watched as the bishop's hand cupped over Robert's head, his form kneeling in line with four boys and seven girls. Twelve of them all together, a holy number, as holy as the day itself was. Robert looked peaceful, his eyes cast down to the hardwood floor, humbling himself for the sacred ritual.

"In the name of *Da Fader,*" Bishop Miller said, as the deacon nervously tipped the water pitcher, a little stream squirting out, hitting Robert's head, splashing upward and dampening the sides of the bishop's hand.

"In the name of the Son, and of the Holy Spirit," Bishop Miller said, as the deacon sent a second and third stream downward.

Slowly the bishop broke the cup of his hands, bringing his hands down over the sides of Robert's head before moving on.

Ella was holding her breath, unable to move. The girl seated beside her glanced sideways. *Let her look and think what she wants to,* Ella thought. *It is done and Robert is now a member of the community . . . of the faith. Come rain, or shine, or snow, or cold, or winter, this can never be undone for as long as Robert shall live.*

The bishop was moving on down the line, repeating the words, but Ella sat drinking in the lines of Robert's face. He wasn't moving, holding as still as the others, waiting quietly. How had the man become like them so quickly? He had shed fully the outward signs of an *Englisha* life, until even to her eyes he looked thoroughly Amish.

Last night she'd had a horrible dream, in which all these weeks vanished like a desert mirage. Yet today it had happened, and no one could deny the water poured on his head. Her Robert was now Amish.

She lay her hand over her heart. This afternoon she would be with him in the buggy. Was such a thing even possible? In the simplest ways of her people, Robert loved her, and even the young bishop had accepted it. From the names circulating, he would surely marry later in the year.

The bishop was moving back down the line, starting back at the beginning, lifting each boy to his feet, kissing him on the cheek. When he came to Robert, he offered his hand, and Robert slowly got to his feet.

The bishop bent his face toward him, and Ella squeezed her eyes shut. It was too much to watch, too holy a moment.

Then, helping the girls to rise, the bishop gave each hand to Bishop Mast's wife, who kissed the girl as the bishop moved down the line. He motioned with his hand after the last one was helped to her feet and kissed, and the newly baptized sat down together, Robert bending his knees in perfect time. Ella glanced away again.

"And now would Mose Mullet, Henry Byler, and John Raber please give testimony on what has happened here today?" Bishop Miller said, sitting down.

Ella shifted carefully on her bench as the low voices droned on, giving their consent to the day's proceedings. Stillness settled over the room. Finally, the song leader called out, "Page four hundred and fifty-five," his voice splitting the reverent silence.

Ella paged through the black songbook as a man's deep baritone broke into song behind her. On the second syllable the whole room joined in, singing with a great burst of joyous sound. Ella sang along, her voice rising and falling with the women around her.

Robert was singing too, his mouth opening and closing as he intently studied the small German words on the page.

Soon he would learn to lead the songs. He would because he was learning everything else so rapidly, and she was sure she would pass out with fright the first time he had to lead out in church. But he would make it with the best of them. His voice would soar and fall with passion, and her heart would race for him because she loved him so dearly.

As the last note died away, Bishop Miller was on his feet again. "And now may the God of Abraham and Isaac and Jacob be with us, and may the grace of our Lord Jesus Christ keep us in the paths of God, and may we always find ourselves with hearts soft and obedient to *Da Hah*'s Word."

The bishop then sat down again, and the front bench of little boys sprang to their feet, dashing away with what speed they dared muster. Behind them the teenage boys followed, and then Robert's row. Ella watched, noting her Robert's erect bearing, the tinge of wetness still in his hair, the way his hand swept down to gather up his hat, and the strength in his body as he leaped down the front steps. Her row of girls rose slowly to their feet, and Ella followed the line out to the kitchen.

"I can help with lunch," she volunteered.

"But you're a visitor," Mary Ellen replied.

"I want to serve the older boy's table," Ella said, feeling the warmth rush up her neck.

"Oh," Mary Ellen said with a twinkle in her eye. "That *Englisha* Robert of yours was baptized, yah."

"Yah," Ella said, "he was."

"The older boys will be in the front room," Mary Ellen said, pointing toward the long line of peanut butter bowls on the kitchen table. "You know what to do then."

Ella nodded and waited in line against the wall, following the other two girls who were assigned to the same table.

Would Robert make the first table? Well, if he didn't, she would also serve the next seating. Her own hunger could wait.

Her eyes lifted slightly from the floor, searching the boys' faces, seeing no sign of Robert as she approached the table. Then there he was, meeting her eyes, looking between the backs of the others, smiling broadly.

Ella glanced away but kept walking toward his section of the table. She leaned over the suspender-strapped backs and set the peanut butter bowls on the table, daring to look up, her heart racing again at the depth in his blue eyes. Quickly she moved away, trying to keep breathing evenly. *How is it right to love a man so much? Yet Da Hah is allowing it, isn't He?* She walked back to the kitchen for more bread and came back to pass the plate in from the end before going back for more peanut butter. She felt his eyes follow her the whole time.

"Come on now, Robert," a boy said, guffawing. "It's time to eat. Sunday afternoons are made for that other kind of stuff."

"That's right," someone else said. "Your wedding's coming soon enough, I'm sure."

"She's a *wunderbar* woman," he said, his voice low and deep.

The whole table erupted in laughter, and Ella kept walking, avoiding the smiles of the girls passing her.

It was worth it! Let them have their fun. Hopefully Robert understood what this meant. He was now one of them, and their laughter was the highest honor they could give him.

After he finished eating, Ella watched as her man left the house for the barn. Robert would go out and get his new buggy ready and then pick her up. She loved that his buggy still smelled of fresh paint even after all these months. It was strange how she noticed that. Eli and Monroe had both driven new buggies, but this was a deeper smell, a poignant odor, as if to add its own flavor to the joy of their love.

"You can get on the next girl's table," one of the girls whispered.

She nodded and moved over to join the others her own age. The bishop announced the prayer, and they bowed their heads, his words lost in the flood of her own thankfulness.

Dear *Da Hah,* thank You so much for the love You have given me again. I'll never understand how it could happen twice or why Aden had to be taken away. But I trust that You do. Thank You that Robert really is who he says he is, and that he hasn't broken my heart, even though I imagined he would. There are times when I can't understand what he sees in me, or even in our people, yet he has become one of us. Thank You.

"Amen," the bishop said, and Ella raised her head along with the others. She wanted to wipe her eyes, but that would draw attention and, no doubt, teasing.

"So Robert made it through instruction class," the girl beside her said, spreading peanut butter on her bread.

"Yah," Ella said, trying to keep her voice clear. "He seems really excited about Amish life."

"It's not often that we have someone join from the outside."

"No, it's not. But Robert is really different. He cares about getting away from the world and starting a new life."

"With one eye on you, of course."

Ella laughed. "Believe me, I couldn't hold him if that was all there was to it."

"You underestimate yourself, if you ask me," the girl said. "Wasn't Bishop Miller after your hand?"

"Let's just say we weren't suited for each other," Ella said.

"Well, he seems to agree with you since he helped Robert out the way he did."

"That's because he sees what a great person Robert is."

"Aw, you would say so," the girl said. "But I must agree he's a nice man."

"He's taken, just remember that," Ella said with a smile.

"Oh I know. What a rotten deal."

They laughed together quietly.

Ten minutes later the bishop's voice boomed through the house. "If we have now eaten, let us give thanks."

They bowed again, and after the prayer Ella stood and helped clean the table, soon catching a glimpse of Robert coming out of the barn, leading his horse. He was a little early, but so much the better. She slipped quietly away and gathered her shawl and bonnet in the washroom. He had the horse hitched and was driving up to the end of the walk when she came out of the doorway.

"Good afternoon," he said, reaching down to take her hand and help her up to the buggy seat.

She took his hand and swung up to sit beside him.

"Amish boys don't help their girls up the buggy steps," she said. "You're going to have to learn that. It will make us soft or something."

"What has that got to do with me?" he asked, slapping the reins, guiding the horse out of the lane, the muscles on his arms rippling under his long shirt sleeves.

She reached over to run her hand from his shoulder to his elbow.

"Hey," he said, "you didn't answer my question."

"Because you're Amish now," she said.

"I guess that's right," he said with a short laugh. "It feels like I've been one for a long time."

"It looks like it too," she said, touching his arm again. "One would think you've been working outside for months already. You've lost all that city fat, and there's nothing left but muscle."

"So that makes a real Amish?"

"It helps," she said, snuggling up against him. "But the baptism was what really did it."

"How am I supposed to drive a buggy if you keep leaning against me?"

"Just keep your hands on the lines. I don't want to land in the ditch."

"Do you think we could land in the ditch?"

"I doubt it — at least not with you driving."

"Then I should be able to drive with one hand, right?"

"We would wreck for sure," she said, pushing his hand off her shoulder and placing it back on the lines. "Just drive."

"Did I do okay today?"

"Do okay with what? Everything you do is okay."

"Act like an Amish man at my Amish baptism?"

"I couldn't have been more Amish myself."

"Well, that's saying something." He beamed.

"Don't get proud now. That's a big, big sin."

"I know," he said, draping his arm around

her shoulder.

She snuggled tighter against him, leaving his arm there.

"I changed my name last week," he said. "To Bontrager, like I said I would."

"You did not," she said, sitting bolt upright and dislodging his arm. "But you had a perfectly wonderful name."

"It's legal now, so there's nothing you can do about it."

"Robert," she said, "I can't believe it."

"Won't you marry me now?" he asked, his arm stealing back to her shoulder.

"I'd marry you if your name were Robert Blight, you know that."

"That's a *gut* feeling," he said, laughing and pulling her close.

"Let's stop here," she said, pointing. "Tie up by that fence post. I want to walk with you down by the river."

"Whoa," he called to the horse, pulling on the lines. "The missus to-be wants to walk by the river."

Ella waited while he tied the horse. Then she took his hand and led him to the water's edge where they listened to the sound of the water running merrily over the rocks.

"It's beautiful here," he said, drawing her close again.

"It's more than beautiful," she said. "But

not half as wonderful as you are."

She lifted her face to his, and he slowly took her in his arms and kissed her. Moments later he held her at arm's length.

"Was that an Amish kiss?" he asked, chuckling softly.

"It was a baptized kiss."

"It's the best I've had yet."

"It had better be," she said, glaring at him before lifting her face again.

After another kiss they watched the water run, the spray from the rocks flying skyward, the light rays seeping down through the trees and sparkling like diamonds.

"There was a time," she said, "when I thought I would never be happy again."

"And I thought I'd never find happiness."

"Do you think we'll grow old together, and have a dozen children gathered around us?"

"Whoa, whoa," he said. "One thing at time! And you already have three girls, so that's a good start."

"And you will be their daett, Robert. Do you know how wonderful that is of you?"

"It won't be hard," he said. "They're wonderful girls. Where are they today?"

"Susanna has them so I could enjoy your baptismal day with you all to myself."

"And now I have you all to myself."

"See," she said, pointing to a tree. "It's a great day, and that cardinal is getting ready to sing a song for us."

"I believe it is," he said, watching the red bird fly to a higher branch. They waited as the minutes passed, the bird bobbed its head, stared at them, and then burst into song.

"Purdy, purdy, purdy . . . sweet, sweet, sweet," it sang.

On the second round Ella burst into tears, sobbing into Robert's shoulder.

"Now, now," he said, holding her tight.

"It's too good to be true," she whispered.

"Perhaps," he said, "but it just is. You and I — we were meant to be."

FORTY-FOUR

Dear Journal,

It's been a long time since I've written to you, a very long time because so much has been going on. The past few months especially were busy with the wedding preparations, the food that had to be made, and all the other little details. Mamm was a true wonder, as always, with her planning skills. She even figured out a way to get everyone in the barn at Seager Hill for the preaching service and filled the house — from the upstairs to the basement — for the meal.

I chose a really dark green for my wedding dress, and a slightly lighter green for my two witnesses. The table waiter girls wore dark brown, and the boys wore brown shirts. The day could not have been nicer if we had ordered the weather from heaven. The house ended up jammed to the limit, but Mamm did it. She is a very gut mamm in more ways than one.

Robert gripped my hand tightly up in the hayloft when the bishop joined mine and his. I don't think he knew Amish people don't do that, but it didn't matter really. I'm sure I saw a little smile on the bishop's face. Robert is like that. He forgets that he's not really Amish-born, and we forget that he ever was Englisha.

I was so glad the wedding could be at Seager Hill. Sure, I would still have been married to Robert anywhere else, even here at the house on Chapman Road, but it was so much better at home, up on the hill, looking down on the rolling valley of my childhood. It was almost like another sign from heaven, a great lifting of spirits, as if I needed it once more, and then the freshness of it all when Robert drove me home after the singing.

It was after midnight, the night still warm, and we had the buggy doors open. I wanted to stop by the little stream to hear the water jingle in the moonlight, but I figured Robert wanted to get home.

Yes, the house on Chapman Road is his home now, as well as mine. How strange that a few words spoken by the bishop and the joining of hands can so change life. I don't think there are many other things with that kind of power.

I waited in the driveway while Robert unhitched the horse, and we walked hand-in-hand toward the house. The girls were at Susanna's for a few days, and Joe and Ronda were gone for a visit to his folks — by design, of course. At the basement door, Robert scooped me up and carried me inside.

I laughed and asked him what he was doing. He said it was an Englisha custom, this carrying of the bride across the threshold. I have never heard of such a thing, but it seemed right that on our wedding night there should be something present from Robert's old world.

Robert's love consumed me that night until I wondered if I loved him too much. I don't know . . . I guess it's possible. I only know that I love this man when not too long ago I was sure I would never love again. Such things are beyond me to figure out.

I am just a simple girl now . . . and happy beyond measure.

DISCUSSION QUESTIONS

1. Is Ella correct in her determination to place the three Stutzman girls' happiness above her own and marry Ivan?

2. Why does Ella's courage fail her when Ivan proposes?

3. Are Ella's fears, stirred by the sight of Bishop Miller leading out at the graveside service, valid? Has the young bishop not forgotten her? And to what means will he go to win her hand?

4. Should Ella have revealed her attraction for Robert Hayes after he shows up at her doorstep announcing his plans to join the Amish?

5. To what degree was Ronda's friendship and advice a help or a hindrance with Ella's desire to untangle her feelings about

her suitors?

6. Is Robert aware of Bishop Miller's attempted maneuvers when he shows up to ask Ella for German lessons?

7. Would Ivan's troubles with the church have led to excommunication if he had not attended the *Englisha* church in town?

8. To what extent did Ivan's dreams of his deceased wife Lois affect his church decisions?

9. Was Ella reckless in taking a meal over to Ivan and sitting down to eat with him after the excommunication?

10. What does Ella's evening with the three girls on the night of Old Christmas reveal about her character?

11. To what extent did Eli's concern and subsequent investigation of Robert aid or hinder Ella?

12. What was the turning point of the story?

ABOUT THE AUTHOR

Jerry Eicher's bestselling Amish fiction (more than 250,000 in combined sales) includes The Adams County Trilogy, the Hannah's Heart books, and the Little Valley Series. After a traditional Amish childhood, Jerry taught for two terms in Amish and Mennonite schools in Ohio and Illinois. Since then he's been involved in church renewal, preaching, and teaching Bible studies. Jerry lives with his wife, Tina, and their four children in Virginia.